I0574135

LOVE LETTERS FOR LADY LARK

BELOW THE SALT SERIES
BOOK THREE

ELIZABETH ROSE

OLIVERHEBERBOOKS

All rights reserved.

No part of this publication may be sold, copied, distributed, reproduced or transmitted in any form or by any means, mechanical or digital, including photocopying and recording or by any information storage and retrieval system without the prior written permission of both the publisher, Oliver Heber Books and the author, Elizabeth Rose, except in the case of brief quotations embodied in critical articles and reviews.

PUBLISHER'S NOTE: This is a work of fiction. Names, characters, places, and incidents either are the product of the author's imagination or are used fictitiously. Any resemblance to actual persons, living or dead, business establishments, events, or locales is entirely coincidental.

Copyright © 2023 by Elizabeth Rose

Published by Oliver-Heber Books

0 9 8 7 6 5 4 3 2 1

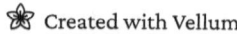 Created with Vellum

CHAPTER I
DEVONSHIRE, ENGLAND, 1374

Love wasn't meant for her.

Lark MacKeefe looked around at the rest of her family during the mass at St. Basil's, feeling the ache in her heart more than ever.

To her right, sat her cousin, Raven, with her new husband, Jonathon. Newly married, they never seemed to stop smiling at each other. To her left was her cousin, and also Raven's twin brother, Rook, with his new wife, Rose. There was no sense in pretending that everyone didn't see the passion in the eyes of those two for each other!

Lark listened to the monks chanting at the other side of the church. The vibrations of their low tones seemed to comfort the turmoil in her heart. Closing her eyes for a minute, she took a deep breath and released it slowly, having learned through the past five years that she needed to keep her head high and her emotions at bay. *Never let them see you sweat*, as her father would always say. However, Lark's past was tarnished and her future didn't look promising either.

1

Breathe deeply. Don't let them see you sweat.

"Mother," came the voice of her four-year-old daughter, Florie, tugging at the long tippet, sleeve of Lark's gown.

Lark's eyes popped open and she bent over to whisper in the little girl's ear. "Shhh," she told her daughter with a finger to her lips. "The mass is just about over, sweetheart."

"But I want to play," complained the child, sitting there kicking her feet, thumping them against the bench in front of her. A pout turned down the corners of her mouth. Raised in the Highlands with the MacKeefe clan, Florie was used to running around in nature, and not being confined for long periods of time.

Lark was a mother on her own, having had a child out of wedlock back in Scotland. Her father was the famous laird and chieftain, Storm MacKeefe, and her mother was an English-woman, Lady Wren Blake. Lark had been visiting her Uncle Lord Corbett Blake in England now for months, needing time away to think. Her parents and daughter had just arrived for the recent wedding of her cousin, Rook. Lark had hoped to get away from her troubles by coming to England, but seeing two of her cousins fall in love and marry now, only reminded her that she would never be so lucky.

No man wanted a tarnished woman such as she.

"Florie, please, hush," scolded Lark, noticing everyone in the church starting to stare. Lark had hoped, in coming to England, that she would manage to escape the judgments and wagging tongues found back in her homeland. Sadly, it seemed the English tongues wagged even quicker and the words about her whispered through the rushes were twice as sharp.

Just on her way into the church this morning, she'd over-heard a little boy asking his mother if Lark was the English whore his friends were talking about.

Lark wasn't a whore! She was only the victim of a silver-tongued devil. A Frenchman who made her infatuated with him only to get her into his bed. Lark's sins weighed heavily on her soul, but there was nothing she could do to change things now.

No man would ever want a ruined Scottish lady.

Lark's daughter would never have the father she deserved, and Lark knew it was all her fault.

"Lark? Lark? Are ye listenin'?" Her father, Storm MacKeefe tapped her on her shoulder, causing her to turn around. The mass had just ended and everyone filed out of the church.

"What is it, Da?" asked Lark, trying her best not to make eye contact with any of the passersby.

"Ye need to discipline yer daughter," he told her in a deep growl. "The lassie has been kickin' at the seats durin' the whole mass, causin' a ruckus. Everyone was starin'."

"Storm, calm down," said Lark's mother, Wren. "Florie is just a child."

Lark's family started to exit the church, but her father kept on complaining.

"The lass needs a father, Lark. It is way past time ye get married."

"Storm, please. Not now." Wren reached over and took Florie's hand. "Come, Florie. Let's wait outside for everyone." She scowled at Storm and walked away with the little girl.

"Mayhap ye need to join a convent, like yer cousin, Eleanor," Storm continued.

Lark looked over at the monks, still sitting there in prayer at the opposite side of the church. They didn't even glance at her like everyone else in the church had. Just one. This monk, although he wore a long cloak and a hood covering his head, wasn't like the others. She could see his long hair hanging down in front of him instead of having the normal tonsure of a ring of hair surrounding a bald head. Odd, but intriguing. It made her want to know more about him.

The man had a handsome face, a small beard and mustache, and dark eyes that drew her in without the edge of judging her. Or at least she thought. She wasn't sure why she felt this way about him, but it was a strong feeling she had.

"Lark? Are ye listenin' to me?" Her father put his hand on her arm.

"Yes, I am," said Lark as they walked to the door together. "Ye want me to get married or join a convent like Eleanor is what ye said. Although, ye realize Eleanor isna a nun. She only works there with the orphaned children."

"Ye can see that the child continues to constantly act up. Somethin' needs to be done."

"If by child, ye mean yer granddaughter, Florie, then I agree. However, me joinin' a convent is no' goin' to do a thing to help that problem."

"Och, then ye'll have to find a man to marry." Storm threw his hands in the air. "I canna go on livin' like this much longer."

"Ye?" Lark stopped in her tracks, her mouth dropping open. "And ye think I enjoy it?" She felt the tears welling up in her eyes, but she blinked them away. Speaking softly, so the others wouldn't hear, she continued. "I ken better than anyone that when I walk by everyone is thinkin' I am naught but a whore."

"Haud yer wheesht, Lark. Dinna say that word in church. We'll be struck down by lightnin' if we're no' careful." Her father looked up at the bright sunlight streaming in through the stained-glass windows of the church as if he thought it was a ray from God directly. One thing about her father was that he was superstitious, even if he tried to convince everyone he was not.

"There isna a cloud in the sky," Lark told him. "And if lightnin' struck me down dead right now, it might be a blessin' in disguise. At least then, all my worries would be over. All the tongues could stop waggin' because they would have nothin' to gossip about anymore."

"What are ye sayin' lass? Blethers, Lark, I didna mean to upset ye like that." Concern showed in Storm's eyes.

Lark felt true compassion coming from her father now. He was a proud man who was respected in Scotland, but here in England he was just another Scott that the English didn't know if they could trust. However, everyone in these parts knew him, since he married Lady Wren, the sister of Lord Corbett Blake. Nay, her father had nothing to worry about at all.

"I think I want to find a tutor for Florie," said Lark as she exited the church, still thinking about the future of her daughter.

"A tutor? Florie is only four," her father pointed out. "Besides, she is a lassie. Only laddies are allowed to be taught."

"I ken that, but it might help stop her from actin' up," said Lark. "At least, this might take her attention and help things until I … I mean if I … ever find a man who will marry me."

"Yer mother and I are stayin' in England for a short while and will help ye with that. I am sure ye will no' have to worry about yer future or the future of yer daughter much longer."

"How can ye be sure? What does that mean?" asked Lark, having a feeling her father was up to something and she didn't like it.

"It only means that yer mother and I care about what happens to ye. We want the best for both ye and our grand-daughter."

"Thank ye, Da." Lark gave her father a hug and a kiss on the cheek. Over Storm's shoulder, she saw the monks leaving the church. They all had their hands folded in front of them, their eyes cast downward, and their heads covered. All except the one monk with the long hair. The handsome one. He stood over to the side, watching her intently. It made her heart jump, but she wasn't sure why.

"Storm, we are waiting for you," called out Wren from the bottom of the church stairs.

"Lark, when this is all over, I want ye to come back to Scotland where ye belong," said Storm.

"It'll never be over," she told him. "And nay, I want to stay here in England for a while with Florie. I like the change."

The MacKeefes had a camp in the Highlands, and they also held Hermitage Castle in the Lowlands on the border too. The clan members could live in either of the places. Storm and his father, who were the two chieftains of the clan, took turns living in the Highlands or at the castle.

"Lark, yer mother is very concerned that ye are alone. So am I."

"I'm no' alone. I'm here with my aunt and uncle and my cousins. And now ye and mother as well."

"Ye ken what I mean. Ye need a husband and a father for Florie. It's time I find one for ye."

"Nay, Da! Please. Give me more time."

"Ye've had nearly five years. How much more time do ye need?"

"As long as it takes," Lark answered with a sigh, feeling as if she'd just about lost all hope.

"Well, I canna wait any longer. And I want ye to realize that everythin' I do is only to help ye."

"What does that mean? Did ye already do somethin'? Please tell me that ye dinna," said Lark, fearing the worst.

"Storm, we are waiting and Florie is starting to fuss," called out Lark's mother again.

"We'll talk," was all her father said before heading down the stairs.

Lark noticed the monk with the long hair still watching her from the door. She turned and followed her father, getting a feeling that something was about to happen in her life and that she wasn't going to like it at all.

CHAPTER 2

Dustin Styles hadn't been able to stop looking at the beautiful Lady Lark from the castle. She took his interest, and he couldn't even focus during the mass. Even now that she'd gone, he couldn't get her image out of his head. He hadn't meant to stare at her during the service or even afterwards, but he couldn't help himself. He'd heard the gossip about the Scottish niece of Lord Corbett Blake. Who hadn't? He'd heard it and hated it because he felt it was a shame that Lady Lark should be talked about in this manner.

Dustin walked back to the cloisters with the rest of the monks in deep thought. Brother Ruford led the way. Brother Ruford was the uncle of Lord Corbett Blake, and also the abbot and eldest monk at the monastery.

The church rose up majestically with high spires atop the stone building. The large bell in the bell-tower rang out loudly, splitting the air, telling all the mass was over. The colorful, stained-glass windows of St. Basil's were an expensive and rare gift to the church. They were from the late Lord Ethan Blake, Lord Corbett's father. A heavy gate guarded the entrance with bars of iron, opened during the day and during masses to let travelers and visitors enter freely. The monastery often housed nobles passing through, as well as priests, nuns, and monks from different chapters.

Dustin wasn't a monk. He was an orphan. He had lived at St. Basil's Monastery his entire life, ever since the day he was abandoned by his family. He was left on the church steps as a baby with nothing but a blanket wrapped around him in the bitter cold. A note had been pinned to his blanket saying *Please watch over my son until I am able to return for him.* The note hadn't been signed, but by the looks of the swirly writing and the ornate little pictures of butterflies that served as dots on the letters I, Dustin figured it was a female who wrote it. Most likely his mother right before she gave him up forever.

It had been twenty-two years now, and Dustin was still waiting for her to return. He knew no one was coming, but part of him couldn't let go of the hope. All he ever wanted was to find out who he really was. Where he belonged. An emptiness engulfed him, and in his heart was a space that longed to be filled ... with family.

Brother Ruford had raised Dustin as if he were his own son. Thankfully, the man had a heart and didn't give Dustin to a peasant family. Brother Ruford had believed at first that Dustin's mother would return, just like he did. But after a few years that hope diminished. By then, everyone at the monastery had become fond of Dustin, and so he stayed and was still there to this very day.

St. Basil's Monastery is where Dustin was raised, and trained to be a scribe transcribing manuscripts all his life. However, he never wanted to become a monk and actually take his vows. He attended the prayer sessions and masses, transcribed manuscripts, and even helped work in the outlying granges, farming the land and assisting the lay monks in tending to the livestock. But that is as far as it went. Brother Ruford hadn't forced him to take his vows or even cut his hair, and Dustin was grateful for his understanding.

"You seem troubled today, Brother Dustin," said Ruford as they made their way through the cloisters coming from the church. The cruciform-style church was connected to the cloisters, covered walkways that led around an open courtyard with beautiful gardens and even a small pond with fish in the center. The monastery had a chapter house for meetings, a scriptorium for the scribes, and a refectory where the monks ate their meals. There was a guesthouse and also an infirmary for the ill and elderly monks. The monks slept in cells, or small rooms in the dormitory on the second floor. However, Dustin lived in a small hut built of wattle and daub, still on the grounds but away from the rest of the monks.

"You know I don't like it when you refer to me as brother," complained Dustin. "And nothing is troubling me."

"I'm sorry, son," said Ruford. "After all these years, I should remember you don't like it, but it is habit, I suppose. Everyone here, layman or monk is called brother."

"Well, not me. And never will I be."

"You are getting older now, Dustin. With no plans to pursue actual monkhood, perhaps it is time you find a life outside the walls of the monastery."

"Really?" Dustin stopped in his tracks. He didn't believe Ruford, who had been like a father to him, would ever say such a thing. "You want me to leave?" Why did the stab to his heart from hearing these words make him feel as if he were being abandoned again? It was silly. He was a grown man. Yet, in his heart he felt something was missing. It was a void that hadn't hurt so much when he'd accepted the monks as his family. But if he left here, that ache would only become worse.

Dustin had given up hope on his mother returning for him

when he was only ten. He still hated the woman for tossing him away like trash. But through the years, even living so simply with the monks, Dustin had finally felt like he belonged somewhere. The monastery was home—the only one he had ever known. Why would he ever want to leave here and be all alone again?

"Nay, of course I don't really want you to leave," said Ruford. He spoke softly since at certain times of the day the monks would remain silent, not speaking to each other until the period was up. "It's just that you are older now, and need a life of your own. If you're not going to take your vows to the church, then there is honestly no reason for you to stay. It would do you good to get out and live your life. Find a woman to marry. Raise a family."

Every year, Brother Ruford tried to talk Dustin into leaving, and every time, Dustin changed the old man's mind before the conversation was over. It wasn't that Dustin didn't want a life beyond the monastery walls. God knew he spent a lot of time in town, visiting taverns and even finding the comfort of whores on occasion. Of course, Ruford knew all about this too, because Dustin had always confessed his sins. The last thing he wanted was to have a blackened soul. Mayhap, living with monks had made him more like them than he realized after all.

"Do you need my cottage for someone else?" he asked.

Dustin had been given the small cottage of wattle and daub that was built in the side garden of the monastery. At one time it had belonged to the old midwife, Heartha, who raised Devon—or Lady Blake. But when Devon and Heartha moved to the castle, the hut remained empty. Devon ended up marrying Lord Corbett and was Lady Devon Blake now, mother of Lord Rook, Lady Raven, and their two younger brothers.

"You've been a loner for too long," said Ruford. "I feel as if you're missing out the best years of your life, and that is not fair to you."

"I still say it sounds like you are trying to get rid of me."

The sound of hoofbeats against the cobbled stone entryway brought to Dustin's attention that they had visitors.

"Someone's here," said Dustin, stretching his neck to see who approached. To his surprise, it was the Scotsman and his beautiful daughter, Lady Lark.

"It's Storm MacKeefe," said Ruford, knowing the Scottish chieftain well since his niece, Lady Wren had married the man. "Laird MacKeefe, to what do we owe this pleasure?" asked Ruford, hurrying forward to greet them.

"Brother Ruford," said Storm from atop his horse, doing nothing to dismount. "I have a favor to ask ye."

"What is that?" Ruford wondered.

"I am visitin' at Blake Castle with my daughter, Lady Lark."

"Yes, of course. Hello, Lady Lark," said Ruford with a slight bow.

Dustin cleared his throat from beside him.

"I'm not sure if you've ever been properly introduced to Brother Dustin," said Ruford, with an outstretched arm.

Dustin scowled at him. "Just call me Dustin. I am not a monk and have never taken my vows," he said, with a bow of respect to the nobles as well.

"Really," said the woman, perusing him with a stoic face. "And yet ye still wear the black Benedictine robes and live here at the monastery? Why?"

"I ... yes, I do," said Dustin, not sure how to answer or if he wanted the woman to be privy to his tale of woe.

"Interestin' that anyone would purposely choose a life like this." The woman glanced around the courtyard. It made Dustin feel uncomfortable and as if she were judging him. He immediately became defensive, wanting her to feel as uncomfortable as he.

"Interesting that others choose to live their lives as if they don't fear God at all," Dustin told her, knowing that she realized he meant her. "I'd call that bold, not to mention defiant, wouldn't you?" Dustin suddenly felt like hell for saying this aloud. After all the gossip he'd heard about the woman, it made him feel no better than those with the wagging tongues. He immediately regretted his words and also his quick emotions that he'd never been able to control.

"Would ye, now?" asked Lark with a sniff. She threw her nose up in the air.

"Laird MacKeefe, what can we do for you?" asked Ruford, breaking in, no doubt to keep Dustin from saying anything else that was considered inappropriate to a noblewoman.

"My daughter is lookin' for a tutor for her child," said Storm.

"My laird, if I'm not mistaken, Lady Lark's child is a girl, is she not?" Ruford so blatantly pointed out.

"Aye, that's right," said Lark, sounding haughty. "Is that a problem?"

"Yes, it is," said Ruford. "The monks only tutor boys. However, if you go to a nunnery, perhaps the nuns will be able to aid you."

"Canna ye break the rule?" asked Storm. "The monastery is close to the castle, but there are no nunneries in this area."

"I wish I could," said Ruford with a shrug. "I am sorry, but I cannot allow that. It would be breaking the rules."

"I see," said Storm. "Well, I wouldna want to put ye in a position that might cause ye trouble. I'm sorry to have bothered ye. Good day." Storm and Lark turned their horses to go.

Dustin watched them leaving and decided to start changing his life, just like Brother Ruford wanted him to do. He was intrigued by Lady Lark, even if she had momentarily made him feel worthless. He supposed he'd made her feel embarrassed by what he'd said as well. Part of him wanted to try to make up for his mistake. "I'll do it," he called out.

"What?" Storm stopped and turned his horse. So did Lark.

"I said, I'll be the little girl's tutor. When do I start?" asked Dustin.

"Ye?" Lark's eyes shot over to her father. "I dinna think so, Da," she whispered.

Dustin realized she didn't want him because he had insulted her, even if it was indirectly.

"Why no'?" Storm asked Lark. "At least this way, Florie will have someone to teach and discipline her before she gets any worse with her behavior."

"Is the child the rebellious sort?" asked Ruford. "I'm not sure this is a good idea, then."

"My daughter, Florie, is high-spirited and that's all," Lark assured them.

Dustin knew better. He'd seen the little girl arrive just days ago while he was out in the field working. She had been crying loudly and having some sort of tantrum. Already, she'd been reckless at mass, and had pulled the tails of the castle's dogs, as well as thrown rocks at the children of some of the servants. Or so he'd been told by the peasants.

"Well, I don't know," said Ruford, looking over at Dustin.

"I don't mind a challenge," said Dustin, his eyes flashing back at Lark once again. "Plus, you just finished telling me that it is time I move on," he reminded the monk.

"Yes, that's true. This might be a good thing for you," agreed Ruford.

"What does this man even ken about teachin' children?" asked Lark.

"I know how to teach a four-year-old, I assure you," said

Dustin, thinking the woman was purposely trying to insult him again.

"Dustin is a scribe," Ruford informed them. "He is also a learned man, very knowledgeable about a lot of things. He is more than qualified for the job."

"A scribe?" asked Lark, considering it, but still not seeming happy about the situation.

"That means, I know how to write, not to mention, read, my lady." Dustin couldn't resist saying this, even though he should have just bitten his tongue. It was a vice of his to speak before thinking sometimes. Once again he was too fast to react, but didn't like the woman insinuating that he wasn't a learned man.

"I ken what a scribe is, ye simpkin," spat Lark. "I just dinna ken if I want ye teachin' my daughter, that's all."

"Lark," said Storm in a deep, scolding tone.

"Mayhap I can tutor you as well, my lady," said Dustin with a smirk.

"Dustin," spat Ruford under his breath.

"The scribe will be fine," Storm answered for the girl, most likely before any more insults could be exchanged between them.

"Da? Really?" asked Lark, seeming shocked that her father would agree to this.

"Excuse me, my lady," said Dustin. "Might I point out that no one else here is willing to do it? Neither will you have an easy time finding someone to teach a bastard of a noble who happens to be a girl. I really don't see that you have any other choice."

Storm's mouth dropped open, and Ruford gasped. Mayhap Dustin did overdo it a bit.

"Well I ... I mean I ..." Lady Lark seemed to suddenly realize that he knew her history, just like everyone else in the area. Her face reddened, and it wasn't from the sun. The woman was embarrassed that her secret life was on display more than she probably had imagined. "Yes, that will be fine," she answered, staring at the ground rather than at Dustin. She wasn't so bold now. Actually, Dustin felt bad for saying this, not meaning to make the woman feel this way. He'd have to confess his sin to Brother Ruford later.

"Be at the castle first thing in the mornin'," instructed Storm.

"Shall I ask for you, my lord?" asked Dustin.

"Nay. Florie is my daughter so ye'll be reportin' to me," said Lark.

"Of course he will. Thank you," said Brother Ruford with a bow, looking over at Dustin, motioning with his eyes to do the same.

"Yes, thank you," said Dustin, bowing as well.

Storm and Lark turned and left. Once they were out of hearing range, Dustin spoke to Ruford.

"What the hell are we thanking them for? Shouldn't they be thanking us instead?"

Ruford's eyes opened wide, then narrowed as he shook his head. "Dustin, stop cursing."

"I'll never get used to that," said Dustin.

"You've had plenty of time to learn that we don't curse inside these monastery walls," Ruford scolded. "I swear, you will never change."

"Well, the wench made me upset with the way she looked down her nose at me."

"Wench? Good sakes, Dustin, you are speaking about a noblewoman, not one of your regular lightskirts. Have I taught you nothing? Have respect for the lady. Mayhap you are the one who needs a tutor, not Lady Lark." Ruford turned and stormed away.

Dustin's gaze focused on the backs of Lark and her father as they rode out the gates of St. Basil's. Even with the girl's attitude and sharp tongue, she still somehow took his interest. Aye, he decided, he was looking forward to this job after all.

"Nay, Ruford you are wrong," Dustin said to himself. "I think there are a lot of things I can teach Lady Lark, after all."

CHAPTER 3

Lark woke the next morning, feeling a breeze on her face. With her eyes still closed, she rolled over in bed at Blake Castle, her arm going around what she thought was her daughter. Then she heard the sound of barking dogs and voices. There seemed to be a commotion outside.

Her eyes fluttered open. "Florie?" she asked, realizing she wasn't hugging her daughter but just a pillow.

She heard the giggling of her little girl and more shouting from what sounded to be coming from out in the courtyard.

"Florie?" she asked again, sitting up in bed and stretching. The light coming in the window was bright. She blinked a few times and rubbed her eyes, looking over to where she heard Florie's giggles. "Florie! Nay!" she shouted, seeing her daughter standing on a chair, leaning out the open window.

"Doggies," said the girl, reaching for them, wobbling on the chair about to lose her balance and fall out the window.

Lark sprang out of bed, bolting across the room, grabbing Florie before she fell to her death.

"Nay! What are ye doin'?" Lark scolded. She held her daughter close to her chest. Florie began to cry.

The door to the room banged open and Lark's cousins, Raven and Robin, rushed into the chamber.

"Oh, thank goodness you have her." Raven let out a deep breath, holding her hand to her heart.

"God's eyes, Lark, we were in the courtyard and saw the girl standing in the window," spat Robin. "She could have fallen to her death."

"I ken that, Robin, but thank ye," she told the man. "As ye can see, I have her now and all is well, so ye are no' needed."

"Why don't you keep a better eye on her?" snapped Robin. "You're not a very good mother."

That comment was like her cousin driving a dagger through her heart. Lark didn't even know how to respond.

"We need to close this shutter." Raven hurried across the room to do so.

"Nay, leave it open," said Lark. "I like the fresh air. Besides, Florie kens no' to do that again. Right, Florie?" she asked her daughter, releasing her from the hug but holding on to her shoulders and looking into the girl's bright blue eyes.

"I'm sorry," said Florie. "Mother, I need to go to the garderobe." The little girl crossed her legs.

"I'll take her," said Raven, scooping up the child.

"I am her mother, I can do it," said Lark, tired of how everyone seemed to think she couldn't raise this child alone. She was doing the best she could, despite the fact Florie had no father, and Lark had no maid to help her. After all, most nobles had a nursemaid to watch after the young ones. Raising children wasn't done by those of status, even if the children were their own.

"You're still in your bedclothes. I'll take her," Raven

answered. "Lark, you need help raising this child. I can send the castle nursemaid up here to assist you during your visit."

"Nay," Lark protested. "I dinna want a nursemaid's help. I can do this. Alone." She held firm with her decision, even though she honestly wasn't feeling strong at the moment. Still, she didn't want to seem vulnerable or helpless because that was the furthest thing from the truth.

"Didn't you have a nursemaid back in Scotland?" asked Robin.

"Of course, I did."

"Why didn't your parents bring her along when they traveled here to see you?" asked Raven.

"The nursemaid in Scotland is the same one my mother had when she had her first child," said Lark.

"Oh, you mean the witch?" asked Robin, his eyes growing large.

"Zara is a gypsy, no' a witch," Lark told him. "I'm sure she would have come if asked, but she is old and it is no longer safe for her to make the journey."

"I still say you need a nursemaid here. You are a noble and shouldn't be doing the work of a servant." Raven shook her head and headed out the door with Florie in her arms.

"What are ye lookin' at, Robin?" snapped Lark, picking up a blanket and holding it in front of her since she indeed was still dressed for bed.

"Not you, if that's what you mean. Raven is right, you know," said Robin. "You do need help raising that unruly child. She is getting way out of hand."

"Take that back," Lark retorted. "My daughter is not unruly."

"Isn't she, now?" Robin raised a brow.

"You are the unruly one," said Lark. "As a matter of fact, ye

21

are startin' to sound arrogant and more and more like Rook every day. And we all ken how irritatin' he can be at times."

"Not anymore," said Robin with a shrug. "Now that Rook is married he's a changed man. The key word here being *married*."

She was about to tell-off her cousin when a page arrived at the open door.

"Lord Robin, this missive just arrived for you," said the boy, handing Robin the letter with two hands which was the proper way for a servant to act around a noble.

"Thank you," said Robin. "You are dismissed." The boy bowed and left. Robin broke the wax seal on the missive, and scanned the contents of the letter quickly.

Lark saw worry crease Robin's forehead. "What is it?" she asked. "Who is it from?"

"It's a missive from my parents in Blackmore," said Robin.

"Och, nay. I hope nothin' has happened to Uncle Madoc or Aunt Abbey."

"Nay, nay, they are fine." Robin continued to read and a small smile turned up his lips. "On the contrary this is very good news after all."

"How so?" she asked, grabbing a cloak and throwing it around her shoulders.

"It seems the Lord of Shrewsbury has died."

"What? That isna good news," said Lark, holding close the cloak in front of her.

"Nay, I suppose not really, but there is more to the missive." A full smile broke out across Robin's face next. "It seems the king has decided to give Shrewsbury Castle to my parents."

"Oh, that's wonderful."

"My parents don't want it. They like living in my grandfather's castle." Robin continued to read. "My grandfather is old and ailing. As soon as he dies, which will be any day now, they'll inherit it."

"So ... I dinna understand. What is so good about all this, then?"

Robin folded up the missive and looked directly at her. "Since I'm the eldest son, my parents have passed the castle on to me and the king has agreed. I am now Lord of Shrewsbury," he said proudly, staring up at the ceiling as if he were already daydreaming about it. "Yes! I have my own castle now." He was so excited that he rushed over and picked up Lark, swinging her around, making her dizzy.

"Stop it, Robin," she shouted, breaking away from him and fixing her cloak again.

"What's the matter, with you? Aren't you happy for me?" asked Robin.

"First of all, ye're the only son of yer parents, no' the eldest, so they had no one else to give it to."

"What does it matter? Didn't you hear me? I am lord of my own castle!"

"I heard ye loud and clear. And since ye were shoutin' so loud, I'm sure the entire castle heard ye as well."

"I can't wait to get there. I'm leaving at once." He hurried to the door, but stopped. Holding up a finger, he turned back to Lark. "Nay, I think I'm going to make a quick visit to Horrabridge first to tell Rook. He'll want to know. He'll be happy for me. Goodbye, Lark." He rushed out the door without closing it, just as Raven walked in with Florie.

"Robin? Where are you going and what's your hurry?" Raven called out after him.

"I have a castle!" he shouted down the hall, making a whooping noise before running off.

"Did Robin just say he has a castle?" Raven closed the door after him while Florie ran over and climbed atop the bed.

"Yes," said Lark. "He inherited it and is now the Lord of Shrewsbury."

"Oh, that is wonderful news," said Raven. "I'm happy for him."

"He's off to tell Rook about it first. To brag, I believe."

"Oh, yes, this is going to make Rook furious." Raven chuckled. "Oh well, at least my brother has Rose with him now to try to calm him down."

"Look at me! Look at me!" called Florie from the bed. When Lark turned around, Florie was jumping on the bed, getting higher and higher.

"Stop that, Florie," scolded Lark, but the little girl wouldn't listen.

Since ropes were strung underneath holding up the mattress and Florie was jumping, the ropes snapped and the mattress fell to the floor. Florie went with it. It wasn't a far fall, but enough to scare the child and make her cry.

"Och, Florie, are ye all right?" Lark rushed over and so did Raven just as there came a knock on the door. Florie cried louder.

The door opened and Lark's mother entered. "What happened?" asked Wren, rushing over to the bed. "Is she hurt?"

"She's fine, Mother," said Lark. "She was jumpin' on the bed and the ropes snapped, that's all."

"Lark, get dressed," said her mother. "The tutor is here, waiting for you in the great hall."

"The scribe? He's here already?" asked Lark, feeling her heart jump into her throat. "But it's so early and I havena even had time to feed Florie yet."

"The monks get up early," stated Raven from the bed, helping Florie from the broken mess. "This is probably late for him."

"He's no' a monk," said Lark, entering the wardrobe, trying to decide what to wear. "Or so he says."

"Oh, that's right," said Wren. "I don't really know him well, but I've heard Brother Ruford talk about him from time to time. I still don't understand why the scribe lives at the monastery if he is not going to become a monk."

"That's what I dinna understand either." Lark chose a bright red dress and brought it back to the bed to don it. "Then again, Aunt Devon lived there too at one time, and she was never goin' to become a monk."

"Oh, Lark. You're not going to wear that, are you?" asked her mother, looking horrified.

"Yes, it's my favorite gown. Why?"

"It's … it's … so bright and vibrant. Mayhap something a little more subdued would be better."

"That gown will make you stand out too much," said Raven, helping to change Florie out of her bedclothes.

"Nay, it's fine," protested Lark.

"I agree with your mother," said Raven. "Why don't you wear a different color for now?"

"Well, Rook wears a red cloak, and no one says a thing about it to him," stated Lark.

"Rook also doesn't want anyone to miss him, and believe me, they don't." Raven finished dressing Florie and stood up and smiled at the girl.

"Why does it matter?" asked Lark. "Are ye both worried I'll stand out too much, and ye're embarrassed because of my bad reputation?"

"Nay, of course not, Lark," said Wren. "It doesn't really matter. It's a pretty gown, so wear it." Wren wore a gown made from the plaid of the MacKeefes, the colors being green and purple. Ever since she married a Scot, she dressed like one too.

25

"Daughter, I only wish you'd start dressing more like a High-lander and less like an Englishwoman someday."

"I am in England, Mother. Besides, ye are English, even if Da is a Highlander. There is no sense in announcin' to every passerby that I am a Scot by wearin' a plaid. That will only give them more to talk about behind my back."

"Lark, you are a fine woman," said her mother with a kind smile. "I am sure someday soon you will find the right man and your troubles will be over." Wren hugged Lark.

"I hope so, Mother," said Lark, seeing how sad Florie looked across the room. The thing Lark wanted most in life, besides everyone to stop ridiculing her for her mistakes of the past, was to have a man to love. Lark wanted a husband who would accept her for who she is, and also be a good father to Florie.

Then again, where in the world was she going to find someone like that?

~

"ORRICK, my friend, so nice to see you again." Dustin walked into the great hall of Blake Castle to find everyone just finishing up the first meal of the day. The castle's sorcerer, Orrick joined him. He was a tall, old man with long white hair, a beard and mustache to match. His eyes were an intriguing color of amethyst beneath his craggy brows.

"Dustin, how are you?" asked Orrick. "I haven't seen you in quite a while."

"I don't have any reason to come to the castle, and have been in the monastery where I always am," said Dustin.

"Ah, yes. I haven't been to the monastery in some time now, so that's why, I guess." Orrick laughed. "Why are you here?" He straightened out his long, purple robe, dressed as usual in an eccentric-looking way. At times, he even wore a tall hat that matched the robe.

"I am here as tutor to Lady Lark's little girl."

"Really." Orrick seemed intrigued. "I thought you were here to replace the castle's scribe who died just last month. We still don't have a scribe, and Lord Corbett has been too busy to find one."

"Castle scribe?" Dustin liked the sound of that. It would get him out of the monastery to live his life, just like Brother Ruford suggested. It would also be a good paying job. Living with the monks, Dustin had very little money. Even though he hadn't taken the vow of poverty, it seemed to have been given to him just because he lived there. "Do you think Lord Corbett would hire me?"

"I don't see why not. He knows you, and likes you. Plus, I'll give him my recommendation since I am his advisor."

"I'd appreciate that, Orrick. Thank you."

"Come up and see me, anytime," offered Orrick.

"Is your chamber still in the east tower?"

"It is. However, I don't have many visitors since most people are afraid of me."

"Well, I'd be more than happy to visit as often as you'll have me."

"Why don't you stay with me while you're tutoring the child?"

"Really?" asked Dustin, excited and yet a little leery of staying with a man who supposedly could conjure magic. "I'll keep it in mind."

"You're not still living in Heartha's old hut of wattle and daub in the monastery, are you?"

"Well ... yes. Since I work at the monastery, there didn't seem much reason to leave there. Plus, I don't have much money and I live there for free."

"You'll be making good money as tutor and scribe. Still, I'd like you to stay with me for a while. I could use the company."

"I might just do that. Thank you."

"Oh, here comes Lady Lark and her cute little daughter now." Orrick walked over to greet Lark, Raven, and Florie. He picked up Florie, and the little girl took a fistful of his beard in her hand and yanked it hard. Dustin saw Orrick make a face and wince before putting the girl back down.

"Horsey," said Florie, running after Raven's two mastiffs.

"Florie, those are no' horses," called out Lark. "They are just very big dogs."

The dogs were huge and knocked into everyone and everything trying to get away from the terrorizing child. Florie was attempting to hoist herself up on their backs and ride them now.

"Nay, Florie! Leave my hounds alone," cried out Raven.

"Raven, what did I say about letting those dogs into the great hall?" called out Lord Corbett from the dais.

"I'm sorry, Father. I'll get them." Raven ran after her dogs.

Pretty much all hell broke loose as Raven tried to catch her dogs and Florie chased them, grabbing for their tails. Some of the ladies of the castle screamed when the dogs put their front paws up on the trestle tables and started to grab food. The men jumped up to catch things the animals knocked to the floor.

Dustin looked back to see Lark just standing there, doing nothing.

"Aren't you going to go after your daughter to stop her?" asked Dustin.

Lark looked up and their gazes interlocked. She had big, round eyes that were a magical shade of green. This close up, Dustin could see her features perfectly. Her face was heart-shaped, her skin perfectly smooth. Dustin found the slight dimple on her chin and her full lips intriguing. Those lips looked just right for kissing. He shook his head, not knowing where the hell that thought came from. After all, he didn't even care much for the wench. Then again, he did like kissing.

"Florie, come here," cried Lark, shaking her head and looking back at Dustin. "She doesna listen to me."

"Perhaps she can't hear you from this far away."

"I dinna see what good it would do to run around in a dither like everyone else, if that is what ye're suggestin'," Lark told him. "When someone catches my daughter, they'll bring her over to me, so I'll just wait."

"My, that's an interesting way to raise a child."

"What are ye sayin', scribe?" Lark's eyes narrowed. "Are ye insinuatin' that I canna handle my daughter?"

"Nay, not at all, my lady." That's exactly what Dustin meant but didn't think it a wise move to upset the woman before he'd even started working for her. Plus, he was a commoner and had no right to tell any noble what to do. He really needed to work on biting his tongue and staying quiet instead of voicing his opinion since it usually only got him into trouble.

"I'm sure ye dinna ken this, since ye're just a commoner, but nobles usually have a nursemaid or send their children away to be fostered by others. So, this is no different in the least."

If she really believed that ignoring the bad behavior of a child while standing right there waiting for someone else to help her was a good idea, then she was even more addled than he thought. Perhaps this is why the father of the child ran and never looked back. Or, at least, that is what he heard through the rushes.

"I beg your pardon, my lady," said Dustin. "Since I'm just a commoner, I'm sure I wouldn't know the first thing about raising noble children." He got down on one knee and whistled, calling the hounds. When the dogs came running to him, the little girl followed. He quickly stood up, snatching two leftover trenchers from the tray of a passing kitchen maid.

Trenchers were flat, stale hunks of bread used as plates. Usually, after the meal, the trenchers were brought to the castle's front gate and given to the beggars and those less fortunate.

"Sit!" he commanded the mastiffs. When they did so, he threw the trenchers to the floor. Each dog picked one up in its mouth and ran off to eat it. Just as Florie was about to follow them again, Dustin scooped her up in his arms, and handed her to Lark.

"Here you go, my lady. One child delivered personally to you without you even having to move."

Lark couldn't believe what she'd just witnessed. The scribe not only managed to stop the chaos, but he also satisfied the hounds and got Florie to refrain from running around terrorizing the dogs. She'd never seen anything like it. What everyone in the room couldn't manage to do, he, a stranger, did in less than a minute.

"That was ... amazin'," Lark told him in awe, holding tightly to her daughter. "Hold still, Florie."

"It's simple once you realize everyone wants something. Once they have it, they'll act the way you want them to," he explained. When the little girl squirmed and started to fuss, he figured he'd better take her attention quickly before things got out of hand again. "I'm Dustin and I'm going to be your tutor," he told the girl. "What's your name?"

"Her name is –" Lark started, but Dustin raised his palm to stop her from answering.

"I am talking to the girl," he told her. "Please, let her answer for herself."

Lark frowned but Florie smiled.

"I'm Florie," said the girl. Then she suddenly became shy and hid her face against her mother's chest.

"That isn't the way to speak to nobles," Lark reprimanded Dustin, the way she should be talking to her child instead. Dustin didn't like it in the least.

"I'm sorry," Dustin told her. "Let me try this again. What is your name, *my lady*?" he asked, speaking and looking directly at the child instead of Lark. Florie burst out laughing but he heard Lark gasp in surprise. He didn't dare look at her right now.

"It's time for my daughter's lesson. We'll be usin' Lord Corbett's solar, so follow me," Lark commanded.

"Of course," he answered, walking behind her instead of at her side.

Lark held her child as she walked, and little Florie peeked over her shoulder at Dustin with wide, curious eyes.

Dustin glanced one way and then the other. When he was sure no one was watching, he made a silly face at the child, closing one eye and sticking out his tongue. Florie's eyes lit up in amusement and she laughed. Every time Lark turned around to see what her daughter was laughing at, Dustin acted normal, and just smiled at Lark and nodded his head.

"In here," said Lark, putting down the girl, stopping outside the room. She looked over at Dustin and waited.

"Oh, you want me to open the door?" he asked, just to make sure.

She nodded slightly.

"I don't get to the castle often, and I'm not used to this." Dustin opened the solar door and was about to step into the room when Lark cleared her throat and made him stop.

31

"We'll get right to the lesson then." She pushed past him, entering first, holding Florie's hand. That told Dustin that servants, and commoners, were always supposed to open doors for the nobles and let them enter the room first. He knew this but supposed he didn't want to remember, so purposely ignored it. Dustin let out an exasperated breath, looking up and down the corridor for a lifeline, but no one was there. With a shrug, he entered the room and closed the door behind him.

As soon as Lark saw Dustin close the door, she ran back over and pulled it wide open.

"Did I do something wrong again, my lady?" he asked, sounding unaware of his actions. Whether or not he was really that ignorant about being alone in the room with a lady, she had no idea. Still, she couldn't allow him to close the door since it would only make rumors about her flourish.

"I am no' sure what goes on at the monastery, but in the castle, when a male is alone with a lady, he must leave the door open," she explained, taking Florie and sitting her at the table.

"I see," he said, scratching the back of his neck. "So, is it true then that on a noble's wedding night, everyone watches them make love, too? I mean, since the door is wide open?"

Lark's eyes snapped upward and her heart jumped. Just having this handsome man mention making love caused her to barely be able to breathe. Why was he saying this? Was he referring to her tarnished reputation again?

"When a man is married to a woman, he can close the door," she answered softly. "Scribe, I hardly think this is something you should be asking me. After all, what I do is none of your business."

"You?" He cocked a smile and laid his bag with the long

strap down on the table. "I thought we were talking about those who are wed. I didn't know you were married, my lady."

"I'm no'," she said, already wishing she hadn't responded so quickly. "I meant that ye shouldna be talkin' about such things ... in front of the child."

"Oh, yes. I see. My fault," he said, pulling out a chair and nodding toward it. "Will you be joining us for the lesson?"

Lark looked at the chair he offered, feeling dumbfounded. No man had ever pulled out a chair for her before.Yet he, the uninformed scribe who didn't seem to know a thing about how to act when in the presence of nobles, was doing something not required at all. She wasn't even sure how to respond. She had been so busy trying to act and sound noble so he wouldn't think of her in a negative way that she was taken aback by his manners. Especially since she'd been convinced up until this point that he didn't have any at all.

"Nay. I'll be across the room. Working on ... my stitchin'," she said, walking over and picking up a basket with stitching in it that she'd found there when she came to Blake Castle and started using this room. She wasn't sure whose it was, but neither did it matter. The distraction would at least keep her away from the scribe.

"What is it that you're working on?" he asked curiously, unpacking his bag. He put a book on the table, as well as a bottle of ink, a quill, and a blank piece of parchment.

"It doesna matter. Just please get to work. I am not payin' ye for idle chatter."

"I wouldn't dream of it," he said. "By the way, we haven't discussed yet what I'll be paid to tutor your child."

Lark's head jerked upward. She had no idea what amount tutors were paid, but she didn't want to admit it.

"Speak to my father about that," she told him.

"I thought you told me I was to report to you regarding the

child. So, that means, you aren't the one paying me for my services after all?"

"What price are ye expectin' to get?" she asked, throwing it back at him.

"Tutors are paid well," he said, not giving her a direct answer. She wasn't sure if this meant he had no idea of what amount to ask, or perhaps he wasn't going to say a price, hoping for more than was sufficient. Either way, she didn't want to handle this. She just wanted the man to leave her alone.

"I assure ye, that ye will be paid accordingly, as I see fit by how much my daughter learns from ye."

That shut him up. His smile faded and he seemed perturbed by the thought that if he wasn't good enough, he'd be paid less. He uncorked the bottle of ink, still looking over at her. She purposely glanced down at the stitching in her hand, trying to ignore him, as well as to make sense out of what it was supposed to be that she was stitching.

"I want to write somethin'," said Florie, standing up on the chair and reaching for his bottle of ink. His hand shot out and he grabbed it just before Florie knocked the ink over.

"Nay," he scolded. "That is for me. Now sit down. You are too young to write. First, I will teach you to read."

Lark's gaze shot over to what was happening, but she didn't say a word.

"I dinna want to sit," said the girl in a huff, crossing her arms over her chest, still standing on the chair. "Mother, I want to write. Tell the man to let me do it."

"Scribe, just let her scribble something before you start the lesson," said Lark, not wanting any trouble to occur. She focused on pulling the colored thread through the cloth with the needle.

"Scribe?" he repeated what she'd called him. "My name is Dustin," he so bluntly reminded her.

Lark should have probably reprimanded him for speaking to her that way, but honestly, she was glad he'd told her his name because she had already forgotten it.

"Dustin," she repeated, still focused on her stitching. "That is an odd name." She kept her head down but quickly glanced up at him. He was still scowling.

"Lark is an odd name too," was his answer.

"Lady Lark," she reminded him with a sigh. This man must have been living like a hermit to constantly forget how he was required to act around nobles.

"Lady Lark," he repeated softly.

"That's better," she said with a nod. When she didn't hear him say anything, she glanced back up to see him staring at her, and he wasn't smiling.

"Is somethin' the matter?" she asked him.

"I think it would be best if I spent the day getting to know Florie first." He corked up the bottle and put it back into the bag. "We can start the lessons tomorrow."

"That's a feather," said Florie, reaching out and grabbing his quill, smashing the delicate barbs in her fist. "Do ye have a birdie?"

"Nay, I don't have a bird. And that is for me to write with, not for you to play with," he explained.

"Fly, fly, fly," shouted Florie, waving the quill in the air, getting ready to throw it across the room.

"That's enough," said Dustin, snatching the quill away from her. His eyes narrowed and his teeth seemed to be clenched.

Florie started to cry and ran over to Lark.

"That man is mean," wailed Florie.

Lark chuckled to herself, almost glad this happened. After all, the scribe seemed to judge her, saying in so many words that she was a bad mother. Then, after he was able to stop the chaos with the dogs so easily, it had impressed but upset her. It had made her wonder if she really wasn't good at being a parent after all. But now, she almost let out a sigh of relief at seeing this. The scribe had become just as flustered around Florie as she felt most of the time.

"I'm sorry if I upset the child. I didn't mean to," he said, pushing the book back into his bag. "I'll leave now and return tomorrow." He slipped the strap of his tutoring bag over his shoulder and headed for the door.

"Ye're leavin'? Already?" asked Lark, standing up, putting Florie down. "Where are ye goin'?" Part of her actually liked having him here. She hadn't met anyone new in a long time, and didn't really have conversations with anyone besides her cousins. It was especially nice to be around a good-looking man. Even if this one was only a simple commoner who knew nothing about life at the castle. Still, it felt good to have someone to talk to.

"I don't feel that we've started off in the best light, or that this is going well at all," he told her, sounding conflicted. "I'd like to leave now and think things over."

"Oh. I see," said Lark, upset that he was leaving. "So, this was all just a waste of time today, I guess."

"Waste of time?" He looked back over his shoulder.

Florie ran over to Lord Corbett's bed and started jumping on it now.

Dustin stood in the doorway, shaking his head. "This is going to be more of a challenge than I thought," he mumbled, not looking at Florie this time, but instead, his eyes were focused directly on her.

"What does that mean, scribe?"

As soon as the word scribe left her mouth, she realized

what a mistake she'd made. She should have called him by his name, but it was too late now.

"On second thought, I think you'd better find another tutor for the child, my lady."

"Another tutor? Whatever for? I have ye."

"Nay, you don't have me, my lady. I quit."

CHAPTER 4

Lark entered the great hall the next morning, holding Florie's hand. Lark had been so upset by the tutor quitting, that she had tossed and turned all night long, unable to sleep.

"There's my little granddaughter," said Wren, coming over to take Florie from Lark. "Good morning, Lark." She picked up Florie.

"Good mornin', Mother." Lark stifled a yawn.

"How did Florie's first lesson go with the tutor yesterday?"

"It didna."

"What do you mean?"

"I mean, the man quit. Now, I have no one to teach my child and will probably no' find another."

"Did I hear that the tutor quit?" Raven walked up, holding on to her husband's arm. Jonathon was a master armorer, but received the courtesy title of lord since marrying Raven.

"The scribe is gone?" asked Jonathon in surprise.

"Yes, he doesna want to teach Florie, and it's just as well," said Lark, not wanting everyone gossiping about this now. She just knew the wagging tongues would turn this around and make it sound like she was to blame or that the man didn't want to be around her bastard child.

"Just as well?" asked Wren. "What does that mean?"

"I'd rather no' talk about this now," said Lark. "I see Uncle Corbett motionin' for us to be seated so the meal can start."

"Oh, yes. You're right," said Wren. "I'll let Florie sit with me for the meal."

Once they were all seated and the meal began, Raven leaned over to talk with Lark.

"What really happened involving the scribe?" asked Raven.

"I told ye. He quit." Lark reached over and took a bun from the tray a servant placed on the table.

"But why did he quit? Something must have happened." Raven took a bun and passed the platter to her husband.

"I didna scare him off, if that is what ye'er thinkin'." Lark held out her goblet and the cup bearer filled it with wine.

"I didn't say that, Lark." Raven waved the cup bearer away so she could talk without the boy listening. "Dustin seems like a nice man. He's handsome, too, in case you didn't notice."

"I might have noticed." Lark chose some vegetables from a platter that a servant held out to her, and Raven did the same before the girl walked away. "What does it matter? He couldna handle Florie and that is what scared him off."

"Really." Raven's tone told Lark that she didn't believe it. "It was just Florie who scared him off?"

"Och, all right, I suppose I could have treated the man a little nicer. Raven, I was so nervous and was just tryin' to act the way a noble is expected to act."

"Mmm hmm," said Raven, taking a sip of wine. "Lark, you don't want Dustin thinking bad things about you, do you?"

"Bad things?" Lark jerked, and spilled a drop of wine. "Do ye really think Dustin is talkin' bad about me?"

"If he quit a good-paying job at the castle, something you did must have really upset him."

"Oh, cousin, I have to admit that I was so scared bein' alone with a man that I guess I might have come across as demandin' or stuffy."

"Scared?" Raven laughed. "Dustin was raised with gentle monks. The man is harmless. Besides, Florie was there too. It wasn't like he was trying to seduce you."

"Nay," she said, forgetting what that was like. It had been so long since a man showed true interest in her that even if the scribe tried to woo her, she probably wouldn't even know it. "I suppose I overreacted. Mayhap the man got the wrong impression of me, after all."

"You'd better go to the monastery and get him back right after the meal."

"Me? Ye think I should go after him? Really?"

"Well, if you don't, he won't return. Ask yourself if you want a tutor for Florie or not."

"I do, but I canna go back to the monastery and seek him out. It wouldna be right. Perhaps I can send a messenger to fetch him."

"Nay, Lark. It sounds as if you acting so far above his status might have been what scared him off in the first place. If you go there yourself, you won't come across as being so high and mighty."

"I agree," said Jonathon from beside her. "Not that I'm trying to eavesdrop, but speaking from experience, a commoner is easily discouraged being around nobles. The lives of the nobles are much different than those who come from below the salt."

"That's true," said Raven. "I know that, because I spent time with Jonathon's family in town before we were married. Commoners have a rough life, Lark. You need to be gentle, caring, and kind with someone who is less fortunate than you."

"Raven, you don't need to make it sound like commoners are pathetic," complained Jonathon from the side of his mouth.

"Sorry, sweetheart. I didn't mean it that way." Raven reached up and kissed her husband on the cheek, making Lark feel even more lonely.

"Will ye go with me to the monastery?" Lark asked Raven.

"I can't," said Raven. "I promised to help Jonathon in the smithy. Today is the day everyone is gathering to celebrate the launch of his new shop. His entire family will be here when the door to the new smithy is opened."

"I see," said Lark, feeling too unsure of herself to go to the monastery alone. "Well, mayhap it would be better if I just waited to see if Dustin returns on his own."

"Nay, Lark. Go and get him. If you don't want to make the trip alone, ask a page to escort you," was Raven's suggestion.

"I'm no' sure," said Lark, looking at all the happy couples sitting around her. If only things could be different, mayhap she wouldn't have to constantly feel like an outcast around her own family. "I think I'd like to be here for the openin' of the new smithy, too," she told Raven.

"What about the scribe?" asked Raven. "You're not going after him to ask him to return as tutor?"

"Mayhap no' today," said Lark, busying herself by pushing her food around her trencher with her spoon. "There are too many more important things goin' on right now."

Lark said the words, but in her heart she felt like nothing short of a liar. The most important thing to her was to find love with a man, and to find a father for Florie.

That thought hit her hard. After all, what did the scribe have to do with any of this? And why had he entered her thoughts of finding a man to love? They were speaking of

Dustin and him tutoring her daughter, naught else. After all, she was a noble and he was just a poor commoner from below the salt.

~

DUSTIN BENT over the manuscript he was transcribing, sitting in the dark of the monastery's scriptorium with nothing but the light of one beeswax candle next to him. After returning here yesterday, he decided that mayhap he didn't want to be the child's tutor after all. Perhaps, in the monastery is where he would stay for the rest of his life. Here, he had time to quiet his mind and live peacefully. Life at the castle seemed busy and very noisy. This was something he really wasn't used to, and neither was he sure he liked it.

The door to the scriptorium opened, sunlight illuminating the room. Brother Ruford walked in, leaving the door open, walking over to see him.

"I thought you took the job at the castle, as the child's tutor," said Ruford in a hushed tone. There were several other monks busy at work in the room, transcribing and illuminating the vellum pages with important works.

"I did, but I quit." Dustin dipped the quill back into the ink well.

"Why?" asked Ruford. "Was my brother not accommodating?"

"Nay, Lord Corbett had nothing to do with this." Dustin scratched a few more letters onto the page, not offering more of an explanation.

"This has something to do with Lady Lark, doesn't it?" asked Ruford. "Dustin, don't let her reputation scare you away."

"What reputation?" he asked, fully aware of what the

monk meant. Still, he didn't see any need to bring it up since it had nothing to do with his situation. One thing Dustin never liked was gossip, even if at times he did listen to it. Then again, it was the only way he really knew what was happening in the world outside of the monastery. Usually, what he learned was from the peasants, whores, and fishmongers when he went to town.

"Won't you give her another chance?" asked the monk.

"She doesn't need or want me there." He continued to write.

"No?" asked the monk. "Then why is she waiting to talk to you right now out in the courtyard?"

"She is?" When Dustin looked up, he saw the bright red of Lark's gown. She stood in the open doorway, peering into the darkness.

"Holy hell, what is she doing here?" groaned Dustin.

"Dustin, please, watch your language," warned Ruford. The other two monks in the room looked up, and then back down to their work again.

"Tell her I'm not interested." Dustin was so upset by this, that a big blob of ink splotched over the page. "God's eyes, nay!" He grabbed a cloth to wipe it up, but Ruford's hand covered his. "I know, I know. Stop with the blasphemy," grumbled Dustin, once again letting loose with his emotions when he should have stuffed them instead.

"You can confess it all to me later. Now, give me the rag." Ruford held out his hand. "I'll clean up your mess here, but you go out there and clean up that mess on your own."

"All right," said Dustin, with a sigh. "But I just want you to know, it is not me making a mess of this situation."

"You can tell God that, but I doubt he'll believe it. Now go."

Dustin wiped off his hands and left the room, stepping out

into the bright sunlight. "My lady," he said with a slight bow. "What brings you to the monastery?"

"What is that room?" asked Lark, trying to look around him. "It is so dark in there."

"That is the scriptorium, where we transcribe and illuminate books."

"Can I see what it looks like?" She said it too loudly, sticking her head into the room. He heard the monks making a shushing sound, since it was forbidden to speak in the scriptorium. Talking would only cause the monks to lose focus on their important work.

"Mayhap later," said Dustin, reaching out and closing the door. "Shall we walk?" He motioned with his arm.

"My page is waitin' for me," she told him, nodding at a young boy standing next to their horses. "I canna be long. Today is the day that the new smithy is openin' at the castle, and there is goin' to be a huge celebration."

"I see. Well, then tell me what brings you here, and I won't waste any more of your precious time, my lady."

"Och, I didna mean it like that. I meant … I mean … mayhap a quick stroll through the cloisters would be all right."

"Right this way, my lady." This time, Dustin led the way, making sure not to get ahead of her, but letting her walk at his side. He headed to the gardens surrounded by the covered walkways of the monastery.

"My lady, shall I come with you?" called out the page standing by the horses.

"Nay, Alfred, I'll be right back," said Lark. "Stay there."

Somehow, Dustin was glad she told the boy to stay behind. It made him feel better not to be leading a procession of those from the castle, traipsing through the secluded area where he lived.

Several monks in hooded robes walked past them.

"Hello," Lark called out to them, but they didn't even look up.

"No' very friendly, are they?" she asked.

"These are Benedictine monks," Dustin told her. "They have certain times of the day that they are forbidden to speak and this is one of them."

"But ye are talkin' to me. And so did Brother Ruford." She obviously didn't understand.

"Brother Ruford is allowed to speak. He is the abbot. I am not a monk, my lady, so the rules don't apply to me. Or haven't you noticed?" His hood was down, and he picked up the ends of his long hair to show her that he didn't have a tonsure like the rest of them.

"Of course, I noticed," she said, seeming to get flustered and flushed in the face. He wasn't sure why.

LARK THOUGHT the man's hair was beautiful. It was oaken brown and almost as long as hers. When Dustin picked it up to show it to her, she felt an odd sort of attraction to him. It made a wave of heat course through her. She didn't understand why, but she supposed it was because she was so close to a handsome man, even if he was ... or wasn't a monk. Ever since she'd been seduced by the Frenchman, Lord Gregoire Chastain, she had been leery of all men. The cur got her pregnant and left, never to return.

"So, did you seek me out for a reason?" asked Dustin, bringing Lark back to the moment.

"Yes," she said, taking a deep breath and releasing it. "I would like ye to come back to the castle to be my daughter's tutor."

"Oh, that," he said, sounding less than enthused to be

revisiting this subject. "I'm not sure it is going to work out, my lady. Perhaps you should look elsewhere."

"I'll pay you more than most tutors. I mean, since ye are teachin' a lassie instead of a laddie."

"You mean, because no one else will."

"Aye. That too," she admitted.

They turned and walked into a private garden behind the kitchen that was really only used for growing food, and not visited by anyone other than the monks who cooked.

"Your daughter needs to be disciplined, or she will never be able to learn a thing."

"I am doin' my best, but as ye ken, Florie doesna have a father."

"Nay?" he asked, looking at her from the sides of his eyes and raising a brow.

"I mean, she does have one but ... but I am no' married. There. Is that what ye wanted to hear me say?" The thought of even admitting this aloud was making her nerves shake. Lark didn't like to talk about this, and neither did she appreciate anyone forcing her to say she had a child out of wedlock. "Mayhap, I was wrong to come here. I'm goin' to leave," she said, quickly turning on her heel, twisting her ankle. "Oh!" she cried out.

Before she even had a chance to fall, two strong arms were around her, bringing her back to a standing position. Dustin stood face to face with her now, his arms around her waist. She looked up into his mysterious dark eyes, feeling entranced. The breeze lifted his long hair around his shoulders, and the scent of ink and parchment, or mayhap books, seemed to cling to his clothing.

"Thank ye," she managed to squeak out, seeing his gaze settle on her mouth. Something inside her came to life. The urge to kiss him almost overwhelmed her, making her feel heady. She closed her eyes and swayed, holding tightly to his arms.

"My lady, are you ill?" he asked, his deep voice right next to her ear. A shiver went through her. It wasn't because she was cold on this warm day. Nay, it was because she wanted, needed, to feel alive again in the presence of a man. However, this was wrong. This man lived in a monastery and was close to being a monk. The last thing he needed was to be with someone like her. Her sins alone could probably make the walls around here crumble.

"I-I'm fine," she said, pushing away from him, not trusting herself to touch him again. If she did, she was going to want to kiss him. God's toes, what was wrong with her? Didn't she learn her lesson the first time around? "I just twisted my ankle, that's all."

"Can you walk?" he asked.

"Sure," she said, taking a step and feeling the pain. She must have winced because he knew it.

"Nay, you are hurt. Come back to the infirmary and one of the monks will take a look at it."

"If ye dinna mind, I'd rather just go back to the castle. Can ye help me to my horse?"

"Of course, my lady. Hold on to my arm."

Lark was reluctant to touch the man again, because she found him attractive and couldn't trust herself anymore to make proper decisions. Her life was a mess from her past decisions. A cacophony of chastising voices filled her head at every minute of the day reminding her of her mistakes. She was constantly judging herself, the inner voices making her feel less than worthy of enjoying even a bit of goodness in her life. She didn't deserve it, is what those dark voices had embedded into her mind over the years.

Dustin lifted her up to her horse, and once again, she

reveled in the feel of his touch. Why did she long for this so much? Why couldn't she just forget all about men?

"I'm coming with you," said Dustin, taking the reins of her horse, walking next to her. The page mounted his horse and followed.

"Ye are? Why?"

"Well, you said there was a celebration going on for the opening of the expanded smithy at the castle, didn't you?"

"Why, yes. I'm sure ye are welcome there. But why do ye even want to join in?"

"I feel it is necessary," said Dustin.

"Ye do?"

"Aye," he answered, looking up at her with a smile. "After all, if I'm going to be your daughter's tutor, I need to start getting her used to me, don't you agree?"

"Och, so ye will return to the job then after all?" she asked, feeling excited about the notion.

"I will," he told her. "After all, I don't want your trip to the monastery to have been nothing but a waste of your precious time."

All of the sudden, Lark began to feel insecure again. This sounded a lot like sarcasm, referring to her comment of him wasting her time right before he quit. Self-doubt reared its ugly head once again and she wondered if Dustin was trying to hurt her.

All she could think was that she hoped she was wrong about him. Lark wanted that more than anything right now, because she really wanted Dustin to stay.

CHAPTER 5

O nce Dustin caught Lark in his arms, he realized he didn't want to let her go. Therefore, he did the only thing he could. He agreed to return to the castle as her daughter's tutor. He was either infatuated with her, or a fool, or mayhap both for agreeing to do this. Still, he thought Lark was a beautiful woman, and he wanted to get to know her better.

He couldn't even imagine how devastating it must be for her to have a child out of wedlock. Being a noble, this was something that could ruin a person's life. Dustin didn't care about her past. The way he saw it, nothing in one's past really mattered. The only thing that counted was if a lesson was learned in the end by the mistakes made. Or, perhaps mistake wasn't even the right word, but it was a troubling situation.

Even though Dustin was raised by monks and had attended most of the masses and prayer sessions his entire life, he was far from being a holy man. He often cursed, bedded wenches, drank heavily on occasion, and even enjoyed the pleasures of life that money could buy. That is, he thought he would enjoy the pleasures of money though he couldn't be sure since he never really had much.

"Lark, hurry, or you'll miss it," called out Lady Raven from the castle, running over to meet them. The courtyard was filled with people and also commotion. "Oh, hello, Dustin," said Raven.

"Good day, my lady," Dustin answered with a bow.

Dustin was familiar with the nobles at Blake Castle, since the monastery was close by and the nobles often visited or asked Dustin to transcribe things for them on occasion. However, he never really had conversations with any of them so he didn't know them well. Only with Orrick did he feel comfortable.

"Are you here for the celebration?" asked Raven. "My husband's new, expanded smithy is finished and will be open for business today."

"Aye, Jonathon is lucky to be the castle's blacksmith," said Dustin, knowing Jonathon as well, who was a commoner and used to live in town.

"I'm a lord now, so address me as Lord Jonathon, or Master Armorer, not blacksmith," said Raven's husband, coming over to greet them, laughing when he said it. "Dustin, so good to see you again."

Dustin clasped hands with the man, not exactly sure how to act now that Jonathon was no longer the town's armorer but the husband of a noblewoman.

"I'm happy for you ... Master Armorer ... Lord Jonathon," said Dustin, tripping over his own words.

Jonathon leaned over and whispered. "I don't really care what the hell you call me, but since it's a big day for me at the castle, mayhap you can just go along with it for now?"

"Of course," Dustin answered, feeling immediately at ease.

Jonathon was still one of them. A commoner, but in nobles' clothing.

"I'm glad I dinna miss the celebration," said Lark, suddenly standing beside Dustin.

"My lady," he said in surprise, not even having heard her approach. "I could have helped you from your horse. Is your ankle still hurting?"

"Did you injure yourself, Lark?" asked Raven.

"I'll be fine," said Lark. "I just twisted it a little, but it is already feelin' better." Her bright green eyes flashed over to Dustin, and he swore he saw a blush color her cheeks.

"Master Armorer," called out Lord Corbett from in front of the new smithy. "We are ready to lift our cups in celebration and open the shop. Please join us."

"I have to go. Are you coming, Raven?" asked Jonathon, excitement and urgency in his voice.

"I wouldn't miss this for the world." Raven took her husband's hand. They hurried over to the smithy together. Dustin could see that the two of them were truly in love.

The old blacksmith's shop at Blake Castle had been small and daunting at one time. When Jonathon and Raven fell in love and married, the position of not only castle blacksmith was given to Jonathon, but the guild also made him a master armorer after he earned the title with his elegant work. Jonathon was skilled in the arts of being a blacksmith, swordsmith, and also an armorer. Therefore, he was in need of his own shop. Lord Corbett expanded the one at the castle for him, building in the luxuries of a bigger forge, gigantic bellows, and a large clean area to work. Dustin hadn't actually seen the improvements, but had heard all about them from Brother Ruford who spent a lot of time at Blake Castle.

There was a room built into the back of the shop to live in, where Jonathon's brother Avery would stay since he was the journeyman. And little ten-year-old Gerold was an apprentice, and would live there as well. Gerold was the son of the late blacksmith whom Jonathon replaced.

"Would you like some heather ale, my lady?" asked a kitchen maid, holding a tray of tankards filled with ale made from the popular Scottish flower, heather.

"Yes, I would." Lark took one, and looked over at Dustin. "Please, raise a cup with us in celebration."

"I'd be honored." Dustin collected a tankard of ale as well.

"I'd like everyone's attention," shouted Lord Corbett. "Today, we are celebrating the new shop of our master armorer who is also the new husband of my daughter, Lady Raven. This is a prestigious position, and a smithy that is well needed by all. Please raise your tankards to celebrate the success of my son-by-marriage, Lord Jonathon Armstrong." Corbett lifted his tankard in the air.

Shouts went up from the crowd and cheery music started to play. There was a blanket hanging over the door to the shop, and Jonathon walked up and pulled it down, getting another cheer from the crowd.

"The smithy is now open, so come inside," shouted Jonathon, holding out his arm to his new shop. His brother, parents, and siblings crowded around him, entering the smithy to get their first glimpses of the improved work area. Dogs barked and children ran around playing. A juggler walked past, tossing small colored bags filled with sand in the air.

"Egads, no one made such a fuss about us like this," complained Corbett's son, Rook, stepping up with a tankard to join them.

· · ·

"Rook? Ye're here?" Lark was surprised to see her cousin and his new wife, Rose, who was the daughter of the late master gardener.

"Of course, I am," said Rook. "Just because I have my own manor now, doesn't mean I'm never coming back to Blake Castle."

"Is that Lord Morcant I see talkin' to Lord Corbett and my father?" Lark stretched her neck to see, sure that it was. "And he has his new French bride with him?" She groaned.

"Yes," answered Rook.

Rook was once betrothed to the Frenchwoman who was anything but nice.

"I wonder who invited them?" asked Lark.

"Rook, be nice," said Rose in a soft voice.

"Och, I see Lady Adeline's parents here too," said Lark, feeling horrified now. Lady Adeline had looked down her nose at Lark and said some horrible things about her.

"Her parents didn't leave yet," Rook told her. "However, I hear they are going back to France right after this celebration."

Lark noticed her Uncle Corbett handing a rolled-up parchment to Lord Morcant.

"What is that parchment your father is givin' Lord Morcant?" asked Lark, curious as to the nature of it.

"Who the hell knows," grumbled Rook. "Hopefully it is a notice telling the French to leave and never return."

"Rook, don't let them bother you. We're married now, so forget all about them," Rose told him.

"Aye, but I still have no desire to see or talk to them at all," he told his wife.

"Well, I am going over there to congratulate Lord Jonathon and Lady Raven," said Rose.

"No matter who is standing there with them, I don't care." Rose was a petite woman with long blonde hair and a cute little turned-up nose. She held the title of Lady now, although she was only a commoner like Jonathon. Rose was a determined woman, and no one was going to scare her off if there was something she wanted to do. Lark liked that about her.

"Rose, it is so good to see ye again," said Lark. She had become close to the woman when she'd recently spent time at Horrabridge Manor. Or Rookrose Manor, as Rook now renamed it.

"She is Lady Rose now," Rook reminded her. "My wife has a title, just like my sister's husband."

"Of course, Lady Rose," said Lark. She and Rose exchanged glances, almost laughing aloud at how insistent Rook was about this. Lark didn't care because she was good friends with Rose either way.

"That's better," said Rook, finally content.

"Did ye see Robin before he left for his new castle in Shrewsbury?" asked Lark, just to shut Rook up. She knew he would be green with envy.

"Yes, I wished him well. Excuse me, but my wife and I need to congratulate Jonathon," said Rook, leaving abruptly, holding Rose's hand.

Lark giggled.

"I sense a little animosity between you two?" asked Dustin.

"Oh, nay, not at all," Lark told him. "I just like to tease my cousin since he constantly gives me a good helpin' of grief. I'm just returnin' the favor. All in good fun, of course."

"Of course," said Dustin, looking totally confused.

"Mother, I want to learn to juggle," said Florie, running up holding three of the juggler's sand bags. The man waved a fist at her from the middle of a group of children, realizing she had stolen them from him.

"Florie, I think we need to return those to the juggler. Excuse me, Dustin, I have to see to my child." Lark put her hand on Florie's shoulder and directed her back to the juggler, scolding Florie, but in a very mild manner.

DUSTIN WATCHED Lark walking away as if nothing was wrong with her ankle at all. Mayhap she had faked twisting her ankle just so he would help her. The idea pleased him, actually. That would mean she was interested in him. He'd never had a noble lady take notice of him before. Dustin was glad to see Lark tending to her child. He was starting to think that mayhap this job as the child's tutor wouldn't be so bad after all.

"Oh, there you are, scribe," said Lord Corbett. He, Lark's father, and the old sorcerer Orrick walked over to join him.

"Lord Corbett, Laird MacKeefe," said Dustin, bowing to them. "Hello, Orrick," he added, nodding to his friend.

"Dustin, since you have returned, does that mean you will be tutor to Lady Lark's daughter after all?" asked Orrick. His eyes sparkled with mischief if Dustin wasn't mistaken.

"Aye, I've decided to give it a try."

"Blethers, that is music to my ears," said Storm, looking happy all of a sudden. "Ye'll be paid well if ye can somehow tame my little granddaughter. She has a troublesome side that is even more worrisome than that of her mother."

"Florie is a delightful child, but just needs attention and understanding," said Dustin, getting a snort from Storm.

"Well, I give her plenty of attention. Too much, actually, between me and my wife doting over her all the time," Storm told him.

"Dustin, Orrick tells me you'd be interested in the position of castle scribe," said Corbett.

"Well, I was considering the position. If it's available," said Dustin, glancing back at Orrick for verification.

"Of course it is," said Orrick. "Lord Corbett, I advise that we

57

hire this man immediately before he gets away. After all, he is the best scribe at the monastery."

"Done," said Corbett before Dustin even had a chance to respond to Orrick's compliment. "Dustin, you'll report to Orrick from now on. He knows exactly what I need. Actually, there will be letters arriving soon from all over, and I'll need you to collect them, record them, and give them to Lady Lark."

"My lord?" asked Dustin, not sure what he meant.

"Lord Corbett is helpin' me to find a suitable nobleman for my daughter to marry," said Storm.

"Really," said Dustin, not having expected this.

"I ken what ye're thinkin', since ye've probably heard the rumors, but no' every nobleman would be against marryin' a lady with a child out of wedlock," said Storm. "We've already sent out missives askin' those interested to join us at a feast bein' held right here at Blake Castle in a month's time."

"That's right," said Corbett. "However, there are more invitations to send out and I'll need you to write them for me, quickly."

"Of course, my lord," said Dustin, not sure he liked the sound of this first job of being castle scribe. He also didn't like the fact they were organizing a feast to try to get a nobleman to marry Lark.

Corbett continued to explain the situation. "This shouldn't be a problem, finding Lark a husband since there are widowers and lords down on their luck, as well as fourth sons of nobles, who would rather marry than join the church. No insult intended," said Corbett.

"None taken," answered Dustin. "Tell me, does Lady Lark know about this plan to find her a husband?"

"No' yet, but she'll be happy about it," said Storm. "Soon, she'll start gettin' letters from noblemen from England as well as Scotland."

"We've asked them to introduce themselves to Lady Lark through letters," said Corbett. "That way, she can feel like she knows them before they even arrive here at the castle."

"Interesting idea," said Dustin, not sure how to respond to this. He had the feeling Lark was going to hate it.

"Actually, to soften the blow, I intend to tell my daughter that she can choose whichever of the noblemen she wants to marry." Storm actually looked proud of this decision, as if it would make everything in Lark's life better. Dustin wasn't so sure about that.

"So, you think there will be a lot of noblemen interested in marrying your daughter?" Dustin asked Storm.

"Och, yes," said Storm with a swish of his hand through the air. "With the dowry I am offerin', I canna see anyone willingly turnin' it away."

The way the men talked, it seemed to Dustin that they were desperate to find a nobleman for Lark to marry and would pay any amount to make it happen. Or bribe them, that is.

"Yes, I am sure a huge dowry would be tempting for anyone, my lords. Even a thief," said Dustin, trying to subtly suggest that they might only be attracting greedy or no-good men by dangling a bunch of money and jewels in their faces. To him, it seemed Lark was an afterthought and this was being done only to save face for the MacKeefe clan. He didn't like the idea of bribery at all. Not when it came to marriage - something he considered sacred in his mind.

"Nay, no thieves," said Corbett. "Since my own son and daughter married commoners, it is important that Lady Lark marry a noble. These noblemen are handpicked and can be trusted."

Dustin felt like snorting aloud at that remark. Living at the monastery, he'd housed many traveling nobles, and some of them were the most dishonorable men he'd ever met.

"Once Lark is married, in time, the gossip of her havin' a child out of wedlock will fade away," said Storm. "Hopefully, eventually, everyone will forget about her tarnished past."

"Yes, I can see how important that would be. To a noble, that is." It was getting harder for Dustin to bite his tongue and not tell these men exactly how he felt. He would be best off right now just walking away.

A few knights came up to talk to the Corbett and Storm, so Dustin silently stepped back from the men, glad this conversation was over. He looked for Lark who was giving the sand bags back to the juggler. Florie, of course, was crying again. The child seemed to do that a lot whenever she didn't get her way. Could no one other than himself see this?

Even so, Dustin's heart went out to Lark. She had her hands full. He couldn't imagine how horrible it must be for her. She'd been used by a noble and now her father and uncle expected her to marry one who would most likely only be doing it for the money involved. Lark deserved better than that. Florie, though a high-spirited child, needed a father. Neither of them needed a greedy man lured into a marriage by the amount of money or jewels he'd gained in the agreement.

"You are upset by what Lords Corbett and Storm are doing," said Orrick, coming up behind him. Dustin had almost forgotten the sorcerer was still there.

"It's none of my business, although I wish I could voice my opinion about the situation," said Dustin, his eyes still fastened on Lark.

"I agree with you."

"What? You do?" Dustin's gaze broke and he looked over at Orrick. "Oh, you mean that it is none of my business?"

"Nay, I mean that I agree with you that Lark deserves

someone better than who she will most likely get for a husband."

"I didn't say that," protested Dustin, shaking his head. A statement like that made by a commoner could land him in the stocks or mayhap even the dungeon.

"I might be Lord Corbett's advisor, but I'm not the girl's father," said Orrick.

"What does that mean?" asked Dustin.

"It means I have no control over what Storm MacKeefe decides is best for his children."

"Aye, no one does."

"Mayhap you can change things, though."

"Me? I'm only a commoner." Dustin's palm hit against his chest. "Why would you think I could do a single thing to change the situation?"

"Well, the way I see it, you have a lot of work to do if you're going to stop Lady Lark from having to marry a greedy noble who will most likely be older than her father."

"I'm sorry, Orrick, I don't know what you're talking about."

"Of course, you do. You have eyes for the girl, it's no secret."

He looked back at Lark. "I cannot deny that I think she is beautiful and intriguing. Even if we seemed to have clashed when we first met."

"If you're going to woo her, you need to do so fast. Those letters will be arriving from her suitors any day now, and in a month's time or less, her father will have married her off to some greedy cur who can never make her happy."

"Woo her?" Dustin's heart jumped into his throat. "Is that what you said?"

"Aye. You heard me."

"Orrick, you are a magic man, you do something to help her. I'm only a commoner. I don't belong with a noblewoman, even if she is a tarnished or a flawed one. Besides, Lady Lark would never be interested in someone from below the salt. I haven't got a shot in hell of ever marrying her." This thought had never entered Dustin's head until the sorcerer just put it there. Now, he wasn't sure if the thought would ever leave.

"Mayhap not, but you are from the monastery, so you, of all people, should believe in miracles."

"I'm sorry to say, old man, that even though I was raised by monks and forced to attend mass and pray, I honestly don't believe in miracles in the least."

"Hmmm," said Orrick, stroking his long beard in thought. "Well, Dustin, mayhap it is time you start believing."

CHAPTER 6

I t had been two full days since Dustin came to the castle to tutor Florie, but Lark had yet to see him at her door. She walked into the great hall with Florie later that evening, meaning to ask Dustin about it, but she couldn't find him.

Seeing Raven talking with her mother, Devon, Lark headed over to them. "Have either of you seen Dustin?" she asked.

"Nay, I haven't seen him," Raven answered.

"Well, he was supposed to start tutoring Florie, and he hasna taught her a thing. I havena even been able to find him for the past two days. I wonder if he went back to the monastery."

"I don't think so," said Devon. "I did see him bringing some of his things up to the tower."

"The tower?" asked Lark.

"Do you mean Orrick's room?" wondered Raven.

"Yes," said Devon. "I'm not certain but I think Corbett and Storm have him transcribing something very important and he is using Orrick's room to do it."

"Nothing is more important than tutorin' Florie, like he agreed," snapped Lark. "I'm goin' to go find him. Would ye two mind keepin' a close eye on Florie for me?"

"Of course, we will," said Devon. "But if Dustin is working, mayhap you shouldn't bother him."

"The only work he should be doing right now is for me."

Lark stormed off, heading up the stairs and to the tower where the sorcerer, Orrick lived. She stopped at the bottom of the spiral stairs that led to the chamber high above. Looking upward, she couldn't help but feel a little nervous. Lark had never been to the sorcerer's room before. Not many had. She hoped she wouldn't be turned into a toad just for knocking on his door. Still, she was so angry that Dustin hadn't even told her he was busy doing work for her father, that she decided she didn't care.

Lark marched right up the tower stairs, stopping at the old gnarled wooden door that had moons and stars and animals carved right into it. It was an interesting door that led to a room where magic supposedly happened. She raised her fist and knocked on it quickly, before she lost her nerve.

When no one answered, she knocked again. "Dustin, are ye in there?" she called out, leaning her ear against the door to hear any answers from inside the room.

Not hearing a response, she decided to leave. When she turned around, she thought she heard the squeak of hinges. When she looked over her shoulder she gasped, seeing the door opened a crack.

"Dustin?" she said softly, turning back and gently pushing the door open. "Dustin, are ye in here? Orrick? Anyone?"

No one answered.

Lark boldly entered the room, looking around with wide, curious eyes. A fire blazed on the hearth, lighting up the place.

Several candles burned brightly from different positions in the room. The light of the moon shown in through the very high window, making a stream of bluish white light that lit up the sorcerer's table in the center of the area.

"Mayhap he's out and I should just wait here for him to return. Yes, that is what I'll do," she spoke aloud to herself, taking a deep breath and releasing it. Slowly, she stepped into the room, leaving the door wide open.

Taking a moment, she surveyed her surroundings.

A tall, four-poster bed was against the far wall under the high, open window. It had long, purple, velvet bedcurtains surrounding a high mattress atop a small dais with two steps. My, she thought. This sorcerer lived like a noble.

Walking across the room, her attention was on the shelves next that held lots of old, dusty books. There were also jars with odd things floating in them that she couldn't identify, and neither did she even want to try. She shuddered and turned quickly, screaming when she saw a large owl staring at her from atop another shelf. It didn't move, and that is when she realized it was naught but a dead, stuffed bird.

There were a few stuffed rodents and even a bat. She held her arms around her, feeling suddenly cold. Then she saw a small desk-like table that was lifted on an angle at one end. The other half of the table was flat. A high stool was placed in front of it. She hurried over to realize it was a writing desk.

A piece of parchment that was spread out and clipped to the angled area, looked like someone had been working on it. On the flat part of the desk was an open bottle of ink, a quill, and at least a dozen or more folded-up missives.

"What's this?" she wondered, picking up a nearby lit candle, holding it up to the parchment to see the page. "It's beautiful," she said, gently reaching out and touching the letters scribed onto vellum. The writing was neat and concise. And running down the edge of the page was a design made of scrolling waves and even a small butterfly or two.

SHE FIGURED this was Dustin's work, since it was the desk of a scribe. As much as she was in awe of the beautiful work, her emotions changed quickly when she read the actual words on the page aloud.

Dearest lord and nobleman,

Your presence is requested at a banquet feast being held at Blake Castle in Devonshire on June 23rd, 1374. You are one of the select few who have been invited and who might be chosen by Laird and Chieftain Storm MacKeefe's daughter, Lady Lark.

"What? Me? And why does it say chosen?" asked Lark aloud. "Whatever are they talkin' about? I'm no' choosin' anyone for anythin'."

She continued to read.

While Lady Lark is unwed and has a bastard daughter, a huge dowry is being offered to the man who will be her husband to compensate for her tarnished past.

The list of money, silks, spices and jewels being offered as her dowry was listed on the parchment as well. "What?" she screeched aloud. "This canna be real."

When she read about the huge dowry being offered, she felt as if her father were desperate to marry her off, and was more or less bribing these lords to take her off his hands.

"Father, how could ye?" She clenched her jaw so tightly that it ached. Then, she finished reading the blasted missive.

You are invited to send a letter to Lady Lark at Blake Castle to introduce yourself ahead of time, since she will be choosing the nobleman who will be her husband. Don't turn down this wonderful offer, because it will never come again.

Laird and Chieftain, Storm MacKeefe.

By the time Lark finished reading the missive, her hands were shaking and her knees were knocking together as well. It wasn't because she was cold or lightheaded. Nay, it was because she was so angry that she was ready to choke someone.

She unclipped the missive from the desk and held it up to the flame of the candle. She meant to burn each and every invitation before they could be sent out.

"Lark, nay! What are you doing?" came Dustin's voice from the door. He ran into the room with Orrick right behind him. "Put that down at once." He ripped the missive from her hand, throwing it to the ground to stamp out the flames.

"How could ye?" Still holding on to the candle, it jerked up and down as she spoke. Hot wax flew in all directions.

Orrick quietly entered the room and closed the door, not saying a word.

"How could I what? And give me that before you burn yourself." Dustin took the candle from her, quickly blowing out the flame before he set it back down on the desk.

"What are you doing in my chamber?" Orrick finally spoke up.

"Yes, why are you here and how did you get in? The door was locked," Dustin told her.

"When ye promised to tutor my daughter and didna show up for the past two days, I came to find ye." Lark crossed her arms over her chest. "What I discovered instead, is ye writin' invites to noblemen, tellin' them I am a whore and bribin' them to marry me with a dowry that is fit for a queen!"

"Now, just a moment," said Dustin, feeling horrible right now that Lark had caught him scribing the invitations for her father. "None of this was my idea. I had to do it because I am the castle scribe and it is my job now. And no one ever called you a whore, so calm down please."

"Well, they might as well have called me that, since the missive tells everyone I am an unwed mother with a bastard child."

"I know," said Dustin, stepping on the burned parchment, stamping out the last of the smoldering flames. "I don't feel good about that part either."

"How could ye betray me like this?" she shrieked, making it sound like this whole thing was his fault.

"I didn't betray you!" he yelled back. "I was only doing my job."

"That's true, Lady Lark," said Orrick in a calm voice, from over by the bed. "It was all your father and Lord Corbett's idea to find you a nobleman to marry."

"This is degradin' and I willna stand for it. I am goin' to stop this at once by destroyin' all the invitations." Lark's face became red. She was so mad now. She reached for the folded-up missives on the table, but Dustin quickly snatched her hand away, holding tightly to her.

"Nay, Lady Lark. Don't do that."

"Let go of me," she fumed, struggling against his hold. Dustin slowly released her.

"I swear, I wanted to tutor Florie, and that is all I wanted to do," he said in his defense. "However, I was told to write these invites first so they can be sent out like the last batch."

"Last batch? There are more? Please tell me this isna true."

"Lady Lark, your father has already sent out the invitations to the noblemen of Scotland, and these are to the nobles in England," explained Orrick.

"Is that all the invitations?"

"Yes, all that I've written," said Dustin. "Why?"

"How many were sent to the Scottish lords?" asked Lark.

"About the same amount," said Orrick.

Dustin watched as Lark stretched her neck, seeming to count the missives from where she stood. There were just over a dozen.

"Why so few?" she asked, almost sounding insulted if Dustin wasn't mistaken.

"Excuse me?" he said to her. "I thought you were upset that any invitations at all went out and now you are wondering why there are not more?"

"How did my father and Lord Corbett decide which nobles to invite?" she demanded to know.

"It is not my position to assume I know the answer to that," said Dustin, not wanting to tell her the truth.

Lark spun around on her heel to face the sorcerer now. "Orrick? Ye are my uncle's advisor, so I am sure ye ken the answer to this."

"Aye, my lady, I do," said Orrick.

"Then tell me."

"Mayhap you should ask your father, instead," Dustin interrupted, not wanting Orrick to tell her and get involved.

"Mayhap ye need to keep yer opinions to yerself, scribe." Lark glared at him now.

Dustin didn't like it when Lark called him scribe. It made the difference in their statuses so much clearer and he didn't want to be reminded he was naught but a commoner and she was a noble. Even as tarnished as she might be.

"Lady Lark, your father and uncle are only doing this for your own good," Orrick told her. "You know better than anyone that you need a husband, not to mention a father for your daughter."

"No noble is goin' to agree to marry an unwed woman with a child born out of wedlock," said Lark. "Even with the large dowry offered, my guess is that these are nobles who are less than desirable themselves. Am I right?"

"Well ... I ..." Orrick looked over at Dustin but didn't answer.

"The truth! I want the truth," she screamed, her arms flailing in the air.

"Yes, Lady Lark, you are correct," said Orrick, sitting down on the bed and releasing a deep sigh. "Most of the nobles would not marry you no matter how much is being offered. This is your father's answer to solving that problem."

"I'm not a problem," said Lark, her bottom lip quivering. Her eyes became glassy and Dustin was sure she was about to cry.

"I'll be there to tutor Florie right after the main meal tomorrow morning," said Dustin, trying to change the subject.

"Fine," she said with a sniffle, picking up her skirts and running out the door.

"Orrick, that didn't go well," said Dustin. "And how the hell did she get into the room when the door was locked?"

"Everything happens for a reason," said the sorcerer, sounding mysterious again and making Dustin wonder if he had anything to do with it. "I think you'd better start wooing her, Dustin. Perhaps this happened for the best after all. It is important she knows what is going on since it involves her and her future."

Orrick walked over and collected the missives, leaving the burnt one, heading for the door. "I'll deliver these right away to Lord Corbett so he can have his messengers send them out. In the meantime, mayhap you should start thinking about how you can calm Lady Lark before she bites off your head again."

Orrick left the room, the door closing on its own. That told

Dustin that Orrick did have something to do with making sure Lark could enter the room and see those missives.

He picked up the burned missive from the floor, brushing it off, feeling like a traitor. Mayhap Orrick was right. If nothing else, there must be something he could do to help Lady Lark feel better.

CHAPTER 7

"Raven, I was horrified," Lark told her cousin the next day as she waited in Lord Corbett's solar for Dustin to arrive for Florie's lesson. "I canna believe my father would do such a thing." She had already explained the entire situation to Raven, looking for a shoulder to cry on.

"Lark, you are overreacting to this," said Raven. "My father and yours are only trying to help you."

"Ye dinna understand how it feels." She glanced over her shoulder to see if Florie was listening. The little girl insisted on dressing herself today, and managed to don her tunic and dress but was having trouble putting on her shoes. Still, it kept the child busy and out of trouble, so Lark decided to leave her for a while before she offered to help.

"I know exactly how it feels," said Raven, opening the shutter, letting in the fresh air. "Or have you forgotten that my father tried to give me away as the prize of a tournament?"

"Nay, I could never forget that." Lark remembered and shuddered.

"You, at least, can choose from the men, which one will be

your husband. I wasn't even allowed that! But I didn't have a child as part of the deal either." Raven leaned against the wall and stared out the window.

"Nay, Raven. Keep the shutter closed." Lark walked over and closed the shutter, locking it.

"But it is a beautiful day. Don't you want to feel the warmth of the sun and smell the fresh breeze in here?"

"Aye, but I also dinna want Florie fallin' out the window tryin' to catch a bird." She let out a deep sigh, looking back at her child who had decided to get undressed now and was standing there only in her long tunic, while her dress lay on the floor at her bare feet. "Florie, nay. Put yer clothes back on. Dustin will be here any minute."

"Mayhap finding a husband will be good for you, Lark. You can't go your whole life raising Florie on your own. It would be good for her to have a father, too."

"I suppose so, but I have a feelin' the nobles those invitations will attract will be boors and curs and men I dinna want touchin' me in the least."

"Then find a man on your own. To marry, I mean."

"Like ye did?" asked Lark.

"Well, sure, why not? Although, I wouldn't suggest falling in love with a commoner. Only because my father and yours will both have a hard time with that."

"I ken. Uncle Corbett thinks all of us should marry nobles only."

"Exactly."

"I'm beginnin' to think that noblemen are less than ideal husbands," said Lark.

"I have to agree," said Raven with a giggle. "Commoners from below the salt have less to prove and therefore they are more sincere. They also make wonderful, passionate lovers."

She whispered the last part behind her hand so Florie wouldn't hear her.

There came a knock on the door, making Lark jump in surprise. "Raven, it's Dustin. He's here to tutor Florie."

"Well, let him in," said Raven.

"I'm afraid to. I wasna very nice to him yesterday and I dinna feel good about the way I spoke to him."

"Just let him in, and stop worrying," said Raven, rolling her eyes. "I'll help Florie get dressed. Now go." Raven gave Lark a light push in the right direction.

Lark made her way to the door, now wishing for a chambermaid so she wouldn't have to face Dustin before he even entered the room. Mayhap she should have a nursemaid for Florie as well. Too late now, she realized, pulling open the door.

"Dustin," she said, smiling at him. Just hearing his name on her tongue took her breath away for some reason.

"My lady," he said with a slight bow, keeping his eyes downcast. "I am here for Lady Florie's lesson. May I enter?"

"Oh. Yes. Of course. Come in." She moved back so quickly that she stumbled slightly but righted herself instantly.

His head snapped around and his gaze went to the floor. "Is your ankle still hurting? Mayhap you need to sit down. I wouldn't want you to fall again."

"I am fine, I assure ye."

"Good, good," he said with a quick nod. Then he cleared his throat as if he were going to say something, but changed his mind at the last moment. "I'll just set up for Florie's lesson here."

"Yes, that will be fine."

He walked over to the table and unpacked his bag.

"Florie is almost ready," Raven called out. "She just needs her shoes."

"I dinna want shoes," complained the little girl with a pout. She sat down on the floor with her arms crossed. Raven looked up at Lark and shrugged, not knowing what to do.

"Florie, put yer shoes on, sweetheart," said Lark.

"Nay!" The little girl continued to pout.

"Allow me, my lady," said Dustin. "Florie, I am ready to teach you. Please come to the table."

"I dinna want to learn. I want to play."

"What do I do?" Lark whispered to Raven who shook her head, having no answer.

"Well, that's a shame," said Dustin, shaking his head as well. "I had a fun day planned, but since Florie isn't interested, I'll just leave then." Dustin started packing up his things again.

"Dustin?" asked Lark, not wanting him to go. He winked at her and she realized it was a ploy to lure Florie over. "All right. Goodbye, and sorry to waste yer time, but Florie doesna want to learn," said Lark.

Dustin was already opening the door to leave before Florie cried out.

"Nay! Wait. I want to have fun learnin'. I'll put on my shoes."

"Good girl," said Raven, helping her.

Florie rushed over to the table and sat down.

"Are you going to listen to your mother now? And not give her more problems?" asked Dustin.

"Uh huh." Florie nodded, sitting there like an angel. Lark's jaw dropped. She wasn't able to believe what had just happened.

"Then, let's get started." Dustin closed the door and came back to the table, talking to Florie as he unpacked his bag once again.

"My, he's good," whispered Raven, her eyes on Dustin as she came to stand by Lark.

"Yes, he is, isna he?" Lark's eyes were fixated on Dustin as well.

"Do you think he'll actually be able to teach Florie anything?" asked Raven.

"I am no' sure but I dinna care. Just as long as he keeps showin' up here, I'll be happy."

～

DUSTIN ENTERED Orrick's tower room later that day, feeling exhausted after just one lesson with the little rebellious girl.

"How did it go?" Orrick had bowls and cups on the table, mixing something up.

"It ...was rough," he said, tossing his bag with the supplies onto his desk. Then he kicked off his shoes and headed over to the pallet on the floor that Orrick had given him to sleep on while he was there. Dustin plopped down on his back and covered his face with his arm.

"Something troubling you?" asked Orrick, his voice old and crackly.

"Nay." Dustin sat up. "She is just so distracting that it is hard to focus on what I'm doing when I'm there."

"Yes, children can be a handful sometimes."

"Not Florie. I'm talking about Lady Lark." He stood up and walked over to the table.

"I see," said Orrick, chuckling softly. "Distracting, is she?"

"Yes, she is. At first, I thought she was haughty when she came to the monastery with her father. But now, I am starting to think it was all just an act."

"An act? How so?"

Dustin sat down on a stool and leaned his elbows on the table. "I honestly think that even though she is a noble, she feels very insecure around people. That mayhap she is not sure how to act."

"Ah. And so she acts haughty to hide it?"

"Yes. I believe so. I mean ... when we are alone, she seems very nice."

"You were alone with her?" asked Orrick, looking up and raising a brow.

"Nay! Yes. I mean, Florie was there, and so was Lady Raven. I just mean, when a lot of other nobles aren't watching, she seems different."

"Has she forgiven you for writing those missives yet?"

"I don't know." Dustin dragged a hand through his long hair. "She didn't say anything else about it. Then again, I was sure not to bring it up in conversation either."

"She'll be receiving letters from potential husbands starting any day now," said Orrick.

"Yes, so I've heard." He stared down at the contents of a cup, wondering what the liquid was inside, thinking Orrick had poured him a drink.

"Lord Corbett wants you to collect those letters that are received, and give them to Lady Lark."

"Ugh," groaned Dustin. "Honestly, I don't want to do it." He swirled the liquid around in the cup.

"You are the castle scribe now, Dustin. It is your job to give her any and all the letters from any and all suitors, and to record the names of those who have written to her."

Dustin noticed the sorcerer stressing the *any* or *all* parts a lot. "If I didn't know better, I'd think you were trying to hint at something."

"God's eyes, really! No wonder you live in a monastery. You are not thinking about women like most the men in this castle do."

"Of course, I am," said Dustin. "Oh ... I think I know what

you're saying." Dustin smiled, picking up a spoon and stirring the contents of the cup. "If I happen to sneak in any other letters to Lady Lark, she'll just think they are from a suitor."

"I didn't say that."

"Mayhap not, but I think that is what I'll do. I like her, and I have the gift of writing, so why not give it a shot while I'm here? What is this, Orrick? Some kind of new drink? He lifted the cup up to his mouth, but stopped when Orrick cleared his throat.

"I wouldn't do that if I were you."

"Why not?" Dustin sniffed the liquid in the cup and make a face. "It doesn't smell that inviting, actually. Mayhap it tastes better than it smells. Let me see." He put his lips on the rim of the cup, about to taste the drink.

"Well, I don't imagine rat pee would smell or taste inviting in the least."

"What!" Dustin dropped the cup and jumped up, sending the liquid running everywhere and dribbling down the leg of the table to the floor. "What the hell are you doing with something like that?"

Orrick burst out laughing. "I'm a sorcerer. I experiment with potions, what do you think?"

"Well, next time warn me what it is before I actually try to drink it."

"I was only having fun with you, that is not what it really is. But next time, mayhap you should wait until something is offered before you decide to just take it."

Dustin wondered if that advice really had something to do with Lady Lark as well.

CHAPTER 8

"I think it would be beneficial to take Florie on an outing today. As part of her studies, of course," Dustin told Lark three days later, as he arrived at the solar for her daughter's lesson. He really wanted to spend time with Lark outside of the castle and away from curious eyes, and this was the only way he could think to do it.

"An outin'?" asked Lark, sounding hesitant. "I'm no' sure about that."

"I want to go, I want to go, Mother." Florie pulled at Lark's tippet and jumped up and down.

"I think the nice weather is making the child restless," said Dustin. "I suggest a day outdoors might be good for her. She can run off some of that extra energy."

"Oh. I suppose ye're right. How long will ye two be gone?" asked Lark.

Dustin chuckled. "Two? You mean three. You are coming with us," he blurted out, seeing her surprised look, realizing mayhap he had spoken too freely once again. "I mean, will you

81

join us, Lady Lark? I'm not sure it would look good for me to be taking the child somewhere by myself."

"Nay, I suppose it wouldna." She looked over at the open window, glancing out. "It does seem to be a nice day."

The sun shone brightly and the scent of wildflowers floated on the breeze.

"Will you join us then?"

"I am no' sure," she said, looking back at him. He knew her hesitance was probably because she didn't want to be alone with a commoner, even if her child was with them. "Where would we be goin'?" she asked.

"Just outside the castle gates. I thought mayhap we could take a short walk in nature."

"Walk?" The idea seemed to displease her. "I dinna usually walk places. Nobles take a wagon or horses to get to where they want to go."

"Well, I don't have a horse or a wagon, since I'm just a commoner," he reminded her. "Besides, if you want Florie to tire herself out, walking is the best thing for her."

"Mother, I want to go for a walk. Pleeeeease?" asked Florie, still pulling on Lark's sleeve.

"There's quite a nice patch of larkspur as well as a field of lavender in bloom nearby," Dustin told her. "I thought I would show them to Florie and teach her about things that grow in nature."

"Ye ken about flowers?" she asked him.

"Why, yes. Of course. I have learned a lot about the land from the monks," he explained. "I farm the land with them as well as take care of the livestock. Mayhap one day Florie would like to even pet a sheep."

"Yes, I want to pet a sheep," cried Florie.

"So, ye think this is somethin' that should be part of Florie's studies?"

"Yes, I do," said Dustin. "I mean, she is learning to read now, but tutoring goes far beyond just that. It is important she learns about everyday life in every aspect."

"Dinna ye think Florie is too young to learn about nature?"

"Not at all. She might be too young for me to teach her about adding numbers right now, and she doesn't have the coordination to dip and hold a quill properly yet, but no age is too young to learn about the gifts from the earth."

"Gifts from the earth," repeated Lark with a smile. "Scribe, I like the way ye word things."

"Please, my name is Dustin."

"Dustin, I want to go. Dustin, take me on a walk." Florie ran over to him now, clinging to his leg and not letting go. She started to sing off-key, really loud.

"It's up to your mother," said Dustin, trying to pry off the little girl's grip, but she held tight. "What do you say, Lady Lark?"

"Pardon me?" Lark looked up and crooked her neck, trying to hear him. "I canna understand what ye are sayin'. Florie, be quiet."

Still, the little girl sang at the top of her lungs.

"I said ... " Dustin realized Lark was never going to hear him over the girl's screeching voice, and he was having a hard time getting Florie to release him. "Just a moment," he told Lark, walking closer to her, dragging Florie along with him every time he took a step.

The little girl thought it was a fun game and started laughing now.

"Will you agree to the outing and come along with us?" Dustin asked Lark once more.

. . .

Lark looked down at her daughter clinging to Dustin's leg, laughing, and seeming happier than she'd ever seen her. She realized laughing was good for Florie. Taking a walk in nature in the fresh air would be good for her too. Lark was a little leery of going with a commoner she really didn't know well, but decided a walk would be beneficial for her as well, to put other thoughts into her mind.

"Yes, I believe I will go with ye."

"Great!" said Dustin, reaching down, still trying to unhook Florie from his leg. "You won't regret it."

"However, I'll require that an escort join us," she told him.

"Huh?" He looked up and frowned, still trying to pry Florie off his leg. "Escort? Whatever for? I'll be with you and the girl."

"And if we come across attackers? Do ye ken how to fight? Do ye even own a weapon? Will ye be able to protect me and my daughter?"

"Well, no, I don't have a sword. But ... Florie, please let go, or we're not going to have time to go on any outing."

"I want to go now. Right now." The little girl let go and jumped up, running toward the door.

"We'll take Raven with us," Lark decided.

Florie reached up, opening the door wider. "Hurry up," she called back to them.

"We'll take Lady Raven?" repeated Dustin. "But she's a girl. When you suggested an escort, I thought you meant a man."

"Raven is a girl who can use a sword better than any man," she assured him.

"I don't know. I don't think that's a good idea."

"Then I'll ask my father to join us instead."

"Nay! Don't do that," gasped Dustin, still not at ease around the rugged Highlander. "I mean, Lady Raven will be fine."

"I'm goin' to look at flowers," called out Florie, running from the room and down the corridor.

"Florie! Get back here," shouted Lark.

"I'll go after her. You find Lady Raven, so we can go," said Dustin, quickly packing up his things and putting his leather bag over his shoulder.

"Ye seem disturbed about somethin'," said Lark. "Are ye?"

"Nay. Nay," said Dustin, shaking his head, hurrying out the door after her daughter.

NOT TWENTY MINUTES LATER, Lark walked over the drawbridge leaving the castle with Raven at her side. Raven's two mastiffs led the way, with Florie running right behind them, most likely trying to ride or terrorize the hounds as usual. Dustin walked ahead of the women, trying to keep up with Florie.

"Thank ye for comin' along to protect us," Lark told Raven.

"Sure," said Raven, her sword swinging at her side. "I hope you don't mind that I brought Copper and Brindy with us. Copper's puppies are weaning now, and I thought it would be good for her to get some exercise and get away from them for a while."

"Well, the dogs do seem to be a good distraction for Florie."

"I figured this way, when your father finds out you left the castle without an escort, he might take it easier on you. After all, the hounds are also good protectors."

"Raven, do ye think it is odd that Dustin wanted to walk somewhere? And that he wanted me to come along when it is supposedly a lesson for Florie?"

"Nay, but you seem to think so."

"I do admit, it feels a little awkward." Lark made her way

from the castle and started to head toward the field of flowers with Raven.

"How so?" asked Raven. "Because Dustin is a good-looking man who seems to like, or want, your company?"

"Nay, that's no' it," said Lark. "It's just that he's different from most men."

"You mean because he's a commoner? You can say the word, Lark. It's not as if you're speaking blasphemy."

"Ye're right," said Lark, letting out a deep breath. "I suppose to someone like ye or Rook, it is nothin' out of the ordinary."

"I'm not sure if that was supposed to be an insult or a compliment," said Raven, shaking her head.

"Neither," said Lark.

"Mother, hurry up! Run! Run! Look at all the flowers," shouted Florie, stretching out her arms and turning a full circle in the field up ahead. Dustin made sure to keep near her.

"Florie, it is not ladylike to run."

"Why not?" asked Raven with a smile. "I think it'll be fun." Raven held her sword to her side so it wouldn't bang against her legs, and gripped her skirt as well. "Let's go." With her other hand she took a hold of Lark's arm and pulled her along with her as she ran through the field of flowers toward Florie.

"Raven! Slow down," shouted Lark, trying to hold up her gown so she wouldn't trip on it. They ran until her heart felt like it would beat right out of her chest. Then they finally came to a halt in front of Dustin and Florie. The dogs barked and jumped, liking the idea that someone was playing with them.

"That was invigorating," said Raven, dropping Lark's hand.

"I can barely catch my breath," complained Lark, holding her hand to her chest.

"My lady, mayhap you need to get out in the fresh air and sunshine more often," said Dustin, not out of breath at all.

"What is this flower?" asked Florie, yanking up a stalk of lavender.

"That is lavender," said Dustin, taking the stalk from Florie. "See all the beautiful little purple flowers? They always reminded me of clusters of grapes in a way."

"What do ye do with it?" asked the little girl.

"Well, the monks use it during holy days, strewn around the floors to help ward off evil spirits," said Dustin.

"Really, Dustin! I hardly think it is appropriate to teach my daughter about evil spirits," scoffed Lark.

"It has so many more uses as well," he continued.

"Like what?" asked Florie, looking up at him with wide eyes.

"Well, it is an ancient symbol for purity, devotion, and love," he told her, glancing over at Lark when he said it.

"That doesna sound like a good lesson at all," said Lark. "What ye are teachin' my daughter is just a bunch of beliefs and silly superstitions."

"Then, let me say this," said Dustin, sniffing the lavender and taking a step closer to Lark. "Lavender is used to scent bath water, used as rushes for the floor, to freshen one's clothes, and even to make one's hair smell even sweeter and more lovely than it already does." He reached up and tucked the sprig of lavender into the side of Lark's long, blonde braid that trailed down her back.

When he did so, Lark looked up into his eyes. The sun lit up his brown orbs, allowing her to see small specks of orange within them that she hadn't noticed before. The breeze made his long hair billow out around him, and when it retreated, she felt the ends of his soft hair brush against her arm. Standing this close to him, she could even smell the leather from the bag he held over his shoulder. Everything suddenly seemed more colorful and so much more filled with life.

Dustin Styles was a handsome man. He was also thought-ful. Never before had any man hinted that her hair smelled sweet and lovely as he just did. Never had any man ever given her a flower, either, yet alone tucked it into her braid. It made her feel special and pretty.

Her heart sped up. The strong scent of lavender, from not only the flower in her hair but also from the field of blooms all around them, filled her senses. The sun felt good on her face, and also atop her head, since she wasn't wearing a head covering of any kind.

"My lady?" said Dustin, holding out another sprig of lavender to her. "Breathe in the scent. It is said to be calming. Relaxing. A true way to conquer the stress of a worried mind. He smelled it and then held it up to her nose. "Sniff it. It will help, I promise."

Lark's eyes closed and she breathed in the scent of flowers ... and also the manly scent of woodsmoke from Dustin's clothes. Her head felt light and her heartbeat rapid. Nothing else seemed to matter but this moment, this second, right here in the field of flowers. Dustin's words were so poetic and if she didn't know better, she'd say romantic as well. Could he be doing this to flirt with her? Because he possibly liked her? She didn't know, but wanted to think so, because it felt so damned good.

"Mother, wake up. Look at the dogs." Florie pulled on her sleeve.

Lark's eyes sprang open, first hearing the barking of the dogs in the distance. Raven's mastiffs were running through the tall larkspur up ahead probably chasing a squirrel or rabbit. She couldn't even see the hounds but could see the stalks of purple, pink and white flowers moving back and forth as the dogs ran in circles.

"Oh, nay," said Raven, shading her eyes from the sun to see where the dogs went. "Copper, Brindy, come here!"

"I'll go after them, my lady," offered Dustin.

"Nay, the dogs don't know you well. I'll get them," said Raven, heading in that direction. "Come on, Florie, you can help me," said Raven holding out her hand for the little girl. Then, Raven did the oddest thing, she looked back over her shoulder and winked. Lark couldn't imagine what that was for.

"Shall we sit down in the field of heather and wait for them to return?" asked Dustin. "I thought this would be a good place for Florie to practice her reading. You can hear the birds singing all around us."

"Sit down?" asked Lark.

"Aye. Or don't nobles sit on the ground?" he asked, in a jesting manner. When she didn't answer, his smile faded. "Oh, I guess I should have brought along a blanket."

"I'm no' a precious little flower that is goin' to wilt if I sit directly on the earth," said Lark, picking up the hem of her gown and plopping down in the lavender. "I am from a Highland clan, ye realize."

"Aye," he said, sitting next to her. "Hermitage Castle. I know of it."

"Well, my father is laird of Hermitage Castle in the Lowlands, but also chieftain of our clan that resides in the Highlands as well," she said, leaning back on her elbows into a reclining position. "Have ye ever been to a Highland camp?" She closed her eyes and lifted her face to the sun.

"Nay, I haven't. I also haven't seen a lady purposely lifting her face to the sun before," he answered. "I thought nobles like white, pale skin because it denotes their status and points out that they don't do back-breaking labor in the sun like peasants do."

"Usually, that's true," she said, her eyes still closed. She could hear the dogs barking in the distance and Florie laughing and Raven talking. Now, she was aware of the musical songs of the birds as well. "I, however, often live at the MacKeefe camp in the Highlands. In cottages built from stone with thatched roofs."

"Really," he said, sounding interested.

"Yes. We have livestock in the mountains and cook over open fires in the outdoors as well."

"You surprise me," said Dustin. "I didn't think you would do something like that."

"I am full of surprises," she said with a smile, starting to finally feel like her old self again. Ever since Gregoire left her pregnant and alone, she had lost her pride and confidence more and more every year as she waited for him to return and marry her, and he never came. After a while, she stopped caring and started hating the man, hoping she'd never see him again.

"Don't move, my lady. There is a bee buzzing around the flower in your hair."

"There is?" She opened her eyes to find Dustin leaning over her, brushing the air, making the bee leave.

"Go after another flower," he told the bee. "This one is already taken."

For a second, she felt as if he was speaking of her, not the plant in her hair.

When he turned his head, his face was right in front of hers. She saw him looking at her mouth. He seemed as if he wanted to kiss her. Lark wanted to kiss him as well.

Their faces moved closer and excitement filled her body. But right before their lips met, he pulled away.

"I am sorry, my lady," he said, looking distraught, brushing back his long hair. "I am not sure what overcame me."

Lark was too near to actually being kissed again that she

didn't want the opportunity to slip away. It had been five long years since a man kissed her. It was time for it to happen once more.

"Dustin," she said, and when he turned to look at her, she put her hands on his shoulders and leaned in and kissed him on the mouth.

Their lips interlocked, and her eyes closed. Her body came to life again after the deep dormancy it had been in from the hardships and trials that had plagued her. She got lost in his kiss. He took her breath away and made her feel as if that bee was back and this time buzzing in her chest, she was so excited.

"Mother, the dogs almost caught a squirrel," shouted Florie, causing Lark to quickly move away from Dustin, but not before once more drowning in the pools of passion that seemed to fill his eyes. Her daughter and Raven were close enough to have seen them kiss, but she didn't think they did.

"That's nice," said Lark, looking down and fixing her gown.

Dustin turned away from the women, fussing with something in his bag.

"I'm glad I brought their leads with me," said Raven, walking up with both the dogs on leads. Raven stopped in her tracks. "Are we interrupting anything?" she asked, her eyes flashing over to Lark.

"Nay," said Lark, followed by her tongue brushing over her lips. Dustin's manly essence still clung to her mouth, and his scent was now embedded in her brain.

"We are ready for your reading lesson, Florie," said Dustin, sitting down and bringing forth a simple book from his pouch.

"I want to read this one," said Florie, reaching into the bag and pulling out another.

"What is that?" asked Raven, stretching her neck to see it.

"Florie, don't touch that," said Dustin, taking the book

from her. He held it in two hands and seemed to treat it reverently.

"Aye, what is that book?" asked Lark curiously.

"It's just one of my books that I read and cherish. It is not for the lessons."

"I've seen that before," said Raven, sitting down and petting Copper who lay down next to her. "I think my father has one like it. Isn't that a book of poems by Geoffrey Chaucer?"

"Yes, it is," said Dustin, looking down at the book and running his hand over the leather-bound cover. "I had the pleasure of transcribing many copies for Mr. Chaucer. In appreciation, he let me keep one. He is a very talented poet."

"Oh, so you like poetry?" asked Raven.

"I do," said Dustin, slipping the book back into his bag. "Mr. Chaucer is thinking about writing an actual story someday. Excuse me, but it is time for Florie's lesson."

Lark found Dustin mysterious and seductive. A commoner who had so much depth to him. She knew he was a scribe, but didn't realize he liked poetic pieces. After all, she just thought he copied mostly holy manuscripts, since he lived at a monastery.

Then again, why should that surprise her? After all, the man was a very good kisser. That alone was not something she expected for someone who had been raised by monks.

DUSTIN WALKED in silence back to the castle, after Florie's lesson was over. Raven kept the hounds on the leads, and Florie was insistent that she was going to walk them. So, the two of them were pulled along up ahead with the dogs, leaving Lark and Dustin alone, following behind.

"Thank ye for suggestin' that Florie have her lesson

outdoors," said Lark. "I think it will help her sleep well tonight."

"Aye," he said, giving Lark a sideways glance. Dustin wanted to say something about the kiss, but didn't know how to approach it. He liked kissing Lark. He liked it a lot. But she wasn't saying anything about what happened either, and that concerned him.

Mayhap she'd been lost in the moment, just like he was. Or mayhap after kissing him, she wished she hadn't. Although any woman who ever kissed Dustin never seemed to regret it, Lark was a lady, a noble. He didn't know how she would react, even if she did seem to initiate the kiss when he was trying to be proper by pulling away.

His head was filled with confusion.

Dustin was starting to have feelings for Lark, and part of him wanted to tell her. Yet another part of him believed if he did so, it could only mean trouble. Still, he wanted to know how she felt about him. The only way to know this would be to come out and ask her.

They were on the drawbridge and he was just about to mention the kiss, when he heard a man call out from behind him.

"Lark, there ye are." It was Lark's father, Storm MacKeefe atop a horse. "I've been lookin' for ye. Where have ye been?"

"Da," said Lark. "I was out in the fields of flowers with Dustin. It was lovely."

"What?" he growled.

"She means, I was giving Florie her lesson out in nature today," said Dustin, before the wild Highlander took off his head with his sword.

"Ye were in a field with my daughter and granddaughter?" asked Storm. "They were unescorted?"

"Nay, Father," interrupted Lark before Dustin could reply.

"Raven was with us, as well as the mastiffs, so we were well-protected."

"Hrmph," snarled Storm. "I dinna like it. Lark, ye are no' to do that again. It is only goin' to cause more gossip, and that is somethin' we dinna want so close to the upcomin' event."

"Da, I dinna like that ye are passing me off to a noble. I told ye before and I'll say it again, I dinna want to marry anyone."

"Lark, we've discussed this, and ye have no choice. I am yer father and I make the decisions. And I'll say it again, dinna go out walkin' in fields so carefree. I dinna like it."

"No harm was done." Lark's eyes flashed over to Dustin and he knew she was thinking about the kiss, just like he was right now. "Ye are gettin' worked up for nothin'."

"Just the same, dinna let me catch ye out alone with a commoner again. It willna look good to the nobles who are yer suitors."

"What suitors? There are none here," said Lark. "I havena seen a one."

"No' yet, but soon," he told her, then turned his attention to Dustin. "Scribe, I hear several messengers stopped by the castle earlier today when ye were gone. They were deliverin' the first of the letters for Lady Lark."

"Really?" asked Lark. "So soon? Ye just sent out those missives."

"Nay, these are the replies from the Scots. I sent out those missives a while ago."

"Oh," said Lark, not sounding at all excited. "Well, where are the letters?"

"The scribe was supposed to be here to collect them. Since he wasna, Orrick took them for now. Scribe, it is yer job to make sure my daughter receives each of the letters from her suitors."

"Da, his name is Dustin, no' Scribe," said Lark sounding cross.

"Mmph. Dustin," Storm mumbled. "Now go! Deliver the letters to Lady Lark, and keep yer eyes open for more arrivin' each day. And Lark, ye be sure to read every one of the letters carefully, because ye will be choosin' one of the men to marry, once they arrive for the celebration feast."

"Yes, Da," said Lark, sounding sad if Dustin wasn't mistaken.

Dustin noticed the sprig of lavender was coming loose from her hair. He raised his hand to fix it, but stopped himself and pretended to be scratching his head instead. The last thing he needed right now was for Lark's father to see him fixing flowers in Lark's hair. If he did that, he was sure he'd find out first-hand why some of the clan were referred to as Madmen MacKeefes.

CHAPTER 9

"All of these letters are for Lady Lark?" Dustin asked Orrick the next morning, holding a half dozen letters from Scotland in his hand.

"Yes," said Orrick. "They are from the suitors who are interested in being Lady Lark's new husband."

"I see," said Dustin, wondering what the letters said.

There was a knock at Orrick's door and Lord Corbett stuck his head inside. "Is Dustin in here?"

"Aye," said Orrick. "Come in."

"Let me in to talk to that scribe," mumbled Storm MacKeefe, pushing past Corbett from behind him and entering the room.

"My lords," said Dustin, wondering what they wanted. He still held on to the letters that had arrived from Scotland.

"There they are." Storm walked over and plucked the letters from Dustin's hand. "Why didna ye give these to my daughter yesterday like I instructed?"

"I figured I would do so today when I went to give Florie her lesson," Dustin answered.

Storm flipped through them, and then opened one and started to read it.

"Excuse me, my lord, but shouldn't Lady Lark see those first? I mean, they are letters written to her, aren't they?" Once again, Dustin was saying things he probably shouldn't be voicing aloud, but he didn't think this was right and was sticking up for Lady Lark.

Storm's angry eyes snapped up to Dustin, and Dustin already felt like kicking himself for his outburst.

"I agree," said Orrick, before Storm could even answer. "Since you've given the girl permission to choose her own husband from the missives she receives, she might think you are trying to force her choice by reading the letters before her."

"I suppose he's got a point," said Corbett.

"Mmph," grumbled Storm, handing the letters back to Dustin. "Fine. When my daughter reads them, it is yer responsibility to record each suitor's name who responds to her. I want to be informed of our progress."

"Is that really my job?" asked Dustin, not really wanting to be part of this process. As a matter of fact, after having to write those invitations, he still felt so guilty that he just wanted to ignore this whole mess all together.

"Aye, it is yer job. Ye're the castle scribe," said Storm. "I also want Lark to answer each letter. Ye will write back to her suitors as she deciphers what she would like to say."

"Really? She is going to have to answer the letters too?" he asked in surprise. "I thought this was just to let her get to know the men before they arrived for the feast where she'll choose one for a husband." This was starting to become too involved for Dustin's liking.

"Have her letters ready to go by tonight," said Storm, turning and walking to the door. "Lark's mother will be leavin' for Scotland tomorrow for a few weeks and will take the missives back with her."

"Aye, my lord. Of course," said Dustin, staring at the letters in his hand. Why did he feel as if he wanted to do anything in his power to stop this from happening? After the kiss with Lark, he didn't want to share her with anyone. Certainly not a greedy noble.

Corbett followed Storm to the door, stopping and turning around, holding a finger in the air. "Oh, Dustin, I almost forgot. My uncle, Brother Ruford, requests your presence at the monastery."

"Really? Why?" asked Dustin. "He knows I am here to tutor the child."

"Yes, of course he does. However, there is a pilgrimage of nuns that have arrived and he thinks you should be there to greet them."

"My lord. I thought my presence here at the castle was my priority."

"It is. However, Brother Ruford said this was important."

"What will I tell Lady Lark?"

"Bring her along with you," said Corbett. "Brother Ruford also told me that Lady Lark's cousin Eleanor is arriving there today and I am sure the women will want to visit. Oh, and also, one of the traveling nuns will be coming back to the castle with you."

"What? Why?" asked Dustin, not understanding this in the least.

"Lark's father decided it would be best if someone watched over Florie to give her more time to study the letters and think about which man she wants to marry. Therefore, one of the nuns, I think her name was Sister Joan, will be watching over Florie until Lark's wedding. The Sister was kind enough to volunteer, even though it will slow down her travels with the pilgrimage."

"Aye, my lord. Of course," said Dustin, not liking this idea at all, and also not knowing how he was going to do everything in one day that the two lords were expecting of him.

The door to the room closed, leaving Dustin standing there staring at the letters in his hand.

"Is something wrong, Dustin?" Orrick walked over and sat down at his table, pouring himself some ale. He propped his feet up on a second chair, and opened an old, dusty book, putting it on his lap to read it.

"Nay, nothing is wrong," Dustin answered, feeling like throwing the letters from Lark's suitors into the fire.

"You seem upset."

"I think this whole thing is ridiculous."

"Obviously, Lady Lark's father thinks it's beneficial."

"I also don't see why this Sister Joan needs to come to the castle to take care of Florie. She'll just be in the way." Dustin was having good results with the child. He also liked the fact that Lark noticed he was able to get Florie to behave. It put him in a better light with Lark. Now the nun was going to show up and ruin everything.

"Mayhap it'll be a good thing," stated Orrick.

"How so?"

"Well, it might give you time alone with Lady Lark."

"Aye. To scribe her letters going out to the men who are hoping to become her husband." He looked down once more at the pile of letters in his grip and shook his head.

"You seem distraught concerning one of these noblemen possibly marrying Lady Lark."

"I have to admit, I am. I guess I'm just being selfish, but I don't really want to share her. I like having her around, and that will end as soon as she marries."

"Well, tell me. Have you done anything at all to woo Lady Lark yet?"

"Nay. Not really. But we did kiss in the field of lavender."

"I see," said the old man, looking up from his book with interest. "And how did that go?"

"I'm … not sure. She seemed to like it, but nothing else was said about it. We were interrupted and it all happened so quickly."

Orrick blew air from his mouth and shook his head. "A wasted opportunity."

"Orrick, why are you so supportive of me trying to woo a lady? I don't understand it. After all, I am only a commoner and nothing can ever happen between us. I mean, not really."

"Aye, just like it couldn't happen with Lady Raven or her brother, Lord Rook?" asked Orrick in a knowing manner.

"You're right," said Dustin, still staring down at the letters but nodding now. "It seemed impossible that a noble would marry from below the salt, yet both Lady Raven and Lord Rook did just that. I suppose mayhap I have just as good of a chance of gaining Lady Lark's interest as any of these men who are sending her letters."

"More so," said Orrick, picking up his tankard of ale and taking a drink. "After all, these men are only words on a piece of parchment, and you are actually here with her."

"Words on a piece of parchment," he said in deep thought, thinking that is exactly what he did every day of his life. "Thank you, Orrick, you have been a big help." He shoved the letters into his leather bag and slipped it over his shoulder, heading to the door.

"Just remember, Dustin, that everything happens for a reason, even if you don't know what that reason is at the time."

Dustin stopped. "What do you mean?"

"I am just saying, don't let people or circumstances

dishearten you. Mayhap incidences, no matter how bad they might seem, are really blessings in disguise."

"That sounds like something I'd hear at the monastery, not in the den of a magic man."

"It's just advice," said Orrick with a shrug of his shoulders. "Would it be easier for you to accept if it looked like a little magic was thrown in with my advice?" Orrick waved his hand through the air, creating a puff of white smoke to explode over his head, rising slowly up to the ceiling.

"What was that?" asked Dustin. "Did you do a spell? Did you conjure something of magic to help me win the eye of Lady Lark?"

"Nay," said Orrick, laughing and shaking his head. "That was only for show, naught else."

"Orrick?" he asked, feeling less than confident that he could actually end up with a noblewoman. "Could you do magic to help me? I mean, if you really wanted to?"

"I'm a sorcerer, what do you think?" Those words gave him hope.

"So, you're saying you would be able to make a love spell or something?"

Orrick's bushy brows dipped together. "Egads, Dustin, you don't need a love spell and neither would I ever give you one because that would work against a person's free will. Plus, Lord Corbett doesn't want me doing magic unless he requests it. It seems to shake everyone up in the castle."

"I'm not afraid of your magic. I mean, if you wanted to use it to help me."

"Nay! I could but I wouldn't. It would not be right and you know it."

"Yes, of course. You're right," said Dustin, lowering his head, feeling bad for even suggesting it now.

"If you are truly interested in Lady Lark, then do something about it yourself. You're a man. Fight for her. Flirt with her. Make her feel special. God's eyes, scribe, stop thinking about it so much and just make it happen!"

"You're right." Dustin held up a hand and nodded. "Sorry about that. I had a weak moment. It won't happen again."

"I hope not, because I am starting to think mayhap Lady Lark would be better off with one of those greedy fools writing her letters, after all."

"Nay! Never," said Dustin, pushing aside his doubts. "I am interested in Lady Lark and will do whatever it takes to gain her interest in me as well."

"Now, that's better," said Orrick with a chuckle. "Just whatever you do, mayhap don't mention that in front of Storm MacKeefe. At least, not right now. It might not go over well with him at the moment."

～

"Florie, what did ye do?" gasped Lark, walking into the wardrobe to find her daughter dressed in one of her best gowns, and wearing one of her expensive headpieces as well. Actually, they were hard to recognize, since Florie had a pair of shears in her hand and had cut them both down to size trying to make them fit her. "Nay! That was bad! Ye ruined my things. How could ye?"

Lark heard a knock at her bedchamber door. She took the shears away from Florie and headed over and pulled open the door to find Dustin standing there.

"Dustin," she said, wondering what he was doing at the door to her bedchamber since they always met in the solar as was proper.

"I am sorry to disturb you, Lady Lark," said Dustin. "However, I have a lot to do today and wondered if we could start Florie's lesson early?"

"Oh. Yes, I suppose that would be fine. I will meet ye at the solar as soon as I get her dressed."

"Dustin, look at me." Florie emerged from the wardrobe, barely able to see through the tattered veil of the headpiece. She almost tripped, dragging the long gown with her, even though it was chopped off in several places and the long sleeves were missing.

"Oh, no," said Dustin, his gaze flashing back at the shears in Lark's hand. "I mean … are you altering one of your gowns for your daughter?"

"Nay, of course no'," spat Lark, looking defeated and as if she were going to cry. "It was one of my favorite gowns and now it is ruined. I dinna ken what to do with her."

Florie sang at the top of her lungs, twirling around in circles.

"Well, I think I have the answer," said Dustin. "Lord Corbett told me this morning that Sister Joan, a traveling nun, will be here to help care for Florie."

"Oh, yes! That would be wonderful," said Lark. "I told my da I didna want a nursemaid, but I changed my mind. I think I do need one. I didna want to have to tell him I was wrong, so this is perfect. I think a nun could be a good influence on Florie dinna ye?"

"Let's hope so," said Dustin, watching the little girl parade around like a queen. It was going to take a strong hand to get Florie to start obeying the adults.

"I'll get her dressed and be right there. Ye can go to the solar and wait for us."

"All right," said Dustin, looking down at his bag. "Oh. I

have some letters from your suitors. Your father wants me to record all their names on a list once you read them."

"Och, it figures. Oh, all right, if it'll make my da happy and get him off my back."

"He also wants me to scribe the letters to the suitors that you will send to them in response."

"Me? I dinna want to write any of those men letters. Nay. I willna do it."

"But you have to. It is what your father ordered."

"I dinna care what he ordered, I told ye I dinna want to write back to these men that I dinna even ken."

Dustin could see now where Florie got her stubbornness. Neither she nor Lark seemed to like to be told what to do. There was a pattern emerging here quickly.

"I'll help you," he offered, not really wanting to do it, but also not wanting trouble between Lark and her father. Plus, it wouldn't look good for him if he couldn't carry out the lord's orders.

"I suppose that will be fine." She looked back at Florie and then at him once more. "Dustin, about the kiss yesterday," she said.

"Yes? What about it?"

Lark noticed Dustin's head snap up and he looked like he was holding his breath.

"I—I think we should both just forget that it ever happened," she told him, feeling that she had been too brash in the field of heather, and that if word got out, she might be called a strumpet. Again. She also figured Dustin would think she was a loose woman now, and that is the last thing she wanted. Lark had been so excited to kiss him, that when he pulled away, she didn't want to let him go. That is not the type of girl she was, and also the wrong image she wanted to portray to Dustin. Even if he was just a commoner.

"Forget about it? Is that really what you want?" he asked, cocking his head, staring at her.

Damn, this wasn't easy. It wasn't what she wanted. Not really. Still, it needed to be done. When he looked at her with those eyes, it made her melt inside and she felt as if she could no longer speak. Instead, she found herself wanting to kiss him again.

But she wouldn't.

She couldn't.

"I think it would be for the best," she said in a mere whisper, looking at the floor rather than into his eyes.

"Yes, I agree," he said, clearing his throat, surprising her with his answer.

"Ye do?" When she peeked back up at him, he was looking down the corridor rather than at her.

"I'm sure you are right. It's for the best. Well, I'll meet you in the solar, ready to scribe letters for your suitors."

He walked away quickly, without even a goodbye. She watched him go, and it made her heart ache.

"Where is Dustin goin'?" asked Florie, peeking out the door after him.

"Never mind," said Lark, pulling her daughter inside the room and closing the door. "Ye have been a very bad little girl, and I am no' happy with ye, Florie."

"I just wanted to be like ye, Mother," said Florie, pouting.

"Like me? Why would ye want to be like me?" The last thing she wanted was for her daughter to end up in a horrible situation like she was in, since making the mistake of lying with a man before she was married.

"If I'm like ye, then Dustin will want to kiss me too," said the little girl, turning and strutting across the room, dragging Lark's chopped gown across the floor with every step she took.

Lark stood there with her mouth hanging open. Her daughter knew she'd kissed Dustin, and that was something she had hoped the little girl had not seen. It was also something she never wanted to have to explain to Florie.

"Let's hurry up and get you changed," said Lark, eager for Sister Joan to show up because Lark realized she was no good at disciplining her child, and nuns were known for being strict. This might just prove to be the answer to her prayers, after all.

CHAPTER 10

"These letters are all for me?" asked Lark, later in the solar. She held the parchments Dustin had given to her, not wanting to read them.

"Aye," he said, busying himself unpacking his bag. He didn't even look at her, and this bothered her immensely. Now, she was wondering if mayhap she shouldn't have said anything about the kiss between them at all. "You can look at them while I give Florie her reading lesson."

"Of course," said Lark, settling the little girl at the table, and then taking the stack of letters over to read by the open window.

"Hello," came a woman's voice from the open door. Lark looked up to see her parents standing there.

"Mother? Da? What are ye two doin' here?"

"I hope we're not disturbing Florie's lesson," said Wren, walking into the room, followed by Storm. "Hello, sweetheart." Wren bent down and kissed Florie on the cheek.

"I want a kiss on the lips like—"

"Florie, that's enough," snapped Lark, realizing her

109

daughter was about to tell her parents she'd kissed Dustin. That would not be a good thing for her father to hear. "What brings ye here?" she asked her parents.

"Lark, since I am leaving for Scotland tomorrow, I had hoped you wouldn't mind if I spent the day with Florie. I want to take her to town with me," said Wren. "They are having a trade fair and I thought she might enjoy it." Wren was English, and Corbett Blake's sister. Even though she lived in Scotland now and dressed like a Highlander, she still spoke like an Englishwoman.

"Oh, I suppose that's fine," said Lark, noticing the scowl on Dustin's face when she said it. "I mean, Dustin, do ye think that would be all right if Florie missed her lesson today?"

"Why in the devil's name are ye askin' him his permission?" growled Storm. "He's only a commoner and will do what we say. Besides, Lark, ye have to read the letters from yer Scottish suitors. The scribe will write the letters to them ye wish to send in return, and yer mother will take them with her when she goes back to Scotland."

"Mother, do you really need to leave?" asked Lark, wanting her mother there since she was soon to be married. Even if her father was hard to cope with at times, her mother always seemed to understand her.

"Well, Hawke and Heather do need me," said Lark, speaking of Lark's younger siblings. "I'll be back for your wedding day though, so don't worry."

"Canna ye stay here and have Da go back in your place?" she asked, getting ready for her father's explosive reaction.

"Lark, stop it," said Storm in a gruff voice. "I am stayin' right here to make sure this weddin' happens. Now, read those letters so the scribe can write yer responses. And be nice to these men. I dinna want ye insultin' any nobleman who is finally willin' to marry ye."

"Storm, that was uncalled for," Wren said, taking Florie's hand. "Why don't you join us at the trade fair?" she asked her husband.

"Will there be a juggler there?" asked Florie. "I want to learn to juggle."

"I don't know, dear, but it should be exciting," Wren answered. "There will be lots of vendors, music, and lots of food to eat."

"I think it would be nice to spend a little time with my wife and granddaughter," said Storm, as soon as Lark's mother mentioned food. Storm looked over at Lark. "Will ye be sure to do as I ask?"

"Yes, Da. I promise," said Lark with a sigh, not wanting to read the letters or have Dustin write the responses, but knowing this was the only way to get her father to leave. Still, the whole idea of the letters seemed awkward to be doing with Dustin now that they'd kissed. Somehow, it almost made her feel like she'd be betraying Dustin in some way.

"Come on, Florie, ye can ride on the horse with me," said Storm, picking up his granddaughter, putting her on his shoulder. Florie squealed in delight and giggled, holding on to the little braid of hair on the side of Storm's head. "Och, lassie, dinna pull my hair. That hurts," whined Storm.

"Storm, don't be ridiculous, it doesn't hurt," said Wren. "You are a Highland warrior, so toughen up and let's get going."

Lark giggled to herself, loving it when her mother put her father in his place.

"We'll see you soon, Lark," said her mother as the three of them left the room.

"Goodbye," Lark called out. "Have fun." She waved to Florie. "Well, I suppose I should read these letters," Lark told Dustin, feeling awkward now being with him there alone.

"Since Florie won't be here, I'll go to the monastery while you are doing that." Dustin quickly packed up his bag.

Lark didn't want him to leave, even if his presence made her nervous. She liked being around him. And now that her daughter wasn't going to be here all day, she finally would have time to spend alone with Dustin to get to know him better. "Mayhap I should go to the monastery with ye," she suggested.

"What for?" he asked, slipping the strap of the bag over his shoulder. "I mean, you have letters from your suitors to read."

"I can do that at the monastery. Ye can write the responses there as well, canna ye?"

"I suppose so," he said, sounding indifferent. "All right, then let's go and get this over with."

"That is an odd thing to say," she told him, not under-standing what he meant. "Ye are actin' as if this is all a task ye would rather no' do."

"I'm sorry, my lady. I didn't mean anything by it. Are you ready to go?"

He was looking right at her again, and all she could think about was kissing him. What was wrong with her? Mayhap spending the day at a holy place with monks and nuns was exactly what she needed. At least then, she wouldn't be tempted to do anything again that she might regret in the future.

"Dustin, it doesna feel right that I ride on a horse while ye walk," said Lark as they made their way to St. Basil's Monastery. "I dinna ken why ye didna just borrow a horse from the castle so ye could ride, too."

"I don't have a horse and neither will I use one of Lord

Corbett's. It's not necessary." Actually, Dustin was now regretting not borrowing one because he realized it would have saved more time. They had a lot to do today if they wanted to have everything done by the time Storm got back from the trade fair. The monastery wasn't far, but still, this was slowing them down.

Lark stopped the horse.

"What are you doing?" he asked.

"Get on the horse with me."

"You are riding sidesaddle," he pointed out.

"It's fine. Just sit behind me, but no' on the saddle itself.We'll be sure to go slow so we don't injure the horse."

He was about to reject her offer, but decided, why not? There was no one here to reprimand them, and this might be the only time he ever had to get this close to Lark.

"All right. Hold still," he said, hoisting himself up to the back of the horse. Once there, Lark was basically sitting in his lap.

"Ye'd better hold on to me since ye are no' in the saddle," she told him. "We wouldna want to lose ye." She smiled, flirting with him if Dustin wasn't mistaken. He liked it.

"Aye, you're right." Dustin slipped his arms around Lark's waist to hold on to her. Her long gown hung down over his leg. Pressed up against her as they rode, his head was nuzzled up close to hers.

"See? This is nice, nay?" she asked him.

"Aye," he agreed. It felt so good to have his arms around Lark that he never wanted to let go.

"I wanted to thank ye for the flower ye put in my hair yesterday," she told him. "That was very thoughtful of ye."

"I had hoped you wouldn't think it too forward of me to do so."

"It wasna any more forward than me kissin' ye in the

heather. I hope ye didna get the wrong idea of what kind of lassie I am."

That surprised him. He had thought she regretted kissing him, but now it sounded as if mayhap she just didn't want him to think of her as some sort of strumpet.

"I didn't see it that way at all, my lady. I actually enjoyed the kiss and had hoped you did too." It was a risk stating his feelings aloud, but one worth taking. In a few weeks Lark would be married to a noble, and he would never again have the chance to say what he felt in his heart.

She turned her head and looked at him. "I did enjoy it. Immensely." Her face was close and she now focused on his mouth. Damn, why did she have to do this? He wanted her now more than anything. Before he talked himself out of it, he leaned forward and kissed her once again. This time, it was him kissing her, not the other way around. He played the part of aggressor so Lark wouldn't have to worry about seeming too forward.

"Mmm," she said with her eyes closed as they rode. "That was nice, Dustin."

"Yes," he said, giving her one more kiss, then pulling away from her. They were close to the monastery, and being seen riding double with his arms around her was already enough to cause a stir. He didn't need kissing a noblewoman added to his list to tell Brother Ruford the next time he went to confession. "Stop the horse," he told her.

Once she did, he hopped off.

"What are ye doin'?" she asked.

"I don't think it will be good for either of us if it is reported back to your father that I was riding with my arms around you."

"Oh. I suppose ye're right."

They approached St. Basil's and waited patiently as two

robed monks pulled open the heavy iron gates at the entrance that was closed between masses and at certain times of the day.

"Thank you, Brother Bertram, Brother Peter," said Dustin with a nod, leading the horse into the courtyard. Once there, he stopped and helped Lady Lark dismount. His hands lingered on her waist and her hands lingered on his shoulders. With her feet on the ground, she looked up with those brilliant green eyes that reminded him of emeralds.

"Thank ye," she whispered, lowering her head a little and looking up with a shy expression. "For everythin'," she added, and he knew exactly what she meant.

"Dustin, there you are." Brother Ruford hurried over to greet them with a nun on his heels. "I'd like you to meet Sister Joan. She is on a pilgrimage and comes all the way from Ireland."

"Hello, nice to meet you, Sister Joan," he said with a nod. The nun looked up at him and he swore her eyes were glassy.

"This is Lady Lark," the monk told the nun. "She is from Scotland, but is staying at her uncle's castle until her wedding in a few weeks' time."

Dustin found it odd that he was introduced before a noble-woman. None of this made any sense to him.

"Lady Lark, it is an honor." Sister Joan folded her hands in prayer and bowed her head.

"Where is the child?" asked Brother Ruford. "Sister Joan is eager to meet her."

"My daughter Florie is at the trade fair with my parents today," explained Lark. "However, she will return to the castle by nightfall."

The bells of St. Basil's rang out loudly, calling all the monks to mass.

"Time for sext," said Dustin.

Lark's eyes opened wide and so did her mouth. "What did ye just say?"

"Sext," Dustin repeated. "It is one of the eight conical hours that denotes a prayer time for monks. It happens at noon."

"Oh," she said with a giggle. "That makes sense now."

"Sister, we need to go," said Brother Ruford. "Dustin, will you and Lady Lark be joining us?"

"Nay," said Dustin. "I have to scribe some letters for my lady, so I think we will tend to that now. It will take some time."

"Well, if you are going to be talking to each other and making noise, don't use the scriptorium," warned Brother Ruford.

"I don't know where else to go," said Dustin.

"Can't you use your cottage?" asked the monk. "No one will bother you there and you can talk as loud as you want and no one will even hear you."

"I can, but won't it cause tongues to wag if I am in there alone with a lady?" asked Dustin, surprised that Ruford would even suggest such a thing. Especially since they were within holy walls.

"No tongues will wag unless you give them reason to do so," said Ruford with a smile. "You have my blessing. Now, Sister, may I escort you to mass?" Ruford held out his arm to the nun.

"Aye, of course," said Sister Joan, looking back at Dustin again. "I am so happy to meet you, Dustin," she said before walking away.

Dustin nodded, but didn't reply. He thought that was an odd thing for the nun to say. Especially since she excluded Lark, a noblewoman, in her statement. It was actually rude, and he felt embarrassed for her.

"I'm sure she meant both of us," he told Lark.

"Of course she did," Lark answered. "Dustin, where is your cottage?"

"It's right here within the walls of the monastery," he explained. "First, we'll drop off your horse at the stable, and then I'll show you.

"OCH, THIS IS SO ... SMALL," said Lark, walking into the cottage made of wattle and daub. "This is where ye lived yer entire life?" she asked in shock. It wasn't any different from a peasant's hut. Then again, it was very similar to the cottages her clan lived in back in the Highlands so she shouldn't have been surprised.

"Yes," he told her. "It was once the home of Lord Corbett Blake's wife, Lady Devon as well. Is something the matter?"

"Nay, no' at all. This will be fine," said Lark, laying the letters on the small wooden table. It was a one room cottage and had only the essentials. There was a hearth on one side of the room with a horizontal pole and a pot hanging over logs stacked for a fire. A small bed was on another wall, and a table and chairs were in the middle of the room. That, and a few trunks was all.

"Did you want to read your letters?" he asked. "Then, tell me what you would like to respond, and I will scribe it for you quickly. We have a lot of them to do." He unpacked his bag, having extra parchment with him, as well as a few quills and ink.

"What will ye do while I read them?" she asked, taking a seat on the opposite side of the table.

"I'll read my book silently while I wait for you." He pulled out the book of poems by Chaucer, leaning back on his chair, placing his feet atop the table. The book was on his lap. Lark wanted to comment on the book as well as his feet, but decided instead to just watch him, while she read her letters from the men back home. Unfortunately, she found it difficult to concentrate on the stupid letters, because Dustin was taking her interest in every little thing he did. Just the way he licked his fingers before turning the pages, to the facial expressions he made while reading through the poems, it all amused her and she found it hard to look away.

With his nose still in the book, his eyes flashed upward. "Anything interesting?" he asked.

"What?" At first, she thought he meant the way she watched him. That is, until he nodded to the letter in her hands.

"The letters. Any interesting men writing them?" he asked.

"Oh, nay," she said, letting out a breath of relief that he hadn't been talking about her watching him. "No' really." Lark sighed and put the last of the letters down on the table.

"What did they say?" asked Dustin.

"No' much." She shrugged her shoulders. "It was all the same thing from one letter to the next. They said they look forward to meetin' me and hope that I will choose them for my husband." She hadn't really read all the letters, just skimmed through them, since none of them interested her as much as watching Dustin.

"Oh. All right." He slipped his book of poems back into his bag and straightened out a piece of blank parchment. Then he opened his bottle of ink and picked up a feathered quill. "What did you want to say to the men in reply?"

"I … nothin' really."

"Well, surely you must have questions for them. Things you want to ask them to get to know them better? I mean, one of these men is going to end up being your husband, my lady."

Lark got up and paced the floor, not caring in the least about these Scottish nobles or getting to know them. The man who took her interest and who she wanted to know better was English and sitting right here in this room. "I dinna have a thing to say back to these men, and neither do I care."

"So," he said, releasing a deep breath and slowly putting his quill down. He leaned forward with his elbows on the table. "Then don't say anything," he suggested.

"I canna do that." She turned to look at him, worried about what her father would say.

"You don't want to marry any of these men, do you?"

"No' the ones who just sent the letters, nay. They all sound stuffy and pretentious. Honestly, I dinna think they even want to marry me at all. I think they only want me for my father's money."

"Hmmm," he said, picking up his quill again and leaning back in his chair. "Well, you'd better say something to them in the letters. I suppose it doesn't matter what, since they'll be sealed and your father will never read them."

"I dinna want to upset my da. He is tryin' so hard to help me. He is laird and chieftain and a very proud man. I'm sorry to say that my actions have embarrassed him."

"I see." Dustin leaned forward on his elbows again. "Do you want to tell me about it, my lady?"

"About ... what?" she asked, her heart beating rapidly. She knew what he meant, but his question made her feel very awkward.

"About your past," he said, kindly, his voice gentle, not pressing. "Only if you want to, of course."

"I'm sure ye already ken all about it." She turned and looked the other way, crossing her arms over her chest.

"I am not one for listening to gossip, if that is what you mean. I would rather hear the true story from your mouth and know how you feel about it all."

"Really?" she asked meekly. No one had ever seemed to

care before what she was feeling, other than her mother. "I suppose I could tell ye. I mean, if ye are really interested." She sat back down on the chair across from him.

"I don't need to know, but I would like to be here for you. To listen. In case you find that talking about it helps to endure the pain. However, it is your decision."

His words touched her heart. This man truly seemed to care about her feelings, and that meant the world to her.

"All right, I'll tell ye." She leaned forward on her elbows now, speaking in a soft voice, even though no one could hear them. Still, she was embarrassed and didn't want to talk about her situation too loud. "It happened when I was much younger."

"Much younger?" He raised a brow. "How old are you?" He looked at her from the sides of his eyes. "And Florie is only five, so it couldn't have been that long ago."

"All right, mayhap it wasn't that long ago. However, I feel as if I have grown up so much since then. I am one and twenty now. I fell for a Frenchman's lies when I was only sixteen."

"I see. And where is this man today?"

"His name is Lord Gregoire Chastain from France. Some of the French had made an alliance with the English at the time. I should have realized I couldna have trusted him, the bastard."

"Were you in love with him?" asked Dustin. This was something that no one, not even her mother, had ever asked her before.

"I—I dinna think so. It was more like I was more infatuated with a handsome man who took notice of me and made me feel special. He said things and I believed him, although I ken now he only said them to lure me to his bed. I didna realize at the time he was only usin' me."

"Does he know about Florie?" asked Dustin.

"He didna ken I was pregnant when he left without saying

a word or a goodbye to anyone," said Lark. "I wrote him a letter telling him when Florie was born. Still, he didna return. Instead, one day I got a letter from him, written by his advisor, sayin' he was married and always was. The man told me no' to write to him anymore because he wanted nothin' to do with me."

"Do you think this is really how Gregoire felt?"

"I didna want to believe it," admitted Lark. "I kept waitin' for him to return, but of course he didna. I was a fool."

"Nay, don't say that," said Dustin, his hand covering hers atop the table to comfort her. It felt nice. "You are not a fool and never were," he told her.

"I wanted to be loved, and I thought that is what I had with Gregoire, but it was only a lie. It was lust and nothin' more."

"He probably never returned because he was married and couldn't marry you. He most likely didn't want your father to kill him," said Dustin with a chuckle. "Sorry, I didn't mean to laugh. It's just that I would never want to be on the wrong end regarding your father. He is a very intimidating man."

"Yes, my father can come across as gruff, but I assure ye once you get to ken him, he has a good heart and is like a big, lovable bear."

"A bear? I never thought of bears as being lovable."

She giggled. "Ye make me laugh, Dustin. I feel so comfortable around ye."

"I feel the same way around you, my lady. Won't you tell me the rest of your story, please?"

"There is no more, really. I got pregnant and had a baby out of wedlock. Now I am raising my child alone, my reputation is tarnished, and no man wants me. Unless he is bribed."

"Your father is going to fix things for you. Hopefully, all the gossip will stop once you marry one of these nobles," he reminded her.

"Yes, but I am no' lookin' forward to havin' to marry someone who is only after the dowry. I swear, I will never marry a man who wants my family's money only, and doesna really want me and Florie."

"Oh, I see," he said, seeming sad for a moment.

"Tell me about you, Dustin."

"I don't have anything to tell."

"Everyone has a story. What is yers? Please. I shared mine with ye."

"Oh, all right," he said, releasing her hand and playing with the quill instead of looking directly at her when he spoke. "I was left on the steps of a monastery as a baby and raised by monks. I never knew my parents."

"Ye were left here at this monastery?"

"Yes," he told her. "This has been the only home I have ever known. Brother Ruford is the one who raised me, so he is like the father that I never had."

"Do ye ken who yer parents were or what happened to them?"

"Nay, I don't. I was found wrapped in a blanket with a note pinned to me."

"A note? What did it say?"

"It seems it was from my mother. And while she never signed her name, she said on the parchment that she'd be back for me. But she never returned."

"Och, nay! So ye were abandoned, just like me."

"Yes. In a different way, but I'm sure the feelings were similar."

"I'm sorry, Dustin. That is a sad story."

"I'm sorry for you, too. I don't believe you deserve any of the turmoil you've been through."

"Thank ye," said Lark, standing up and leaning over the table, giving him a quick kiss on the mouth. She glanced out the window, seeing someone in the distance through the open gate that led to the cottage.

"Och, I see my cousin, Eleanor, out there. She must have just arrived."

"Is your cousin Eleanor a sister to Lady Raven?" he asked.

"Nay. Eleanor is the daughter of Lord Garrett and Lady Echo. Lady Echo is my Uncle Corbett's sister."

"I see. And your mother, Lady Wren, is his sister too?"

"Yes. He also has a brother, Lord Madoc, who is my cousin Robin's father."

"Do you have any siblings, Lark? I mean, Lady Lark. I'm sorry, I meant no disrespect." He held up his hands in surrender.

"No disrespect taken," she told him with a smile. "Honestly, I like it when ye just call me Lark. It makes me forget that our statuses are so different."

"Yes. I suppose so, although I'll never be able to forget that you are a noble and I am from below the salt."

There was an awkward moment of silence. "Three," she said.

"Three?" He looked up, seeming confused.

"Ye asked if I had siblin's. I have an older half-brother named Renard and a younger brother named Hawke. The youngest is my sister, Heather."

"Oh, I'd like to meet them all someday."

"I'm sure they'll be at my weddin'. Ye can meet them then."

"Yes, I guess so." He cleared his throat and picked up the feather pen, dipping it in the ink while holding his other hand over a piece of parchment.

"What are ye doin'?" she asked.

"Your father is going to want a list of the men who wrote you letters, so you'll have to tell me who they are."

"All right. I can do that. But I'd like to go out there and greet Eleanor first."

"We have to write them back. I mean, you do. This is important and we cannot wait. I can help you decide what to say to them if you'd like."

"Ye can? Ye would do that for me?"

"Aye, it is my job as scribe."

"So, what should I say?"

"I think you should just keep it simple. Thank them each for the letter they sent, and say you're looking forward to meeting them."

"Ye really think I should say that? But I dinna want to meet any of them and am no' lookin' forward to it."

"I think if you tell them the truth, it'll only cause problems between your suitors and your father. Lord Storm is going to a lot of trouble to make this work, so I think you should give him what he wants. For now, at least."

"If you believe so," said Lark, feeling a heaviness in her heart. For some reason, she thought Dustin was going to object to her sending letters to these men. She secretly hoped so. After the kisses they'd shared, she thought for sure he was interested in her. But if so, why was he trying so hard to get her to write to these men in return? Mayhap she read Dustin wrong after all.

"I'll stay here until ye are done, and then go greet my cousin." She sat back down, feeling a heaviness in her heart.

Mayhap Dustin didn't really have feelings for her after all. She supposed it was better if he didn't because she didn't want him hurt in the end.

Even if he did have true feelings for her, nothing could ever come of it, so what did it really matter? Her father would never allow her to marry a commoner from below the salt.

CHAPTER 11

L ark watched Dustin stamp the last of the wax seals on the missives he'd written for her, still wishing these letters weren't going back to her suitors in Scotland. While she didn't know what to say or write, Dustin was wonderful with words. He made the letters sound respectable without saying anything personal to the men in one way or another. Therefore, the letters wouldn't cause trouble for her father, but neither did they give the men any real encouragement that she wanted to marry them either.

"It is amazin' how ye can be so good at writin' a bunch of nothin' and makin' it sound like possibly somethin'," she told him.

"Ah, well," he said, blowing on the wax seal to dry it. "I can say a lot of something instead of nothing and mean it as well."

She giggled, since it all sounded so funny. "Ye are so funny, Dustin. Florie likes ye too. Ye are such a good tutor. Someday ye'll make a good father and husband to some lucky lassie."

His hands stilled and he said nothing. Then, he answered

so softly that she could barely hear him. "I would like it if I made some lady feel lucky."

She noticed he said lady instead of woman, but figured he didn't mean it in a titled way.

"Thank ye, Dustin," she said, reaching out and touching his hand. His gaze traveled to her fingers.

"For what?" he asked.

"Ye make me feel lucky to ken ye. Even if it is just for a little while."

"What does that mean?" he asked.

"It means, once I'm married, I will be movin' back to Scotland and we'll never see each other again."

"Oh," he answered, slowly placing the letter on the table. He slid his hand out from under hers and picked up the candle he'd used to melt the wax for the seals, and blew it out. When he did, Lark heard a knock at the door.

"Someone's here," she said, quickly pulling back her hand and standing up.

"Come in," he called out, standing as well.

"Lark? Are you in here?" Lark saw her cousin Eleanor poking her head into the cottage.

"Eleanor!" Lark ran to her and embraced her in a hug. "It is so good to see ye."

"Good to see you, too, cousin," Eleanor replied. "I just arrived and was looking for you since someone told me you were here. Then I saw Brother Ruford and Sister Joan coming from the church and they told me where to find you."

DUSTIN WATCHED the two women embrace, and part of him felt jealous in a way. They were family. He had no family. He couldn't even imagine how it felt to see a relative, or to give them a hug. Dustin could feel the strong bond between the cousins, and that only made him feel lonely.

Did he have siblings or cousins somewhere he wondered? What were his parents like? Were they weak or strong or rich or poor? And why in heaven's name did they abandon him as a baby? The thought of parents abandoning their baby made him angry now.

"Who is this?" asked Eleanor.

"This is Dustin Styles," Lark introduced him. "He is Florie's tutor and also the castle scribe. Dustin, this is my cousin, Eleanor Blackmore."

"Nice to meet you, my lady," said Dustin with a half-bow.

Eleanor looked to be about the same age as Lark. However, she was not Scottish, she was an English lady. She was dressed in the gown of a noblewoman, but wore a big crucifix on a chain around her neck. She had bright red hair tucked under a small headpiece and ringlets of fire hung down the sides of her face. In Dustin's opinion, this woman was far too elegant and pretty to be living in an abbey, even if she wasn't a nun. Then again, wasn't he in a very similar situation?

"Dustin," Eleanor repeated his name. "Oh, aren't you the orphan boy that Lord Corbett's uncle, Brother Ruford, raised here at the monastery?"

"Yes," he said, dropping his gaze. "That would be me."

"I would love if you came back to visit the other orphans at St. Anne's Abbey someday," said Eleanor.

"What? Why would I do that?" he asked, feeling as if this were a demeaning thing to do.

"I think what my cousin means is that ye have a good life and it will help make the orphans feel as if they have a chance, too. Eleanor helps to find good homes for the orphans at St. Anne's Abbey in Hythe."

"Yes, you can give the children hope," said Eleanor.

"Well, mayhap someday," said Dustin. "However, I am very busy here in Steepleton. Lady Lark, we need to get back to the castle. Your father will be returning from the trade fair soon and he'll want these letters."

"What are those letters?" asked Eleanor, eyeing them on the table.

"Da is makin' me respond to all the suitors who send me letters," explained Lark.

"Aye, I heard from my parents that you are to be married by the end of the month. I wanted to be here to support you, Lark. I also wanted to tell you that you did a brave thing by raising Florie on your own. Most ladies in your position would have given up their babies instead. I still cannot believe anyone could possibly abandon their baby on the steps of a church!"

"Eleanor, please," said Lark, glancing over at Dustin.

This was a very awkward situation, and Dustin no longer wished to be here.

"I'll go to the stable and get the horse," he told Lark, packing the letters and items into his bag and heading to the door.

"Oh, excuse me," said Sister Joan, almost bumping into him as he tried to leave the cottage. "Dustin," she said his name with a smile.

"Yes, Sister. My name is Dustin." She stood in the doorway so he waited for her to move. "I need to fetch the horse so we can leave."

"I have a horse-drawn wagon that the sister and I can use to get to Blake Castle," Eleanor told him. "The stable boy should have it ready."

"I can tell Brother Ruford that we'll be leaving," offered the nun, still not moving.

"I'm so glad ye are comin' to the castle, Eleanor," said Lark.

"I am nervous about this marriage, and ye can help me decide which of the suitors to choose."

"Me? I know nothing about men," stated Eleanor. "Mayhap you should ask Raven since she is the married one."

"Nay, she is married to a commoner, just like Rook," Lark reminded her. "If I marry a commoner, Uncle Corbett, as well as my father, will have my head. The only way I can redeem myself from my mistakes of the past is to marry well, and with someone of my own status."

"You're right," agreed Eleanor. "You'll have to marry someone of your status. You don't have a choice."

"Excuse me," said Dustin, pushing past the nun and taking off for the stable at a near run. He didn't want to hear any more of this conversation. It only made him feel worse about himself than he already did.

Why couldn't life be different for him? Why couldn't he have cousins and siblings and be happily titled and looking for a wife with whom to raise a family?

If he wasn't just a poor commoner from below the salt, he could be like the suitors, writing letters to Lady Lark right now, trying to persuade her to choose him for her husband.

He stopped at the door to the stables, and looked down at his bag containing the letters. Why couldn't he be one of these men? Lark didn't know any of them. All she knew was what they wrote to her in the letters. So far, she wasn't impressed with any of them either. Then again, he read the letters and they were the most pathetic writings he'd ever seen.

None of these men had love in their hearts, and it showed in what they wrote. All they really wanted was the money, just like Lark said.

"What if she got a romantic letter?" he asked himself aloud. Yes, he decided. He loved poetry, and he knew how to write. What if he wrote her letters, pretending to be one of her suitors? A secret admirer? This would be a true way to find out how she really felt about him.

Lark deserved a romantic man, not one of these pompous nobles who only cared about themselves and what they could gain by the marriage. None of them would ever treat Lark the way she deserved to be treated. Plus, he was sure all of these men would send Florie away to be fostered as soon as they said the wedding vows. Florie was all Lark had, and her daughter should never be taken from her.

"What if I did it?" Dustin asked himself, deciding whether or not to write love letters to Lark in secret. He could tell her exactly how he really felt about her, but she wouldn't know it was him. Then, he would discover if perhaps there was really a way they could be together. If she fell in love with him through the letters, not letting the fact he was a commoner distract her, perhaps she would find him the love she'd been looking for her entire life.

Mayhap, so would he.

"Dustin? Didn't you hear me?"

Dustin turned to find Brother Ruford standing there with a bewildered look on his face.

"I'm sorry, Brother Ruford. Did you say something?"

"I wanted to talk to you before you left for the castle. However, you seem to be involved in another conversation, but with yourself."

"I'm sorry," he said. "What was it you wanted to speak to me about?"

"It's about Sister Joan," he told him.

"What about her?"

"She's been asking a lot of questions about you, and I don't know why."

"Questions? About me? What kind of questions?"

"She wanted to know all about when I first found you on"

the steps to the church. About when you were a baby."

"That's odd," said Dustin. "But she's probably like Lady Eleanor, and cares immensely that all the children have good homes. Lady Eleanor wants me to talk to the orphans. Perhaps Sister Joan wants that as well."

"Mayhap," said Brother Ruford. "But she kept asking to see all the records from the past. To be precise, she was asking about boy babies left on the steps of the church twenty-two years ago."

"What?" Dustin's head snapped up. "Were there a lot during that time span?"

"Nay, Dustin, there were not. As a matter of fact, you were the only boy."

"So, this Sister Joan was asking about me personally, then?"

"When she found out the information, she was very interested in meeting you. She even offered to go to Blake Castle as a nursemaid for Florie."

"What does this mean?" asked Dustin. "I don't understand."

"Dustin, I can't be sure yet, but I have a suspicion that this nun might actually know something about your mother."

"Nay. Really?" Dustin's heart sped up. On one hand, he wanted to know about his mother and father and who they were. But on the other hand, he was angry with them for abandoning him as a baby. He wasn't sure what to think about this newfound information or what to do with it.

"Mayhap you should ask Sister Joan if she knows anything about your parents," suggested Brother Ruford.

"Me?"

"Yes. I was going to ask her about it, but I wasn't sure if you wanted to know, so I thought it should come from you instead."

"Aye. Nay. Oh, hell, I don't know." Dustin dragged a weary hand through his hair in thought, confused as to what to do.

"No swearing, Dustin. You're in a monastery and under the scrutiny of God's eyes," grumbled Ruford.

"Yes. God's eyes, what if she really knows who my mother was? Or is? What if my mother is still alive?"

"When I mentioned God's eyes, I didn't mean for you to use it in blasphemy," said Ruford through his teeth. "Dustin, just ask her."

"I am not sure I want to know. Sister Joan is a stranger to me. What if she really knows something but is mistaken about it? Or God forbid, lying? I won't be able to live with that."

"Then, just get to know Sister Joan first and see if you can trust her. However, Dustin, I must point out that she is a nun and does the work of God like I do. Of course you can trust her."

"I have a hard time trusting people and you know that, Ruford."

"*Brother* Ruford. You need to call me Brother in the monastery and in front of others."

"Mayhap I should be calling you father since you're the only father I ever knew. I'm not sure I want to know my real father. I'm not sure about any of this." Suddenly, he was changing his mind about wanting family. After all, what if his parents were horrible people? Mayhap he was the son of a thief, a whore, or even a murderer. If so, he wasn't sure he really wanted to know.

"Then pray to find your answer," suggested the monk, like Dustin knew he would say. Brother Ruford's answer to everything was prayer.

"I have something else on my mind right now that is more important." Dustin saw Lark and Eleanor and Sister Joan heading toward the stable.

"If it's Lady Lark on your mind, then remove that thought right now," Ruford warned him.

"Why?"

"You are a commoner and that is all you will ever be," said Ruford. "My nephew is upset that his son and daughter just married below their status. He might not be able to change that, but he can stop any of his siblings' children from making the same mistake."

"Do you think it's really a mistake?" Dustin asked Ruford. "That Lady Raven and Lord Rook married from below the salt?"

"It is not for me to judge," said Ruford. "But the only advice I want to give you is to watch your step, and for heaven's sake, think before you act."

"In what way?"

"I mean, Lady Lark already has a child out of wedlock, and her father and uncle would never let her marry a man who wasn't noble. So don't put yourself in a position that will end up with your neck on the chopping block."

"So you're telling me, don't get her pregnant?"

"I'm saying, don't break the girl's heart, Dustin. She has already had such a hard life. Although she acts strong, she is very fragile. Don't do anything to lead her on, because you know you two don't belong together and nothing can change that."

"So sure about that, are you?" asked Dustin, not liking to be told what or what not to do.

"The only thing I'm sure about is that you have a mind of your own, and you always have, ever since you were a child. That is what worries me the most. I'm afraid before this is all over, one of you, or perhaps both of you, are going to end up broken-hearted."

CHAPTER 12

Dustin finished writing a love letter to Lady Lark the next morning, blowing on the ink to dry it.

"What are you doing?" asked Orrick, sitting up in bed and stretching.

Dustin didn't mind staying with Orrick. The man was not really bothersome in the least. It was also nice to have company—someone to talk to about his troubles. Orrick might be an advisor to Lord Corbett, but he also gave Dustin advice regarding Lady Lark, and Dustin appreciated it.

"I've written a love poem to Lady Lark. I am going to slip it in with any letters that arrive here today from her suitors."

"I see." Orrick stood up and shuffled across the room, lighting another candle. "Did you sign it?"

"Nay!" The idea seemed preposterous to Dustin. "Of course, not. I can't let her know it is from me."

"Then why do it?" asked Orrick, smoothing down his long beard.

"I am doing this because I want to see if she is attracted to me. Through my writing. If so, in time I will tell her the letters came from me. Mayhap." He folded up the parchment and slipped a band around it. He didn't want to use the wax seal, or she might recognize it and he'd be discovered. "I haven't really thought that far ahead."

"Well, good luck," said Orrick. "I hope you find what you are looking for."

"Me too."

There came a knock at the door, and Orrick crossed the room and opened it. A page stood there with something in his hand.

"I have letters that were delivered to the castle this morning," said the boy. "I was told they are for Lady Lark and that I should bring them here and give them to the scribe."

"Oh, thank you." Dustin grabbed his letter and his bag and shot out of his chair. He hurried over to the page, taking the letters from him. There were only two today, but at least he could slip his into the pile when he gave them to Lark to read.

"Off to work, I suppose?" asked Orrick.

"Aye," said Dustin with a smile, not able to wait until Lark read his letter.

LARK PACED THE SOLAR, waiting for Dustin, wondering where he was this morning. Florie was already acting up, since she had nightmares all night long and Lark got very little sleep at all.

There was a knock at the door, and she ran over to greet him.

"Where have you been?" she asked as she opened the door. She stopped from saying more when she realized it was Sister Joan, not Dustin.

"My lady, I am here to care for the child," said the nun. Her hands were folded in front of her and she slowly nodded her head in respect.

"Well, the scribe is arriving at any minute to tutor Florie," explained Lark, looking back at her daughter who was yawning, sitting on the stool at the table, swinging her feet back and forth.

"Oh. Did you want me to return later, then?" asked Sister Joan.

"Nay, I suppose you can come in and wait." Lark moved aside and the nun entered.

"Hello, Florie, I am Sister Joan," said the nun, speaking in a soft tone so as not to frighten the child. She walked in a gliding motion over to Florie who looked at her curiously.

"Why do ye wear that robe? Why is yer head covered?" asked the girl. "What color hair do ye have?"

Florie was always asking questions, and sometimes it became overwhelming to others around her. The last thing Lark wanted was for her daughter to scare the nun away.

"Florie, stop asking her so many questions," said Lark, leaving the door open and heading over to the table. "Sister Joan is here to help take care of you, so be nice to her."

Florie crossed her arms over her chest and pouted.

"I don't mind your questions," said Sister Joan. "Would you like to see my hair?"

"Yes!" Florie looked excited.

"I suppose it wouldn't hurt to show you, although nuns are supposed to wear their wimples everywhere they go." Sister Joan removed her wimple to expose her brown hair tied up atop her head.

"My hair is yellow," said Florie.

"Yes, it is golden, like a princess, and very pretty." The nun reached out and gently ran her hand over Florie's head, making the little girl smile.

"I would like to be a princess. That would be fun," said Florie.

"Good morning, I am sorry I am late." Dustin walked in, but stopped when he saw the nun.

"Oh, excuse me," said Sister Joan, turning away and putting her wimple back in place.

Dustin stood there, staring, and Lark didn't understand why.

"Are ye feelin' ill?" she asked him.

"Nay." He shook his head. "Nay, I'm fine."

"Oh, ye have more letters for me," said Lark, looking down to the parchments in his hand. "Let me read them." She took them from him and headed across the room.

"There are only three today," he told her, putting his things on the table. He seemed nervous for some reason. Lark decided it must be because the nun was here and he wasn't used to having a lot of people watching during his lessons.

"I hope ye dinna mind that I told Sister Joan she could stay for Florie's lesson?"

"Nay. Of course not." He didn't even look up when he spoke.

"I thought I'd take Florie for a walk through the orchard later," said the nun. "Florie, have you ever picked apples and eaten them right off the tree?"

"I dinna think so," said the little girl.

"Would you like to do that?"

"All right," said Florie.

"Time for your reading lesson." Dustin opened the book he'd brought with him. It had simple stories made for children learning to read. He pushed it across the table to the girl.

"I dinna want to read this." Florie hopped off the chair and ran over to her mother. "I want to read those letters." She pointed to the ones in Lark's hand.

. . .

"WHAT? NAY." Dustin's head snapped up as he saw Florie climbing atop her mother's lap. Lark sat on the bed with the letters in her hand. The nun opened the shutter and peered outside, breathing in a breath of fresh air with a smile on her face. "Florie, this is what you need to read over here. Those letters are for your mother," Dustin said, trying to bring the little girl back to the table, but she wouldn't listen.

"Och, I dinna mind if she stays here," said Lark, unfolding the first letter. "These men are simpletons and dinna write anythin' that is hard to read, I'm sure."

"Let me see, let me see," said Florie, ripping the letter out of her mother's hand. "I want to read."

"All right. What is this word?" asked Lark.

Florie looked at it and made a face. "D-D-Dog?"

"Nay," said Lark with a giggle. "It is *Dear*. Mayhap this writing is a little too messy to read. Let's try another one."

Dustin saw her opening his love poem next and swore he was about to swoon like a blasted girl. Why did this have to be happening? The love poem he wrote was only meant for her eyes, not the eyes and ears of a child and a nun. What was he going to do now?

"Florie, come here," he said in desperation, but the little girl was too interested in her mother's letters to listen to him.

"Oh, this one seems to be a poem. That should be easy to read," said Lark. "I'll read it aloud and ye follow along with me as I point to the words, Florie."

"God's eyes, nay," Dustin mumbled under his breath. This was the worst thing that could possibly happen. Could this situation get any worse?

"Did I hear you mention God?" asked the nun, having overheard him curse.

"Nay. Yes. I mean ... God is good to give us ... this time to teach a child." Wow, did that sound addled! He squeezed his eyes closed and when he opened them, he saw Lark holding up the letter he wrote, pointing out the words to Florie as Lark read it aloud.

"*Lady Lark,*" she started, smiling widely. "That's me," she told her daughter.

"Lady Lark," repeated Florie, pointing at the words on the page.

"*Yer smile is the warmth that melts my heart,*" she read, looking closer at the page. "*Like the sunshine that opens a bud, my love for ye blossoms every day.*"

"Oh, my," gasped the nun from across the room. "Is this someone you've already met? It sounds so personal."

"I—nay," said Lark, her smile disappearing. "I wonder who it is from." With her finger she scanned down the page. "I dinna see a signature at the bottom. It just says, *Yer Secret Admirer.*"

Dustin watched as Lark's cheeks turned bright red. He was sure his face was as red right now too, but from embarrassment on his part. He didn't think anyone but Lark would be reading his poem of love.

"Read more, read more," said Florie, excitedly bouncing up and down on the bed, sitting next to her.

"I think we should start your lesson," said Dustin.

"I agree," said Sister Joan. "What these men are writing is not for the ears of a child."

"I want to hear more, Mother," whined Florie.

Lark scanned the parchment, looking flustered. "Well, I'm sure there is nothin' here that is really inappropriate," she commented. Then, to Dustin's dismay, she continued to read aloud.

"*Yer voice is like the sweet chirpin' of the meadowlark.*"

"That's a bird, right, Mother?" asked Florie.

"Yes, a meadowlark is a bird, that's right," she answered.

"Read more." Florie clapped her hands together in excitement.

"Well, all right." Lark continued to read. *"I long to taste yer sweet lips and–"* She stopped abruptly and quickly folded the letter back up. "Mayhap it would be best to start your lesson now after all, sweetheart. We have kept Dustin waitin' too long already."

"Yes," said Dustin, clearing his throat. "I think that would be best."

Damn, if he had known this would happen, he wouldn't have put the letter in with the others. He felt like hiding under the table right now. Thank goodness she didn't know he wrote it. His words were meant only for Lark, and he felt as if his soul was bared right in front of a child and a holy woman. Egads, could this be any worse?

Florie ran over to the table and sat down for her lesson.

"When the lesson is over we can record these letters and who they are from," Lark told Dustin.

"Aye. Of course," he said, just wanting this day to be over.

"Of course, this love poem is no' signed. I guess I'll have to show it to my da and ask him who he thinks it could be from."

"Nay! Don't do that," said Dustin, almost shouting. He could just picture Storm MacKeefe reading the words and vowing to kill whichever man wrote them to his daughter.

"Why no'?" asked Lark.

"I—I think mayhap you should wait." He needed a good reason, but couldn't seem to think at the moment.

"Wait? Whatever for?"

"In case your secret admirer sends another letter. I mean … mayhap then he'll sign it. Yes, that's it. Give him a chance to tell you who he is."

"I dinna ken." She stared down at the letter in thought. "I am no' sure I should wait," said Lark.

"I agree with Dustin," said Sister Joan, surprising the heck out of him.

"Ye do?" asked Lark, furrowing her brow.

"Yes. After all, it sounds like this man is possibly different from the rest."

"Aye. He writes like none of the others," agreed Lark.

"Mayhap just wait, like Dustin said," continued the nun. "If you have to choose a husband, get to know him through his letters first. Does your father really need to know?"

"I suppose I can wait to tell him. Ye're right. I might just keep this to myself for now," Lark finally and thankfully agreed.

Dustin could have kissed the nun right now for helping him out, whether she'd meant to do so or not. "Let's start our reading lesson with something that is more appropriate for children," he told Florie, opening the book.

From now on, he'd have to be more careful so others would not see his private love letters to Lady Lark.

"LARK, what is that you keep looking at under the table?" Raven asked during the main meal later that day.

"It's nothin'," said Lark, folding up the love letter, hiding it on her lap. She couldn't stop wondering which nobleman might have sent it.

"You've got a letter!" said Raven, reaching out and snatching it away from her.

"Let me see," said her cousin, Eleanor, who was sitting next to Raven.

"Nay! Give it back to me." Lark reached out for it, but Raven turned her shoulder and read it along with Eleanor.

"Oh, my!" said Eleanor. "Someone really seems to like you."

"Let's see who it is from," said Raven, scanning her finger down to the bottom of the parchment. "Oh, it just says a secret admirer. How mysterious and exciting."

"He compares your voice to a meadowlark?" asked Eleanor, putting her hands to her heart. "That is so sweet."

"And he wants to kiss your sweet lips and ... oh my," said Raven, reading through the letter with wide eyes. "He says his body burns for ye."

Raven and Eleanor giggled.

"Give me that, and dinna let my da hear ye." Lark yanked the letter away from them, her gaze quickly darting over to her father. Thank goodness he was busy talking to her Uncle Corbett and didn't notice.

"Lark, this is exciting, having a secret admirer," said Raven.

"Yes, I can't wait to find out who he is," said Eleanor. "I have never had any man say such romantic things to me."

"Ye live in a nunnery," Lark pointed out, pushing the missive into a pouch attached to her waist belt. "Ye are no' goin' to find any men there except for monks."

"I don't live there all the time," said Eleanor in her defense. "Sometimes, I go back to my father's castle in Hythe. Besides, I am not looking for a man to marry, but you are."

"Eleanor, you just don't want any man since you can't have the one you still love after all these years," said Raven.

"Ye mean that boy named Connor that she was once betrothed to?" asked Lark. "The one who is an executioner now?"

"Yes, that's the one," said Raven.

"Nay, you're wrong," cried Eleanor with glassy eyes. "It's

Connor's father who is the hangman, not him. And I don't want to talk about him anymore. We're talking about Lark now." Eleanor cleverly turned the conversation back to Lark. "Cousin, when you find out who the nobleman is, the one who is your secret admirer, are you going to choose him to marry?"

"I dinna ken," said Lark, looking down and running a loving hand over her bag with a smile on her face. "I have never had a man say such sweet things to me before. I truly hope he is handsome and that he writes to me again. However, I must say he is at the top of my list so far for becoming my husband."

Dustin downed another tankard of ale, sitting below the salt with the other commoners, but keeping an eye on Lark up at the dais. He was sure he saw her showing her cousins the love letter he wrote to her. Bid the devil, he was just stirring up trouble by doing this. He never should have written anything at all to her.

He could no longer watch. Dustin got up from the bench, making his way back up to the tower, so he could be alone and think about his situation.

"Where are you going?" asked Orrick, almost bumping into him in the corridor.

"Hello, Orrick. I need to get away. To think."

"Does this have anything to do with that letter you wrote this morning?"

"It has everything to do with it," he said, feeling a heaviness in his heart. "I am not a noble and never should have written it. Now, Lark thinks some noble is wooing her, and she seems to like it. Damn, I might have just made a big mistake."

"Well, go think things over, then. I'll leave you alone. But remember, everything happens for a reason, Dustin. Just give it some time and mayhap things will work out without you even trying to fix them."

"I highly doubt that," grumbled Dustin, climbing the stairs.

He entered the sorcerer's room at the top of the tower and plopped down on his pallet, throwing his arm over his face in despair. Flames burned on the hearth, and the only sounds in the room were his breathing and the crackling of the wood on the fire.

He had just started to doze off, when he thought he heard the creak of the door opening. He glanced over, and to his surprise, he saw Lark poking her head into the room.

"Dustin?" she called out silently, looking around.

"Lady Lark!" He bolted upright to a sitting position. What the hell was she doing here?

"Och, there ye are," she said with a smile that made her look so pretty. She boldly entered the room and closed the door behind her, making Dustin feel extremely uneasy.

"What are you doing here? You can't be here!" He jumped to his feet. "What if someone sees you? Why did you close the door?"

"Calm down, Dustin," she said, making a face that told him she thought he was overreacting. "No one was payin' attention to me leavin' the great hall. Even if they were, I'm sure they thought I was only visitin' the garderobe."

"This is not right," said Dustin, realizing how much trouble he'd be in if anyone knew she was alone with him and especially with the door closed. In a magic man's room, no less. Wasn't she the one who told him they needed to keep the door open when they were alone together? Suddenly, she didn't seem eager to follow the rules.

"Everyone is still eatin', and we are no' doin' anythin' wrong," said Lark, waving a carefree hand through the air.

"Not yet," Dustin mumbled under his breath.

"Just relax. Ye are much too tense."

Egads, this woman had nerves of steel.

"I am relaxed," he told her, feeling as if he could barely breathe, the air was so thick right now.

"Besides, I saw Orrick having a conversation with my da and uncle, and those tend to be quite lengthy."

"Well, why are you here?" he demanded to know. "What do you want?" All he had wanted was time alone to rest and try to forget about the girl. But now she was right here in the room with him. There would be no forgetting anything now.

"I saw ye leave the great hall before the meal was finished. Ye looked upset, and I was worried about ye, that's all."

"You were?" No one had ever worried about him before. This was new to him and he wasn't sure how to react.

"Aye. Are you ill?" She reached out and laid her hand on his forehead. "Ye do feel a little warm."

Damn, it felt good to have her touch him. How could he tell her that he wasn't warm but burning up with desire for her? Just feeling her hand on his forehead caused him to stir below his belt.

"You'd better not do that, my lady," he warned her, gently pushing her hand away.

"Why no'? Does it bother ye?"

"Aye, more than you know."

"I'm sorry." Her smile turned to a frown. "I suppose I should leave then."

"Wait," he said, reaching out and taking her arm. "Don't go. That's not what I meant."

"All right. I will stay for a while then." Her smile was back again.

"We can sit at the table, and talk," he suggested, with an outstretched arm in invitation.

"Of course." She walked over to the table and Dustin quickly pulled out a chair for her.

"My, you spoil me," she said with a giggle, taking a seat.

"You deserve to be spoiled," he told her. "If you were mine, I'd-" He stopped in mid-sentence, wanting to hit himself for voicing this aloud.

"What would ye do if I were yers, Dustin?"

"Nothing. I'm sorry. That was improper and I never should have said it. Forgive me, my lady." He couldn't be so close to her anymore because he was making bad choices. He started pacing the floor.

"Tell me, Dustin. Please. I want to ken." She was standing right next to him, and when he turned around quickly, he bumped into her.

His hands went to her shoulders to keep her from falling. He stared deeply into her green eyes getting lost in the swirling depths. It was as if he felt he were looking into her very soul.

"It's not appropriate of me to voice my feelings aloud."

"Why no'?" she asked, blinking twice in succession. "Because I am a noble and ye are a commoner? Is that what is worryin' ye?"

"Isn't that reason enough?" He shook his head.

"Nay," she said defiantly. "It's no' enough, and I dinna care about status right now."

"Since when? You clearly pointed out to me before how important it was to remember that you are a noble and I am not."

"I changed my mind about that."

"I really don't know what to say."

"Well, I do. I want to say I enjoyed our kiss and hope to experience it again."

"You did? You do?" This was leading somewhere that

147

neither of them should be going. He should end this right now and send her away.

But, of course, he didn't.

"Yes, didn't ye enjoy it too?"

"Well, of course I did."

"Then kiss me again, and stop bein' so afraid of me. I willna bite ye. I might be a lady, but I am still a woman with wants and needs and desires."

"Desires," he repeated, feeling some of his own right now. This woman was making him very aroused, and he was at the point where he wanted to do something about it.

Ever since they'd kissed, all he could do was think about kissing her again, wishing to do it and so much more.

With no more talking, their lips met in a deep and passionate kiss, wanted by both of them. It felt like heaven to Dustin. He was living a dream, holding a beautiful lady, kissing her, and feeling like he'd never felt before.

LARK LOST herself in Dustin's kiss. He held her gently, but securely at the same time. His lips were soft and sensuous. His kiss was filled with life and extreme passion. She found herself melting in his arms. This man made her feel like nothing else mattered. His kiss had awakened something within her that had died the day Gregoire left her pregnant and alone.

"Dustin, when ye kiss me, it feels ... right. It makes me feel so good, that I canna explain it," she whispered.

"Lady Lark, I like it too."

"Please, dinna call me lady when we are kissin'." The last thing she wanted to be reminded of at a time like this was that they were not of the same status. "Just call me Lark."

"I don't know if I can do that."

"Please?" she asked, pulling back and looking into his

hooded eyes. "I want ye to think of me as no different from any other lassie right now."

"Damn it, Lark," he ground out, using her name, even though she wished he hadn't done so with a swear word attached to it. "You don't know what you're doing to me."

"Then tell me." She playfully ran her hands down his chest, delighting in the feel of his muscles and firm body hidden beneath his coarse tunic.

He groaned.

"You are so beautiful that I can't stop thinking about you and wishing that our circumstances could be different." He cupped her cheek with his palm, kissing her again. And when he dropped his hand, it grazed against the swell of her breast, making her gasp out loud.

"I'm sorry. I shouldn't have done that. I'll stop now."

His words of ending all this made her feel panicked. She didn't want him to stop, and neither did she want him to walk away from her right now. Lark needed to feel loved. It was something that was missing from her life, and she doubted she'd really gain that by marrying a greedy old nobleman. A strong pulsing feeling deep within her brought her to life, and she wanted to explore that sensation more. This might be her one and only chance to experience what she'd been wanting for so long to feel.

"I like ye, Dustin," she said, taking his hand and laying it atop her chest, silently giving him permission to continue. "I dinna want ye to stop. No' ever."

"God's eyes." He squeezed his eyes shut and then they popped open again. "You don't know what you are saying. If we don't stop right now, Lark, I won't be able to because you are driving me mad with want."

He pulled her closer to him instead of pushing her away. His words said one thing, but his body actions said another.

She felt his hard erection pressing up against her stomach and realized he wanted her badly. It made her heart leap into her throat, and her breathing deepened.

"Oh!" She looked down and saw the bulge, and such a strong urge overcame her that she couldn't stop herself from reaching out to touch it. When she skimmed her fingers over his hardened form, right through his clothes, he gave a sharp intake of breath.

"I'm sorry. Did I hurt ye?"

He laughed. "Lark, you could never hurt me. You are like a siren calling to me, and I am helpless to stop from wanting your charms."

He surprised her, as well as pleased her with his words. They were so imaginative and she liked being compared to a siren of the sea. Lark felt both his hands skim over her breasts now, and then close over them in a quick squeeze.

"Ooooh, that feels good," she whispered, throwing back her head as he nuzzled her neck and continued to kiss her all the way down to her cleavage.

"Stop me, Lark," he begged. "Please, stop me, because if you don't, I am going to make love to you right here."

She inhaled sharply, becoming more and more excited by the thought of making love with the handsome scribe named Dustin.

"I want ye, Dustin," she whispered. "I want to ken how it feels to make love with ye."

"But you're getting married soon," he reminded her, his hand trailing down her neck, his fingers dipping into her cleavage, brushing against her bare breast. A delightful shiver ran through her.

"All the more reason," she replied. "I have never been so excited by a man before as I am by ye, right now."

"Never?" he whispered into her ear, his hot breath followed

by his tongue, tracing the outline of her lobe. Her breathing deepened, and his hand slid lower. She felt him cupping her entire breast and it about drove her mad with want. His thumb flicked quickly over her nipple, and she swore she felt it go taut at his touch. She cried out in a soft, lust-filled whimper.

"Oh! Dustin, please," she begged him now. The tears welled up in her eyes from being so aroused and excited. "The last time I coupled with a man, it was far from satisfyin' and left me with a bairn."

"Are you saying you've never found completion?"'

"Nay, never," she whispered, about ready to burst. He slowly pushed aside her bodice and slowly lowered his head, all the while his eyes being interlocked with hers. His mouth covered her nipple. She felt the wet, intimate warmth as he suckled her like a bairn, using his lips and tongue to excite her. Lark moaned, reaching out and pulling his head closer, all the while pushing herself deeper into his mouth. "I want to ken how it feels to let myself go." Her chest heaved as she struggled for air, feeling as if she were on fire. Her head dizzied. "I want to make love with you and shatter in your arms." There was no holding in her thoughts or feelings anymore. Not that she ever wanted to, when it came to this sexy, talented man.

Dustin's head came up and he cupped her chin, looking deeply into her eyes again. "Lark," he whispered her name, his voice alone almost making her shatter. "I want this, too. More than you'll ever know."

"Yes," she whispered with her eyes closed, sure this would be the moment they both surrendered and made love.

"But this is wrong," he continued, making her eyes pop open.

"Wrong?" she repeated, at a loss for words. Was he really planning on stopping? Now?

"It will ruin your reputation."

That made her laugh. "Dustin, my reputation was ruined long before I ever met ye. Dinna fret about that."

"You're not afraid of being a ... a naughty girl?" he asked with a raised brow.

She played with him in a flirtatious way. "Would ye spank me if I were?"

"Only if you wanted me to."

She saw his tongue shoot out to lick his upper lip. He liked the idea as much as she did, and it was no secret. Damn, why did every little thing he did make her feel more and more lusty?

"Ye dinna see me stoppin' ye, do ye?" She smiled coyly.

Dustin gripped the hem of her gown, slowly pulling it higher and higher. Then he slipped both his hands under her skirt and around her hips to her buttocks.

"Oooooooh," he moaned, taking her bare cheeks in his hands, squeezing her bottom end like he was kneading dough.

"It would be so easy to take you right now," he said next to her ear, his hot breath causing her to tingle. "We wouldn't even have to remove your clothing since you are naked beneath your skirt."

"True," she said, feeling her excitement growing. "But I thought ye were goin' to spank me for bein' naughty."

"Is that what you want?" he asked.

"Mmmm," she moaned, looking up at him and running her tongue over her top lip now. "If you feel it is needed."

He turned her around and bent her over the table, throwing her gown up over her head. She felt the cool air drift past her, doing nothing to quench the fires burning within her belly. And when he playfully slapped her bare ass, the sound of skin against skin about drove her over the edge. She was so excited now that she could no longer hold in her lustful passion.

She turned around, smiling at him, feeling like the devil

and not caring that she was about to give herself to a man she barely knew. She needed this. She wanted this. Even if it was a one-time occurrence, all that mattered was what she was feeling right now.

"Do it," she commanded.

"Argh," he grunted, running a hand through his long hair and looking up at the ceiling. "You don't know what you're saying." He was still holding back, although she knew he wanted this as much as she. Mayhap he only needed a bit more persuading.

She reached out and untied his trews, freeing his erection, and releasing his clothes. His trews dropped to the ground, pooling around his feet.

"Oh, now that was bad," he said in a playful manner. "Very, very, naughty."

"No' as naughty as this, I bet." She reached out and took his hardened form in her hand, closing her fingers around him and squeezing slightly. He felt like silk over steel, and smooth, as she slid her hand up and down his manhood.

"Ooooh, Lark. "I want you so bad right now, that I am going to burst."

"Then take me."

"I can't. You're a ... a lady."

"Nay," she scolded. "I told ye, tonight I am just like any other lassie ye've bedded. Now, do to me what ye would do with any other lover."

"Are you sure about this?" His lusty eyes drank her in. It was as if he were a wild animal and she his prey, and she wanted to be devoured by this dark wolf.

"No regrets," she told him. Before she knew what had happened, he picked her up and her legs were wrapped around his waist, her backside slightly resting on the table. He kissed her, holding her higher against him as he turned and walked, and then her back was up against the wall. His manhood poked at her entry, and then she felt him slowly slipping his length into her.

"Ooooh," she cried as he moved his hips, finding a rhythm. He held her up, but slowly slid her down his shaft, little by little until he filled her completely.

"Is this too much for you?" he asked, as if he truly cared.

"I want more," she told him, and he continued to thrust in and out, guided by her own liquid passion.

"Nay, this is too rough for you. I don't want to hurt you," he said, carrying her over to the pallet on the ground and laying her down gently.

"I want more, Dustin," she said through ragged breathing. "I am so close to the brink of release, and I need to ken how it feels. Please, dinna deny me what I long for. Help me to find my completion."

"I cannot deny you anything, my love." He straddled her, pushing up her gown once again. And when he entered her, they did the dance of love just like any two lovers would do. Dustin turned into an animal, and she ... she loved every minute of it.

Climbing higher and higher, Lark felt euphoric. This was a feeling she had never felt in her life. With each thrust, she was brought closer and closer to the precipice of desire, and then colors, beautiful colors, exploded behind her closed lids as she let herself go. Lark screamed out, releasing all the pent-up feelings she had buried deep inside herself for so many years. She found such satisfaction and completion with Dustin, that she never wanted it to end.

Lark heard him moan and saw him shaking his head like a dog trying to dry off. She giggled and squealed and then squealed out loud again.

Then, sated and spent, they lay next to each other, not

saying a word for a minute or two. Lark stared up at the ceiling with a smile on her face.

"That was ... that was amazin', Dustin. Thank ye."

"Yes, it was," he said, and she wished he had stopped there and not continued talking. "Oh, Lark, what did we do?" he asked, sounding as if he felt guilty.

"We did exactly what we wanted to do, and no one stopped us."

Just when she said that, there was a small knock at the door.

They both looked at each other and Dustin held his finger up to his lips to tell her to be silent. He hurried over and donned his trews while she sat up and fixed her gown.

"Lark? Lark, are you in there?" came a woman's voice from outside the door.

"It's Raven," said Lark, jumping to her feet.

"Your father is asking for you," said Raven through the door. "Lark, if you're in there, you really need to leave now, before he comes looking for you."

"Thank ye, Dustin," said Lark, kissing him once more and running for the door.

This was a night Lark would never forget for as long as she lived.

She pulled open the door and stepped out, closing the door behind her.

"What were you doing in there alone?" Raven asked her.

"I wasna alone, Raven. I was with Dustin."

"Doing what?" gasped Raven.

Lark looked at her and smiled, not saying a word. Then she hurried down the tower stairs, humming to herself.

CHAPTER 13

Dustin found it hard to even look at Lark the next day when he walked into the solar for Florie's lesson. Guilt gnawed at him for having made love with Lark. While he had enjoyed the experience immensely, he now wished he had been stronger and turned her away. This couldn't end well for either of them if word got out about it.

He heard voices and looked up. Dustin froze, seeing not only Lark and Florie there inside the solar, but also Sister Joan, Raven, and Eleanor. God's eyes, why did they all have to be here?

"What's going on?" he asked, walking in with the letters of the day in his hand. He hadn't had time to write another poem for Lark, and now he was glad he didn't. If so, it would only be read aloud again by Lark or Florie.

"I want to read another letter." Florie ran over, jumping up, trying to touch the letters in his hand.

"Now, Florie, that isn't polite." Sister Joan hurried over and escorted the girl back to her chair.

"I'll take those," said Raven with a smile, holding out her hand.

His gaze shot over to Lark at the other side of the room.

"It's fine. You can give them to her," said Lark.

He handed them over, and went to the table to unpack his tutoring supplies.

"Quick, look at them, Lark. See if there is another one from your secret admirer," said Eleanor.

Dustin's head snapped up. "You ladies ... know about that?" he asked, feeling uncomfortable and like he wanted to leave.

"Of course we know about her secret admirer. Lark tells us everything," said Raven.

"Everything?" Now his gaze shot over to Lark who was smiling at him.

"Well, mayhap no' everything, but only what I want them to ken," said Lark, making Dustin wonder if Lark had told her cousins that they'd coupled. God's feet, he hoped not! He was so nervous that someone would find out that he couldn't even concentrate on why he was there.

"I don't see any letter from your secret admirer among them," said Eleanor, leaning over to look at the letters in Lark's hands.

"Neither do I," said Raven, picking up a few to inspect them.

Lark let out a deep sigh, throwing the letters down on the bed. "Nay, there isna one. Only mindless clishmaclaver from noblemen who sound stiff."

"And that's a bad thing?" asked Raven with a grin. She and Eleanor giggled and looked over at Dustin.

Dustin dropped his gaze to the table, not wanting to look back up. They knew. He could tell that Lark had told them about them making love.

"Stiff with their words," Lark corrected herself. "I had really hoped there would be another romantic poem from my secret admirer. Oh well, mayhap tomorrow." She brushed her hands together.

"Aren't you going to read any of them?" asked Eleanor.

"Nay," Lark answered. "There is nothin' important in them. Dustin will write simple responses to all the noblemen for me. Right?"

"Oh, right," said Dustin with a nod. "As you wish, my lady."

"I really wanted another love poem from my secret admirer," said Lark. "He sounds like such an interestin' man."

Dustin suddenly felt jealous. This was ridiculous! He was her secret admirer, he didn't need to be jealous of himself. Didn't she realize he wrote that letter? He thought after making love with her yesterday, she would know it had been him. He also didn't think he really needed to write the love poems anymore. But now, it seemed as if Lark was disappointed that she didn't get one. She must really like her secret admirer. Damn, Dustin was hoping she would feel that way about him instead.

Did she honestly think the love letter was from a nobleman? And if so, did it make her want to marry him? In his haste to convey his feelings for her and sneakily try to figure out if she liked him, mayhap he'd only made things worse. Bid the devil, this woman was complicated. Lark hadn't even said anything to him about their little affair when he saw her in the great hall this morning. Did it mean nothing at all to her? And after making passionate love with him, was she really still planning on marrying a noble that she didn't even know?

Of course she was, he realized. What she had with him was nothing more than her last chance of doing anything crazy before she was tied down as the wife of a noble.

The door opened and Lark's father entered the room.

"Excuse me, ladies. And scribe," said Storm, looking over at Dustin. "I need to interrupt."

"What is it Da? Is anything wrong?" asked Lark.

"Actually, I am here to speak with the scribe." Storm's eyes bore into Dustin, and he didn't like it. It certainly got his attention. Dustin had a feeling things were about to become heated. He hoped to hell that Storm hadn't heard about what he'd done with the man's daughter.

"Da, his name is Dustin," said Lark. "Call him that, no' scribe."

"Sorry. Dustin," said Storm, seeming like he did it only to please his daughter.

"Yes, Lord MacKeefe?" asked Dustin. "How can I help you?"

"Walk with me," he said in a gruff voice.

"Da, Dustin is givin' Florie her lesson," protested Lark. "Canna this wait until later?"

"Nay. Today there will be no lesson. Ye are all dismissed," said Storm with a wave of his hand. "Let's go, scribe."

"Da! Dinna call him that," cried Lark.

"Dustin," Storm corrected himself under his breath.

Dustin collected up his things, looking over at Lark with anxiety filling him. Their eyes met and she seemed as concerned as he felt at the moment. Still, there was nothing she could do to help him. Dustin was on his own now. He had made the decision to make love with Lark, and now he had the horrible feeling he was about to pay the consequences for his action.

"Mayhap I'll come with ye." Lark jumped to her feet.

"Yes," said Dustin, hope flooding him. Mayhap with Lark there too, things wouldn't be as bad.

"Nay," growled Storm. Dustin's hope diminished as quickly as it had come. "Ye stay here and read over those letters from the suitors. Actually, let me see them." Storm walked back over to Lark and held out his hand.

"Why?" asked Lark, picking them up and holding them to her chest. "These are my letters."

"I want to see what the men are saying to ye." He snatched them from her, shuffled through them, and after a satisfied grunt, he gave them back to her. "Have ye found one of the nobles ye would like to marry yet?"

"Nay. No' yet," said Lark. "And it will depend on meetin' them, of course. After all, words on a page tell me nothin' about a man."

"Only if he's romantic," said Raven softly.

"What did ye say?" asked Storm.

"Da, please leave us alone," begged Lark.

"I'm goin'. Come, scribe," said Storm, making Dustin want to correct him like Lark had, but he decided it would be better to keep quiet and let the man call him whatever he wanted.

Once out in the corridor, Storm spoke.

"Lord Corbett would like ye to write a letter for him. He wants to invite a friend of Lord Morcant's to the feast even though it is last minute."

"Was Lord Morcant invited to the feast too?" asked Dustin, remembering seeing Corbett hand the man a missive the day of the grand opening of the smithy.

"Yes, he is a neighbor and Lord Corbett invited him."

"But he's no longer a single man since he married that Frenchwoman who was betrothed to Lord Rook."

"Nay, but Lord Corbett wants to keep things friendly between them."

"Oh, I see. All right, I will go to Lord Corbett anon."

"Wait." Storm cleared his throat and stopped in the corridor. He waited until a few servants walked by before he continued. "There is something else I need to ask ye." He didn't look particularly happy. "It is in regard to my daughter."

"What is it, my lord?" Dustin felt his palms sweating. Here it was. Storm must have found out his secret somehow. He would now be chastised and thrown in the dungeon. Or mayhap condemned to death.

"I hear things through the rushes."

"Yes?" asked Dustin, holding his breath, knowing there was no getting out of this now. He'd be lucky not to end up drawn and quartered.

"I heard that some man is ..."

Dustin froze, not breathing or talking or even moving in the least.

"Some man is sendin' my daughter silly love poems, and I dinna like it."

Dustin breathed a sigh of relief. "Oh, is that all?"

"Aye. What did ye think I was goin' to say?" Storm looked at Dustin from the corners of his eyes.

"I wasn't sure," he said, trying not to say too much, nor to make eye contact. He didn't want Storm to read his mind.

"Well, I want ye to find out who this cur is, so I can do somethin' about it. I dinna need some addlepated dreamer wooin' my daughter. She needs to marry a good fightin' man. Someone who will keep her safe and make a proper alliance with the MacKeefe clan. This secret admirer is only goin' to confuse her. Blethers, now I wish I hadna given her permission to choose her own husband from these nobles after all."

"Pardon me, my lord?" asked Dustin, taken aback by what he'd just heard. "You are going to try to stop a man from wooing your daughter? I thought that was the intention of this whole feast. That suitors would try to win her hand in marriage."

"Nay, no' at all. It's to find her a husband who is willin' to have her. No' one who will spout silly nonsense. It's no' an easy task, ye realize. No' when a lassie has a bad reputation and a child as well. No' many men will accept that! I am payin' dearly, and I dinna want my money bein' wasted and goin' to the wrong man."

Dustin could no longer stay quiet. He felt as if he wanted to defend Lark. She was a wonderful woman and didn't deserve to be belittled, especially not by her own father.

"If I may speak freely, my lord, I think any man would be lucky to have Lady Lark as his wife. And Florie as his daughter, too. They are both delightful to be around."

"I didna say ye could speak freely, scribe. And it doesna matter what ye think. Ye are no' goin' to be marryin' my daughter, so what does it matter to ye? Ye are only the scribe and tutor, and have no say in the matter."

Dustin wanted to tell Storm right then and there that he was in love with Lark. He wanted to say he had just as much right to marry her as any of these second-rate nobles he was trying to lure in with a big dowry. He also wanted to tell him that he and Lark coupled and that he wouldn't allow any other man besides himself to touch her. Yes, he wanted to tell Lark's father that she deserved so much better than any of these greedy nobles, and that she also deserved to find love and happiness in her life.

Then he realized, he had nothing at all to offer Lark. He was only a commoner, and was more pathetic than all the second-rate nobles put together who Storm was trying to lure in. Dustin hesitated because he also had no idea if Lark had feelings for him ... other than lust. She had seemed so disappointed when she didn't receive a letter from her secret admirer today, that he wondered if she had no desire to even be with him again. It sounded as if she wanted a romantic nobleman instead. His head spun and he wasn't sure what to do or say.

So, sadly, he said nothing.

"Well, why are ye still standin' there?" Storm snapped. "Go. Lord Corbett awaits yer services."

"Aye, my lord," said Dustin, turning and walking away, feeling like he'd let himself down by not saying how he really felt toward Lady Lark. Had he let her down as well? Perhaps now he'd never know.

LARK CLOSED the door to the solar as soon as Sister Joan left with Florie.

"Lark, why do you think your father wanted to speak with Dustin?" asked Eleanor.

"Do you think he found out that you and Dustin made love yesterday?" Raven wanted to know.

"No' unless one of ye told him." She looked at both of her cousins in turn.

"It wasn't me," said Eleanor, shaking her head. Red ringlets of loose hair framing her face bounced back and forth.

"It wasn't me either. I'd never tell your father something like that, believe me," promised Raven with a roll of her eyes.

"Hmmm," said Lark. "Then, I really dinna ken what my father wants with Dustin."

"Tell us more about you and Dustin making love," said Raven excitedly, sitting down next to Lark on the edge of the bed.

"Yes, do. You didn't go into details. I'd like to hear more, too." Eleanor sat on the other side of her. Both women fixed their gazes on Lark and leaned in so as not to miss a word.

"I am no' goin' to tell ye two anythin' too personal," said

Lark. Then a smile spread across her face as she remembered how good it felt to be in Dustin's arms. "All I will say is that what we did was excitin', wonderful, and also a little naughty."

"Naughty?" That got Raven's attention. "How naughty?"

"Well ... let's just say I received a little spankin' on my bare backside for bein' a naughty lassie."

"Oh, my." Eleanor held a hand to her mouth, sounding shocked.

"Did you do anything else naughty?" asked Raven, seeming to like the idea of getting a spanking. "I mean, now that I'm married, Jonathon and I often have many new ways to couple. Although, I musts admit that we've never tried that!"

Both of the girls looked at her with wide eyes, waiting for her to answer.

Lark giggled. "Well, he picked me up and my legs were wrapped around his waist. We made love standin' up against the wall, and then lying down on his pallet as well."

Squeals of excitement went up from all three of them.

"Lark, how do you feel about Dustin?" asked Eleanor. "Do you like him a lot?"

"Like him? How about are you in love with him?" asked Raven.

"I am no' sure," said Lark. Her smile disappeared. "I mean, I have strong feelin's for the man. He is kind and thoughtful and very good to me, as well as to Florie. He's also smart and handsome. As well as an excellent lover."

"Mayhap he's the one you should marry," said Raven.

"Nay. I canna." Lark shook her head. "My da would never let me do such a thing. I need to choose from the men who are writin' me these letters." She nodded to the letters on the bed.

"Oh, do any of those men catch your interest?" asked Eleanor.

"Just one. The secret admirer." Lark pulled that letter out of her bodice, shocking both of her cousins that she would be hiding it there. "I wonder who he is?" asked Lark, opening the letter and staring at it. "Whoever he is, he is soooo romantic. He sent me a love poem, and no one has ever done that before. I really like it. No man I ken has ever been so creative with his words. It makes me wonder what he is like in person."

"Lark, I just had a crazy thought," said Raven.

"What?" asked Lark.

"Do you think that perhaps Dustin wrote that letter?" asked Raven.

"Dustin?" Lark made a face. "Why would ye say that?"

"Well, he is a scribe. And he likes to read poems by Geoffrey Chaucer. I saw the book he was reading. It isn't something every nobleman would have or read."

Lark hadn't really considered that the scribe might do something as risky as this. Then again, he did make love with her, and that was much riskier than writing a love letter. Still, these letters were only from the nobles invited to the feast. Dustin was a commoner who worried too much about what the nobles thought. He would never do such a daft thing. She didn't think he had the nerve to even try.

"Nay. Why would he do such a thing?" asked Lark. "He kens his place as a commoner, and this wouldna be right to be pretendin' he was a noble."

"Neither is bedding you, but yet he did it anyway," Eleanor pointed out. "Mayhap the man has true feelings for you that go beyond lust. Did you ever consider that?"

"Nay, I dinna think so." Lark shook her head. "I mean, I have to admit, I tempted him in a way where he couldna say no. He did try to back out of it, but I convinced him. He was an aroused man. It was just lust between us, I'm sure."

"You tempted him? Why would you do that?" asked Eleanor. "You are about to get married."

"That is the exact reason I did," explained Lark. "I wanted to experience makin' love and enjoyin' it before I am shoved off to some old, ugly noble who only wants me for the dowry that Da is danglin' in front of his fat face. How could I ever enjoy makin' love with someone like that?"

"I see your point, and I can't say I blame you," said Raven.

"Well, I don't understand this at all," said Eleanor, sounding a little disgusted.

"Nay, I dinna suppose ye would, Eleanor." Lark felt as if she were being judged by her cousin. "After all, ye decided to push all men aside to be a nun, so what would ye ken about men or lust or makin' love?"

"I am not a nun," Eleanor protested. "Besides, I do not push all men aside, no matter what you think."

"Eleanor, she's right," agreed Raven. "You need to forget about Connor and move on with your life."

"We are talking about Lark here, not me." Eleanor always seemed to change the conversation. She also never got over losing the man she loved. "Now, let's get back to talking about the scribe."

"Dustin is a wonderful man," said Lark. "However, I really dinna believe he wants to woo me. I'm sure he would have said somethin' to me personally if this were true. He had plenty of opportunities to do so. I mean, he didna even say a thing about the night of passion we shared together, so there is yer answer. It meant nothin' to him but a release for his lust. I believe it was a one-time thing only. However, this secret admirer has a true way with words and seems to really want to marry me." She held up the missive and smiled. "This man makes me feel like a queen. I need to find out who he is, or it is goin' to drive me crazy."

"Mayhap your father can find out," suggested Eleanor.

"Nay! I dinna want him involved. My da is no' romantic,

and willna understand this. Just ask my mother if ye dinna believe me. I will just wait until the feast and find out then, since I'm sure the man will be here."

"Oh, so you wrote him back, like you did with the other nobles trying to win your hand in marriage?" asked Eleanor.

"Well, nay," said Lark, frowning at the letter. "I couldna do that since I dinna even ken the man's name or where he is from."

"Forget about your secret admirer, Lark. I think Dustin really likes you," Raven continued to try to convince her.

"I'm sure he does. I really like him, too," said Lark, nonchalantly. "But nothin' can ever come of it, and he kens it. Because of my mistakes of the past, me marryin' a noble who will accept me and my child is the only way to make all the waggin' tongues stop once and for all."'

"Do you really believe that?" asked Eleanor. "That the gossip about you will stop once you're married?"

"Well, if I marry a commoner like Raven and Rook did, I guarantee the talk behind my back will only worsen. I canna live like that anymore," Lark told them, feeling upset by the way people looked at her and spoke to each other behind their hands when she passed by. They were still doing it here in England, just not as much as back in her homeland. "It is too sad and hard to bear. Besides, I dinna want Florie to have to grow up with people talkin' bad behind her back as well. That will only determine her future too, and she may never marry because of it. Dinna ye see? I have to do this for Florie, as well as myself. I have to marry well, because if no', my life will be naught but a livin' hell forever."

CHAPTER 14

Dustin looked through the missives that arrived for Lark the next day, making his way to the solar. When he got to the door, he looked up and down the corridor, then quickly reached into his tunic and pulled out a letter he wrote for Lark as her secret admirer. Slipping it into the pile of letters, he knocked and entered the room.

"Good mornin'," said Lark, wearing her traveling cloak. She was the only one in the room.

"Good morning," said Dustin, looking around. "Where is everyone?"

"We will no' have a lesson for Florie today," she announced. "Instead, I will be takin' her with me to visit my cousin, Lord Rook at Rookrose Manor."

"Oh. All right. I understand." He felt a little disappointed since he was looking forward to spending time with Lark and Florie. "Here are the letters for today." He handed her the letters from the suitors that had arrived this morning from messengers from every direction. The guard at the gate had a box where he collected them, and Dustin picked them up every day.

"My letters," she said, sounding excited. She hurried over to him, taking them and ripping them open, throwing each on the bed after barely glancing at it. When she got to the one he wrote, she stopped and read it carefully. A smile lit up her face.

"Is there a letter from a suitor that pleases you?" he asked, walking closer to her, but leaving the solar door wide open as was proper.

"Yes, there is," she said, almost looking like she was going to jump up and down she was so excited. "It is from my secret admirer," she told him. "He is such a romantic man."

"Really. What does it say?" Dustin acted interested and as if he didn't already know.

"It's a love poem," Lark explained. She sighed and held it to her heart. "He says I am like the goddess Persephone. When I walk the earth, everything blooms and birds sing. But like Persephone, when I am not here, the world is dark and dreary and void of life. Isna that the most romantic thing ye've ever heard?" She stared off into nothingness with a dreamy smile on her face.

"Aye. I guess so. I mean, yes, you are like a goddess, I agree," he told her, meaning to tell her he wrote the letter, trying his best to lead into it. Before he could say more, Lord Corbett and Lord Storm arrived at the solar.

"Lark, the others are waitin' for ye out in the courtyard," said Storm. "Why the delay?"

"Da!" Lark turned away from him, but Dustin was close enough to see her shove the love letter he wrote under her cloak, hiding it from her father. "I was just waitin' for Dustin to bring me the letters for today from my suitors."

"Letters?" Storm stepped in front of Corbett and hurried over to the bed. "Let me see them." He shuffled through them quickly, then threw them down on the bed, the same as Lark had done.

"What are ye doin'?" asked Lark.

"Nothin'. Nothin' at all."

"I have two guards escorting your traveling party to Rookrose Manor," said Corbett. "However, I didn't realize Raven, Eleanor, and Sister Joan would all be going with you and Florie as well. Mayhap I should assign another man to travel with you. We can never be too careful."

"Nay, Uncle Corbett, that willna be necessary," said Lark.

"I agree. Another man along would be beneficial for yer protection," said Storm. "Corbett and I have previous commitments or I'd go with ye myself."

"If it's another man along that will make you two feel better, then I will accompany Lady Lark and the others," offered Dustin, feeling this would be a good opportunity to get Lark alone to explain to her that he was her secret admirer.

"Ye?" asked Storm with a chuckle. "Ye're just a commoner, and a simple scribe. I'm sure ye canna even swing a sword if the ladies get in trouble and need protectin'."

"My lord," said Dustin, not wanting Lark's father to think less of him. "I assure you, I am capable of protecting the women. I might not own a sword, but I do have a dagger. I might have been raised in a monastery, but I am not a monk. I assure you, I can fight with my bare hands if need be. I can protect your daughter and the others, so you need not worry for their safety."

"I dinna ken," said Storm, not sounding like he was going to accept Dustin's offer.

"My lords," Dustin continued, not willing to give up the fight. "I think it would be best not to skip too many of Florie's lessons since yesterday's lesson was already canceled and she'll miss more of them while visiting Rookrose Manor. With your permission, I'd like to join the group on their journey. That way, I will be there and be sure to continue teaching the child once we arrive."

Storm didn't answer, and this made Dustin nervous. He didn't know what else he could possibly say to try to convince the man that he was more than capable of protecting the women.

"Da, Raven will be with us too," said Lark. "Ye ken she is better with a sword than any man."

This didn't make Dustin feel any better to hear this, even though Lady Raven was quite different from any of the other noblewomen. Still, if Storm turned down Dustin now, it would be a highly embarrassing situation.

"I still dinna like it," complained Storm.

"I'll send Jonathon along as well," suggested Corbett, speaking of Raven's husband.

"Jonathon? The blacksmith?" asked Storm, his brows dipping in frustration.

"Aye," answered Corbett. "Lord Jonathon served as a mercenary for me on several occasions. He is handy with a sword, axe, blacksmith hammer, or anything you throw at him. You don't need to worry."

Dustin noticed how Corbett had called Jonathon, Lord, even though he was only a commoner. Dustin realized it was a courtesy title since he married a lady, but Dustin wished for a courtesy title as well someday. However, a scribe and tutor wouldn't earn one, so he wouldn't hold his breath that his life would be changing anytime soon.

"Well, I guess so. Go on, then," Storm finally agreed, nodding at Dustin. "Well, hurry up ye two. Everyone is waitin' for ye. Dinna be gone more than a day or two at most. Lark, there is a lot to be done to prepare for when yer suitors arrive. I had hoped ye would help Lady Devon in planning this important event."

"Of course, I will, as soon as we return," Lark assured her father.

"Thank you, my lords," said Dustin, with a bow to the men. Then he quickly followed Lark out of the solar. "I promise, I will lay down my life for the ladies if need be," he told the lords over his shoulder.

"Leave that to the fightin' men," growled Storm. "A quill is the only thing ye'll ever have in yer hand and we all ken it."

Dustin left the room feeling as if Storm didn't like him in the least. Dustin also hoped that Storm would never discover that he recently had his daughter in his hands, not just a quill. If only the man could be fond of him, then he might have an actual chance to be with Lark, even though he was naught but a commoner. Dustin would have to do something fast to change Storm's mind and win his favors. Unfortunately, he had no idea what that would have to be.

If only he was a fighting man, even if he wasn't a noble, then this would be so much easier.

LARK MOUNTED HER HORSE, still smiling because of the love poem from her secret admirer that she'd received today. It was even better than the previous one.

"Lark, why are you smiling so much?" asked Raven, riding up next to her. Sister Joan was seated on the bench seat of the wagon with Eleanor and little Florie. Albert, the thirteen-year-old castle page was with them and would be driving. The two guards who were escorting them positioned themselves one in front of the wagon and the other next to it.

"I'm just happy. I received another letter from my secret admirer today," Lark told her cousin.

"Are we ready to leave, my ladies?" called out one of the guards.

"We are just waiting for my husband," Raven told him.

"And Dustin," added Lark, looking over to see both Jonathon and Dustin approaching on horseback. "Oh, here they are now."

"Move on out," called out the guard, leading the way with the wagon right behind him.

"What did the letter say?" asked Raven, riding close to Lark and talking softly so no one else would hear.

"In today's letter, he compared me to a goddess," said Lark, feeling elated that any man would think of her as such, since most men only thought of her as a whore. "Raven, this is the man I will choose to marry," said Lark, her heart feeling light and happy.

"Really?" asked Raven. "But you don't even know who he is, nor have you met him yet. Mayhap you should wait before making that decision."

"Nay, I'm sure of it. Any nobleman who can write in this manner is the best choice for a husband. I am sure I will like him."

"What are you two talking about?" asked Jonathon as he and Dustin rode up to join them.

"Lark has chosen her husband already," announced Raven, shaking her head since she didn't agree with it.

"You have?" Dustin's head snapped up. "Who? Who is it you decided to marry?"

"I dinna ken his name. No' yet," said Lark. "He is the man who writes me love poems and refers to himself as my secret admirer."

"That sounds interesting," said Jonathon. "Don't you think so, Dustin?"

DUSTIN HEARD this and his heart stood still. He groaned inwardly. How could Lark be so infatuated with a pretend suitor and simple words on a piece of parchment? After all, they'd made actual love. Dustin was real. He thought she'd have more feelings about him instead.

"Dustin?" asked Jonathon.

"Aye, yes," he said, clearing his throat. "It is great that Lady Lark has chosen her future husband."

"The best part," continued Lark, "is that I'll be married to a nobleman who no' only seems to already respect me, but then others will do so too, once they find out about this. My reputation will be saved. That is all that matters to me right now."

"Yes. It's the most important thing," repeated Dustin, feeling like he'd been punched in the gut.

"Mother, ride up here by me," said Florie, standing on the seat of the bench. Dustin saw the little girl's action and realized how dangerous it was. If the wagon hit a bump, she could fall right out.

"Florie, sit down," warned Dustin, quickly directing his horse over to the side of the wagon.

"I want to ride a horse, too," whined Florie.

"Sit down, please," said the nun, but Florie wouldn't listen.

"Why don't you come here and you can ride with me?" Dustin realized if something didn't happen quickly, Florie was either going to fall and get hurt, or cause a scene and start crying. He didn't want any of that. He had hoped this would be a quiet trip.

"I want to ride with Dustin," said the girl, climbing over

the nun and then atop Eleanor's lap since she was sitting on the end of the bench seat.

"Do you want me to stop the wagon?" asked Albert.

"No need," said Dustin coming up close to them, and reaching out and scooping up the child. "I've got her." He put her in front of him on the horse, wrapping his arm around her in a protective manner as he held the reins with the other. His concern was that the girl was secure.

"I like ye, Dustin," said Florie, looking back at him. "Mayhap ye can be my new father."

That took Dustin by surprise, and he wasn't sure how to answer. However, by the silence of the others, he knew he had to say something.

"I don't know about that," said Dustin, looking over at Lark. "After all, I am only a commoner. Besides, it seems as if your mother has already decided on the nobleman she wants to marry."

LARK'S HEART melted when she saw Dustin protecting her daughter as if the girl were his own. He was good with Florie and her daughter seemed to really like him. Dustin had started to fill that void in Florie's life lately. Lark had never seen the girl smile as much as she did when she was with him.

Dustin also had the patience of a saint. No other man would be so gentle and caring with a child who caused so much havoc. This made her start to think. Would whichever nobleman she married be as kind to her daughter as Dustin was? Her secret admirer had written many nice things about her in the love poems, and that made her heart soar. But if the man she married didn't like or want a bastard child, what would happen to Florie? Lark couldn't allow anyone to take her daughter away from her. Florie was the most important person in her life.

"Did you want to tell me more about this secret admirer that you've decided to marry?" asked Raven from next to her. "Tell me exactly what he wrote in today's letter. I want to know."

"Nay. No' now, mayhap later," said Lark, her gaze roving back to Dustin and Florie again. The excitement and happiness she'd felt from the letter now diminished. Instead of bliss, she felt empty and sad. She had all but dismissed the memory of what happened between her and Dustin because she realized it couldn't go anywhere and that she needed to marry a noble.

Who was she fooling? Dustin was the man who truly made her heart soar. Perhaps she needed to stop fighting these feelings she was having for him. She had thought if she focused on the secret admirer instead, in time she would forget what she was truly feeling for the scribe. But now, she wondered if she could be happy with anyone besides Dustin. Damn it, why was he a commoner instead of one of her noble suitors? This made everything more difficult.

Still watching Dustin and Florie, she saw them talking and laughing. Dustin pointed out birds and ground squirrels to Florie, teaching her about them as they rode. He even grabbed a low-hanging branch and plucked off a leaf. He gave it to Florie, and told her what kind of tree it was from.

Suddenly, everything changed. Lark felt confused and torn. She needed a nobleman, but wanted a commoner. Why did this have to be happening in her life?

Letting out a deep sigh, she rode in silence. Now, her heart felt even emptier than it had for nearly the last five years.

CHAPTER 15

"Raven, Lark, so nice of you to visit." Lord Rook, the twin brother of Lady Raven, met them in the courtyard of Rookrose Manor. His new wife, Lady Rose, was with him. Rose had been the daughter of the late master gardener, but now she was married to a nobleman.

"Hello, Rose. I mean, Lady Rose," Lark called out from atop her horse. Lark liked the woman. They had become close friends recently when Lark spent time here while Rose and her gardening team were fixing up Rook's gardens.

Lark was about to dismount, when Dustin came up next to her with Florie at his side. "Allow me, my lady," he told her, holding out his arms.

"Thank ye." As Dustin lowered her to the ground, Lark felt her body trembling. It wasn't because she was frightened by him. It was because she felt powerless, but in a good way, when she was in Dustin's arms.

"Mother, Dustin told me he would teach me all about flowers today," said Florie, jumping up and swatting at a butterfly that fluttered past her.

"Be nice to the butterfly, Florie," Dustin told the girl in a gentle voice. "The garden is their home and we have to remember that we are only the visitors here."

"Sorry," said Florie, holding out her arm. "Nice flutterby," she said, making both Lark and Dustin laugh. Then, when the butterfly actually landed on her hand, they were all surprised.

"What do I do?" asked Florie, not moving, seeming suddenly scared.

"Ye dinna need to do anythin', Florie," said Lark. "The butterfly is sayin' hello."

"Hello," said Florie, staring at the butterfly on her hand and smiling from ear to ear. "Do ye want to eat a flower?"

"They drink the nectar from the flowers," explained Dustin as the butterfly flew off.

"What is nexter?" asked Florie, making them chuckle again.

"I see we have a lot to cover today." Dustin took Florie's hand and looked back at Lark. "My lady, would you care to join us for Florie's lesson that will be in the garden today?" asked Dustin.

"Aye. I'd like that," Lark told him, thankful and happy to be included.

"Florie, perhaps you can ask Lady Rose if it is all right if we spend time in her garden," Dustin told the little girl.

"All right, I will. Lady Rose, Lady Rose," she called out, running over to Rook and Rose. Sister Joan hurried after her.

"I think I need to start spendin' more time with my daughter," Lark told Dustin, surprising him that she said this.

"I agree. I think it would be a great idea," Dustin answered.

"Just since ye've been tutorin' her, Florie seems so much calmer."

"She is. Spending time with Sister Joan seems to have helped her too," said Dustin, looking at the nun holding

Florie's hand. "I believe all the little girl really needed or wanted was attention."

"Yes. I suppose so," said Lark, realizing that Dustin was right.

"I think perhaps that is what everyone needs. To be included in things and to feel needed, respected, and also appreciated."

Lark got the feeling Dustin was no longer talking about the child. After all, the words *needed, respected and appreciated* were not normal ones to describe the wants of a child. Did he mean her? Or was he speaking of himself? The man was good with words. He was also skilled at saying things in a way that hinted at what he meant without actually coming out and saying it. Still, at times it confused her.

"Lady Lark, did you mean it when you said you were going to marry the suitor who is your secret admirer?" asked Dustin.

Suddenly, Lark didn't feel as sure of her decision. She also didn't want to talk about this with Dustin. They'd made love, and she was afraid he would think she used him. That wasn't at all her intention. Or was it? Now she felt even worse. She had acted rash, giving in to her desires without considering how Dustin might feel. This didn't make her feel good about herself at all.

"I'd rather no' talk about that right now. If ye'll excuse me, I need to greet my cousin and his wife."

"But—" Dustin started to say something, but she could stay with him no longer.

As she walked away, she had the feeling he wanted to talk about what happened between them. Neither of them had said anything more about it, and she supposed she owed it to him as well as to herself to discuss what had happened.

She turned around to tell him mayhap she wanted to talk after all, but he was already in a conversation with Jonathon.

Lark supposed it would have to wait until later. That would probably be the best since she had no idea how to tell Dustin what she was feeling in her heart.

How in the world could she admit to a commoner that he would be a better husband than any nobleman? It pained her, and she didn't want to hurt Dustin. But nothing could change the situation. She had to marry a noble to clear her name and reputation, that much was evident. Lark needed to do it for Florie and for her own future as well. Didn't she?

She looked back at Dustin. Florie ran over to him. He scooped the little girl up into his arms as she laughed and tried reaching for a dragonfly buzzing over her head now. Holding her on his hip, Dustin ran after the dragonfly as the two of them chased it through the garden.

Why was she losing her heart to this man? And how long, she wondered, could she continue to fool herself by saying she would marry a noble when Dustin was the only one for her?

LATER THAT DAY, Lark and all the others made their way into the labyrinth of bushes to Rose and Rook's pleasure garden. They carried baskets of food as well as cider, ale, and blankets to spread on the ground.

It was a beautiful summer day. All the flowers were in bloom. The scent of lilies of the valley, wild roses, and irises drifted past in the air.

Lark had been impressed by how many types of flowers Dustin had been able to identify and point out to Florie. Living at the monastery must have been a lifetime of learning for him. After all, monks were very learned men. They had not only book knowledge, but also knew all about the land they farmed and the animals and plants of the forest.

"Where did ye want to sit to have lunch, Florie?" Lark asked her daughter. It was Florie's idea to eat outside. While Rook had grumbled at the idea, his wife, Rose loved nature and the outdoors, so she decided they would all eat their meal in the pleasure garden today.

"I want to eat on the swing." Florie ran over and jumped atop a swing that Lark hadn't seen the last time she was here.

"Rose, is that a new swing?" asked Lark.

"Yes and no," said Rose with a giggle.

"It looks familiar," said Raven.

"I like the arch of flowers over it." Eleanor walked over to sniff the roses covering the archway above the swing.

"Don't you recognize that old bench?" asked Rook.

"That's the bench?" asked Lark in surprise.

"The one you carved your name onto when you were a child?" asked Raven.

"That's the one," said Rose. "It's now painted and turned into a swing, thanks to my gardeners, Thomasina and Phineas. My cousin Georgiana helped too."

"I would have done it, but they enjoy manual labor," said Rook, taking a blanket and spreading it over the ground. He was fooling no one. Rook had always been lazy and tended to overuse his powers of being a noble to get others to do things for him. Lark almost laughed aloud. She just had to say something about it.

"Rook, I dinna believe for a moment ye'd do anythin' yerself that ye thought was the job of a servant," said Lark.

"Rook is changing," Rose told her. "Just yesterday, he helped me pick herbs in the garden."

"Really?" asked Raven, overhearing them.

"Don't say that too loud, Rose. I don't want my household to get the wrong idea of me," Rook told his wife. "It'll kill my reputation."

Rook started to sit down, but before his butt hit the blanket, Bandit, their dog, raced into the pleasure garden. The hound gripped the blanket in his teeth and took off, dragging it through the garden. Rook's bottom hit the dirt and he groaned.

"If the damned dog wasn't so cute I'd yell at it right now," Rook told the women.

"I'll get him," Dustin called out, easily collecting the blanket from the dog. It seemed the man was good with children and animals too. Lark liked that about him.

"Thank you," said Raven, collecting the blanket from him and setting up the lunch.

DUSTIN STOOD at the far end of the pleasure garden with Jonathon.

"Lord Jonathon," he said. "Can we talk?"

"Sure," said Jonathon. "Dustin, you don't need to use my title when the others aren't listening." They had known each other for years. "Honestly, I feel kind of odd when anyone uses it, but it helps me to come across as being more noble, I guess. To Raven and her family, I mean. I still don't feel noble in the least."

"Can I ask you a question about you and Raven?"

"Of course. Go ahead."

"Did you let her know your feelings for her before you were married? Even though you were a commoner?"

"Everything happened really fast, and I swear it is nothing but a blur in my head, but I'm sure I must have. Why do you ask?"

"Oh, no reason." Dustin's gaze wandered over to Lark. She was placing food in front of Florie and they sat together on the blanket. He liked the fact that Lark said she wanted to start spending more time with her daughter. After all, if he had ever known his mother, he wished she would have spent time with him, too.

"You like her, don't you?" asked Jonathon, grinning as if he knew a secret.

"Who?" Dustin turned to face him.

"You know exactly who I mean. Has anything happened yet between you and Lady Lark?"

Dustin released a deep breath of air. "All right, so you are on to me. Yes, I have strong feelings for Lady Lark, and something did happen between us."

"Coupled, did you?"

"Why would you say that?"

"I know that look on your face. I had it too, when I had intimate relations with Raven while she was destined to marry a noble."

"How did you tell her you loved her? And how did you tell her father?"

"Telling the girl isn't half as bad as trying to tell her father you want to marry her, if that is what you mean."

"Now wait," said Dustin, holding up his hand. "I never said anything about wanting to marry Lady Lark."

"You didn't have to, it's obvious. Does she know how you feel?"

"Well ... I am not really sure. She seems to like me and all, but I'm afraid she has her heart set on marrying a nobleman. I didn't want to say anything. Not yet."

"Then when?" asked Jonathon. "When she is already married to one of her suitors and it is too late to change things?"

"I've been trying to change things, I assure you. I am not just doing nothing about it. I have a plan in action and it is actually quite romantic."

"Romantic? Wait a minute," said Jonathon with a smile,

holding up his index finger. "Are you by any chance Lady Lark's secret admirer who keeps sending her love poems?"

"Oh, you know about that?" Dustin was surprised to hear this, since he thought Lark had been trying to keep the letters from the others.

"Sure, I know about the secret admirer. Raven can talk about nothing else. It seems women like that kind of thing."

"Then, Lady Raven told you?"

"She did. She's my wife." Jonathon shrugged. "We have no secrets from each other."

"Do you think I did the wrong thing by sending Lark love letters?"

"Nay, not really. If I were you and had the skill of writing romantic poems, I would use it, just like you did, I suppose. I mean, unless you just signed your own name instead, which would have been better."

"I thought of doing that, but really couldn't," said Dustin. "If her father found out, he'd kill me for sure. He doesn't seem too fond of commoners. Especially me."

"Well, you can't keep your identity a secret forever. Eventually, Lord Storm MacKeefe is going to have to know the truth. That is, if you're serious about his daughter."

"Oh, I am," said Dustin, thinking back to the letters again. "Did your wife tell you what Lady Lark said about the man? The secret admirer writing the love letters, that is."

"She and her cousins all think the secret admirer is romantic," said Jonathon. "I swear, it is making it difficult for the rest of us."

"How so?"

"Well, now Raven wants me to try writing love poems to her. Can you believe it? I'm not a writer. I work in a smithy banging on iron and sweating from the hot forge. For heaven's sake, I made the woman a set of armor. Isn't that enough? I swear, Dustin, every man is going to want to wring your neck as soon as they discover the secret admirer is you."

"Why?" asked Dustin.

"Because, you make the rest of us seem lacking. Don't you know that every woman wants to be wooed the way you're wooing Lark?"

"Really? They do?"

"Of course, they do. I swear, living in a monastery has made you oblivious to the wants and needs of women. Wait a minute," said Jonathon. "Since you're the one writing the love poems, mayhap I'm the one who needs to learn more about women." He chuckled.

"Believe me, women are a mystery to me as well," said Dustin. "And living in a monastery, it's not like I'm around them enough to have figured things out."

"Well, after listening to Raven, it seems women like it when men say flowery things to them and about them. I swear, Raven is changing. I didn't think she would care about that kind of stuff since she has never acted like the other ladies of the castle."

"I suppose you're right, about all this," said Dustin, pondering the thought of romantic wooing, and wondering what else he could do.

"If you ever need to talk to me regarding Lady Lark, I'm here for you, Dustin. Even though, I'm not sure how much help I'll actually be."

"Do you really mean that? That you're here for me?"

"Of course, I do. After all, us commoners need to stick together. Excuse me, now. I think I might just go and pick a flower and give it to Raven. Even though we're married, I need to work at keeping our relationship fun, exciting, and alive. Thanks to you," he added with a chuckle, walking away.

As soon as he left, Sister Joan approached, handing him a cup of ale. "Here you go, Dustin. You look thirsty."

"Thank you, Sister," he said, taking the cup and downing the ale. He couldn't get his mind off of Lark, nor could he stop wondering what to do about his situation.

"My, you really were thirsty," said the nun with a giggle.

When he looked back over at her, the sun was on her face. She looked so much prettier and younger than all the nuns he knew from living at the monastery. This one didn't really seem like a nun for some reason but he didn't know why. Something about her was almost familiar.

"Where are you from, Sister Joan?" he asked, thinking about what Brother Ruford had told him and how she might know something about his mother.

"I came here on a pilgrimage from Ireland."

"You don't have an Irish accent at all. You sound more British to me."

"You do have a keen ear, Dustin." Her voice was soft and calming. For some reason it made him feel more at ease. Or mayhap it was chugging the ale that did it. "I am from England, but many years ago moved to Ireland," she told him.

"What for?" he asked. "Didn't you like it here?"

"Why, yes, I did. Very much so." A sadness seemed to coat her words. "It wasn't my choice to leave, but it was something I needed to do."

"I don't understand," said Dustin.

"Let's not talk about me. What about you?" Her smile was back again.

"What about me?" he asked.

"Tell me about your family."

"I don't have a family." His gaze went back to Lark and Florie again, as well as Raven and Rook and Eleanor. They were a family, and in a way it made him jealous. No matter what their troubles were, they were there to support each other. They also seemed to overcome any obstacles in their way. He longed for that. Dustin never thought he wanted to get married and have children, but lately, his heart was telling him otherwise.

"I hear from Brother Ruford that you were an orphan," said the nun. "He took you in and raised you?"

"Yes. And even though the monks are my family, I am still an orphan and will always be."

"Why do you say that? Did you give up hope of ever discovering who your parents might be?"

This would be the perfect opportunity to ask her if she knew something about his parents. Part of him wanted to do just that. But a stronger part of him decided he wasn't sure he really wanted to know. What if he discovered his mother was a whore or his father had been a thief or even a pirate? It was hard enough living with the fact he was a mere commoner. Could he bear it if he was even less? And what would Lark think of him if he discovered his parents were horrible murderers or something? He didn't need anything making it harder for him to catch Lady Lark's eye. Plus, his parents couldn't be anything good if they abandoned him and never returned. Aye, he decided, he was better off never knowing.

"I don't need or want parents," he spat. "Not anymore." The feeling of bitterness flooded his heart.

The nun jerked backward, as if his words shocked her. "Dustin, how can you say that?"

"Sister, my parents abandoned me. They left me on the steps of the church when I was a baby, and never even looked back. Why would I want to find them now after all this time? What does it even matter? I hate them for what they did to me, and will never forgive them as long as I live."

"My, those are harsh words, Dustin. I am sure you don't really mean them."

"Yes, I mean them. I've been deprived of the simple things in life such as growing up with parents, and having a family. That is something that tends to darken a man's heart forever."

"Oh," she said, looking as if she were taken aback and not sure what to say. "I'm sorry to hear that hatred has filled your heart for people you don't even know."

"I know enough," he told her. "I know that they didn't love me."

"How can you say that?" asked the nun in challenge. "Every mother loves her child."

"Nay. Not mine. My mother did not love me or want me. Now, if you'll excuse me, sister, I no longer care to dig up my devastating past."

He walked away, not wanting to be reminded of everything he'd been deprived of, especially the thought of never having had a true family. He sat down next to Florie. She plopped down atop his lap and held a sweetmeat up to his mouth.

"Eat this. It's good," she said, chomping on another. Her fingers were all slobbery from being in her mouth.

"Florie, dinna do that. Dustin doesna want it." Lark tried to stop her.

Bandit barked and ran over. The dog's nose moved toward the sweetmeat, but Dustin took it and popped it into his mouth before the hound could get it. Bandit whimpered and wagged his tail, hoping for another chance to get something to eat. Florie and Lark both laughed.

"Oh, you are so wrong, Lady Lark," said Dustin. "I love sweetmeats and I wanted it very much," he told her, feeling his heart swell with happiness being here right now. He reached over with one hand and petted the dog on the head.

Dustin wanted it all right, more than anyone could know.

It wasn't just about the sweetmeat. It was about Lark and Florie and her family. In a way, these people were starting to feel like his family, too. They were like the family he never had, and they helped to fill that gnawing void in his heart that he'd lived with his entire life.

Being with Lark and her family felt right, and he wasn't going to let it pass him by without putting up a fight. Dustin wanted Lark as his wife. Yes, he was sure of it now. He also wanted Florie as his daughter. He decided he was ready to get married now and have a family of his own. Mayhap someday he'd even like to get a dog. It was time to move forward and to leave his sad past behind.

He looked over at Lark and her sparkling, happy eyes interlocked with his. No man would ever treat her as good as the way he would, even if they could all give her things he could never afford. The one thing he could give her was love, and lots of it.

It was then and there that he decided before they returned to Blake Castle, he would tell Lark exactly how he felt about her, and also that he was her secret admirer.

CHAPTER 16

"Good night, sweetheart," said Lark, kissing Florie on the cheek as Sister Joan held the little girl's hand. "Are ye sure ye dinna want to stay with me tonight?"

They were spending the night at Rookrose Manor, and heading home first thing in the morning.

"I do, Mother, but Lady Eleanor is goin' to tell me a story," said Florie with a yawn. "She said she works with children my age and kens lots of stories that I'd like. I want to hear one before I go to sleep."

"All right then," said Lark. "Sister, are you sure Florie willna be a bother?"

Eleanor and Sister Joan were sharing a room. Raven and her husband had another. Lark had her own room. Dustin, since he was a commoner, would spend the night with the servants, sleeping in the great hall by the fire.

"She's no bother at all," Sister Joan assured her, leaving with Florie still talking about stories.

Lark went to her room and lit a candle, closing the door behind her. It was dark already, and everyone was going to sleep for the night. She'd had such a wonderful day that she didn't even want to leave tomorrow. It felt good to spend time with her family, her daughter, and most of all, Dustin.

"Dustin," she said aloud, followed by a sigh. She couldn't seem to get him off her mind now.

Lark put the candle down on the bedside table, and changed into her nightclothes. Not really sleepy, she walked over to the window and pulled open the shutter, staring out at the nighttime sky. Stars twinkled in the heavens, making the night sky look magical. The full moon shone brightly, lighting up the garden and labyrinth down below.

She noticed movement in the garden, and peered out trying to see who it was. The person stopped in front of the entrance to the labyrinth. As the man looked back over his shoulder, Lark could see his face lit up in the bluish-white light of the moon. It was Dustin.

"I wonder what he is doin' out in the garden this time of night?" she said to herself as he turned and entered the labyrinth. She waited for a few minutes. When he didn't return, she decided he must be sleeping out there in nature, rather than with the servants in the great hall. Lark wanted to go after him, but she couldn't. It wouldn't be proper. Instead, she decided to go to bed.

She climbed into bed, laying down and hearing a crunching noise under her pillow. When she moved the pillow, she found a folded-up piece of parchment under there.

"What is this?" she asked, sitting up with the parchment in her hand. She brought the nighttime candle closer, and carefully unfolded the letter.

Even before she read it, she knew who it was from. It was another love letter from her secret admirer. However, this one didn't have a poem inside. Instead, it just said to meet him in the pleasure garden under the light of the full moon so he could gaze upon her beautiful face and they could meet in secret. It was signed, her secret admirer.

At first, it alarmed her. She worried that this man was stalking her and it frightened her. Had he been in her room? Was he still here now?

Then, she took control of her silly thoughts, realizing no one had followed her here at all. Her secret admirer was someone who was already here at the manor, although she had been trying so hard to believe it was from a nobleman who had yet to arrive.

Despair filled her, and she realized she needed to stop lying to herself and accept the truth. There was no nobleman wooing her. She had no secret admirer who she could choose to marry. Raven's words echoed in her head with her suspicion of Dustin having written the poems.

"Dammit," she spat, not wanting to accept the fact it was him. This only complicated matters.

Confused because she had lied to herself since the first letter, she still found herself wanting to believe this secret admirer was the answer to all her problems ... not the cause of them.

Not bothering to change out of her nightclothes, she grabbed her traveling cloak and wrapped it around her. Then, she took the candle from the bedside table, and headed out the door.

DUSTIN WAITED in the pleasure garden, pacing back and forth. He'd left a letter for Lark under her pillow and was sure she must have found it by now.

He didn't sign his name because he didn't want Rook or

someone else in the manor to find it. If so, it could mean trouble for him.

Dustin figured if he signed it from her secret admirer, she would know it was from him. After all, how else would the letter get here, otherwise?

He was going to tell her tonight exactly how he felt about her. He would admit to being her secret admirer, and tell her that he loved her and wanted to marry her.

All of a sudden doubt reared its ugly head, and the whole thing sounded so addled to him that he groaned. What in heaven's name was he doing? Lady Lark would never want him. He'd heard her say she needed to marry a noble to clear her name. He was the furthest thing from a noble or what she really needed in her life right now.

Then Dustin had another thought, and it wasn't a good one. If she thought some secret admirer was really in the plea-sure garden waiting for her, she would never venture out here at night alone. She would report it to Rook or the guards and not come looking for him without an escort.

Holy hell, he'd made a horrible mistake! He needed to get out of here now, before he was arrested and accused of things that would land him in chains.

"Dustin?" came the sweet voice of an angel from the entrance of the labyrinth. "Dustin, are ye out here?" Lark stepped out from the bushes and the moonlight hit her, illumi-nating her body. Wearing a long hooded cloak and holding the candle, she looked like nothing less than an angel.

He didn't see any guards with her, so he stepped out into the moonlight to make his presence known.

"Lark. You came," he said in a deep, soft voice.

She looked up and their eyes interlocked. "Yes. I found a note under my pillow saying to meet my secret admirer here."

"Of course," he said, wetting his lips because right now

his mouth was so dry that he could barely swallow. "That was me, Lark. I am your secret admirer and have always been."

For some reason, she seemed hesitant, almost as if she didn't want to believe him.

"Prove it," she challenged him, causing him to shake his head in disbelief.

"Lark, don't you know that those love poems were from me all along? Not even now, as I stand here and admit it to you?"

"Nay, ye're no' my secret admirer," she spat, almost seeming angry with him or unable to accept it.

"I am."

"If ye are, then why didna ye sign yer name to them?" Now, she sounded a little betrayed or hurt, and this made him feel even worse for what he did.

"If I had, you wouldn't have taken them to heart. I needed to know how you really felt about me. You would have discarded those letters if I had signed them, or mayhap had me arrested for trying to woo you when I had no right."

"I lost my heart to the man who wrote those words. He was the man who was goin' to set me free from my horrible past."

"Lark, I know I am just a commoner, and you said you needed to marry a noble. But please, don't be angry with me for trying to show you through my words what I felt in my heart. I don't want to see you marry a nobleman that won't care for you the way I know I can."

Now, she was silent. He could have kicked himself for saying anything about marriage. What the hell was the matter with him?

"It is late. I shouldna have come out here alone. I am goin' back to bed." Lark turned to go, and Dustin panicked.

His heart ached for her and he couldn't stand to lose her this way.

He couldn't let her walk away now. Not after he'd bared his soul to her. Or had he? Mayhap he hadn't done quite enough.

"I love you, Lark," he called out, causing her to stop in her tracks.

She spoke to him over her shoulder, not facing him at all. "I need to marry a noble," she reminded him. "It is the only way to clear my name."

"I know, but who? Who will you marry?" he asked, slowly making his way across the garden toward her. "The secret admirer?"

"My secret admirer wants me for his wife," she said, and he heard the quaver in her voice. "That man is romantic and makes me feel special and pretty and like a queen."

"Or a goddess?" he asked, coming closer. "You are like the goddess, Persephone, walking the earth and making every little thing spring to life." He repeated what he had written in the letter.

"I told ye what that letter said," she cried, never turning toward him. "Ye are no' my secret admirer, Dustin, so dinna pretend that ye are."

"Why are you fighting what you know is true?"

"Nothin' can ever come from what happened between us. Never!"

"Your voice is like the sweet chirping of the meadowlark," he repeated, not willing to let her walk out of his life like this.

Still, she didn't turn around. Lark just held the candle that flickered in the breeze, staring in the opposite direction.

"Ye heard me read that aloud, too," she said softly.

"I long to taste your sweet lips that make my heart beat faster and my body burn for the sweet, sweet touch of your skin against mine," he repeated more of the poem that she hadn't read aloud.

"How do ye ken that?" She spun around and faced him now. "Ye read my letter, admit it."

"Nay, Lark. I know what the love poem said because I was the one who wrote it. In your heart you know it is true, but you are too afraid to admit it. Am I right?"

He walked right up to her now, putting his hands on her shoulders and staring down into her eyes.

"Oh, Dustin," she said, her bottom lip trembling, as if she were about to cry. "I do ken it is ye, and I think part of me realized it from the very start. I was afraid to fall in love with a commoner. I have made the wrong choices in the past, and all I wanted for myself and my daughter was to have a fresh start. Dinna ye understand? I canna afford to make any more mistakes. Ever."

"I love you, Lark. I am not afraid to say it, even if you don't want me only because I am a commoner, not because I am wrong for you. I want to marry you and make you my wife."

"I canna. Tongues will wag." Her words were clipped and sharp.

"I don't care about gossip and reputations, and neither should you. If you love me the way I love you, then that is all that truly matters. I want to love a woman, and I finally feel like I do. I also want a family, Lark, and have been feeling like I am already a part of yours."

"I ken," she said, her eyes filling with tears. "I have felt it, too."

Dustin continued to pour out his feelings for Lark, telling her everything that was in his heart. "I also want Florie as my daughter. I want to be the best husband to you and the best father to Florie that I can be. This is something I have always longed for and never had. That is, until I met you."

"Dustin," she said, barely above a whisper. The candle fell from her hand, hitting the ground and extinguishing itself. "I love ye, too. Part of me always kent the love letters could be from no one but ye. But I tried so hard no' to believe it."

"Why? I don't understand."

"I denied that it could be from ye, because I didna want it to be true."

"Y-you didn't?"

She shook her head, tears trailing down her cheeks. "I didna want to fall in love with a man I could never have, because it hurts too much. I guess I convinced myself my secret admirer was a nobleman, because then I had hope. Hope that my life could be better."

"That's what I want for you, too, Lark. For your life to be better."

"My da will never let me marry a commoner, so I pushed those feelin's about ye away. I didna want to feel the hurt anymore, Dustin. Neither did I ever want to hurt ye." She reached up to gently stroke his face.

"Lark, I'm sorry that I tricked you and that I let you down. I never meant to hurt you by pretending I was someone else. I just didn't know how to tell you exactly how I felt about you. I–"

Dustin's words were cut off as Lark threw herself into his arms and kissed him with so much passion that it took him by surprise. He wasn't expecting this at all.

"I love ye too, Dustin, and I am glad ye are my secret admirer." She continued to kiss him in the moonlight. "I love bein' around ye, and the love poems ye write. I love the way ye are kind to my daughter and how ye never judge me for my past. I also love the way ye make me feel. Instead of feelin' ashamed, I am proud when I am around ye. Ye treat me like I'm a goddess, and no one has ever done that before."

"Slow down, Lark," he told her with a chuckle, as she

continued to kiss him and hold him tightly. "Mayhap we should go back to the manor and talk this over."

"Nay," she said, pulling off her cloak and throwing it to the ground. Her night rail was thin and white, and in the moonlight he couldn't help but notice her hard little nipples poking out from under the cloth.

This excited him, and immediately he became aroused.

"Lark?" he asked as she reached out and started pulling off his tunic. "What are you doing?"

She stopped. "Dinna ye want this as much as me?" she asked.

"Of course, I do. Probably even more than you."

"Then stop talkin' so much, Dustin, someone might hear ye."

"Hear me?" he chuckled as she continued to remove his tunic. "It's the middle of the night and we are inside a labyrinth of bushes that block us from sight and any sound."

"Good," she said, pushing him down atop the cloak. "Then take off yer trews, and hurry. I canna wait much longer."

"I love it when you are demanding in this way. It excites me more than you know."

Before he knew it, she was standing there naked in the moonlight looking like the Goddess of Love, Aphrodite. He wanted to give this goddess of a woman loving like she'd never known.

Pulling off his trews, he flipped them to the side, and held out his arms.

"Come to me, my goddess of love and temptation."

He let her take the top position, and wasn't sorry about it. Since she wasn't trapped under his weight, she moved her hips more freely as he entered her and they made love right there in the pleasure garden.

It didn't take either of them long to find their release. And when they were finished, he cradled her in his arms and they stared up at the moon and stars, listening to the peaceful sound of crickets in the night.

"Now we know why it is called a pleasure garden," he said with a chuckle.

"Dustin, I love ye," she told him. "I love ye and I want to be with ye for the rest of my life."

"I love you, too. I could lay here all night with you in my arms staring up at the night sky."

"It is so magical," she told him. With Lark pressed up against him, he could feel the rapid beating of her heart. "But I dinna think it would be a good idea to stay here too long."

"I know you're right." He was about to get up when Bandit's nose appeared before him and the hound started licking his face.

"Bandit!" Lark shot up to a sitting position.

Dustin laughed. "It's just a dog. Don't sound so upset."

"He's a dog who likes to steal braies. Fast, get yer clothes on before they are gone."

He thought she was jesting at first as she hurriedly pulled her night rail over her head. But when he saw Bandit standing there in the moonlight with his trews in the dog's mouth, he started getting a little concerned.

How would he explain this? The last thing he wanted was to be caught bare-assed in a pleasure garden with a noble-woman in the middle of the night.

"Dustin, the dog is heading for the entrance of the labyrinth with yer trews. Do somethin', fast. We've got to stop him."

When she looked like she was about to run after the hound, he held up a halting hand.

"Nay," he told her. "Being chased is exactly what Bandit

wants. Just turn around and ignore him. Don't give him any attention at all."

"Ignore him? Really?"

"Do it. Don't look at him or even talk to him. Understand?"

"If ye say so." Lark turned around, picking up her cloak from the ground.

Dustin donned his tunic and turned his back to the dog too.

"Mmmm, this sweetmeat is good," said Dustin, pretending like he was eating something. "Did you want a bite, Lark?"

"Dustin?" she whispered. "Ye are no' holdin' a thing."

"Aye, but Bandit doesn't know that," he whispered back.

"Och, I see. Oh, yes, I would like a sweetmeat," she said, peeking back over her shoulder.

"Don't look. Turn around," he told her. "Wait for it. Wait."

Sure enough, the pitter-patter of the dog's paws on the ground could be heard. Then, Bandit walked in front of them and dropped the trews from his mouth, looking up at Dustin and barking.

"Thank you, Bandit." Dustin grabbed his trews and donned them. The dog continued to bark.

"Dustin, Bandit is goin' to keep barkin' and will give us away," said Lark with concern in her voice.

"Don't worry. I have it handled."

He opened a pouch that was attached to the belt on his trews and pulled out a sweetmeat that was leftover from their meal outdoors.

"Ye really have a sweetmeat?" asked Lark in surprise. "Why?"

"I told you before when Florie offered me one, that I really like sweetmeats." He held it out and Bandit slobbered his hand taking it, gobbling it down. Then, the dog sat there silently like an angel, wagging his tail and waiting for more.

"I guess ye're no' the only one who likes them," said Lark with a giggle. "Ye must love sweetmeats more than anythin'."

"Not more than anything," he said, leaning over and kissing her on the tip of her nose. "I love you, Lady Lark, much, much more."

CHAPTER 17

A week passed by quickly, and still they hadn't left Rookrose Manor. Lark decided she didn't ever want to go back to Blake Castle. Since they were here, Florie hadn't acted up at all. Lark had convinced even Eleanor and Sister Joan to spend more time out in the gardens since the place was so beautiful as well as peaceful.

"Hurry, Florie, Dustin is goin' to read ye a new story." Today, Lark sat on the swing in the pleasure garden with Dustin. Florie chased Bandit around, actually getting close to catching the dog once or twice.

Raven and Eleanor were at the other end of the garden talking with Rose and Rose's cousin, Georgiana. Rose's gardeners and good friends, Phineas and Thomasina weeded around the gravesites of Rose's parents.

"I want a story about a princess," said Florie, running over to them and crawling up onto Dustin's lap. Lark's eyes opened wide when Florie dropped down on Dustin and he cringed.

"Florie, gentle," he told the girl, repositioning her on his lap.

"I want to hold the book," said Florie, holding out her hands.

"All right," said Dustin, opening the book and letting her hold on to the covers.

Dustin had a book of blank pages he always carried with him, and had made it into a book of stories for Florie to enjoy. He'd been very busy this past week. Between Florie's lessons and making the book for her, he also made sure to leave a love poem under Lark's pillow every night.

Lark had a pile of the love letters now, all tied together with a red ribbon from her hair. These meant to world to her. She would never get rid of them as long as she lived.

"Read, read," said Florie, squirming around in excitement.

"Well, Florie," said Dustin. "You know how to read now, and I made sure to use easy words. Today, you are going to be the one reading the book to me and your mother."

"Really?" asked Florie with wide eyes. She looked so surprised that it made Lark giggle.

"Go on, sweetheart," Lark told her daughter. She and Dustin and even Sister Joan had spent so much time with Florie this past week that Lark felt like they were an actual family.

Florie looked down at the page and squealed in delight. "Look, Mother, there are flutterbys on the page, and flowers."

Lark and Dustin thought it was so cute when she referred to butterflies that way, that they hadn't been correcting her, but someday they would.

"Really? Let me see." Lark noticed the wonderful decorations on the page. Dustin's drawings were breathtaking.

"Dustin, it was so nice of ye to put butterflies on the pages since ye ken how much Florie likes them."

"I do, I do like them," shouted Florie.

"Well, I like them too," said Dustin. "They have always been special to me."

"Why?" asked Lark.

"Let's just say that I saw one somewhere once when I was a boy, and now they remind me of someone."

"Who? Who do flutterbys remind ye of? Is it me?" asked Florie.

"Yes, you certainly are one of those people I think of when I see a butterfly," he told Florie. "Now, start reading right here, and just go slow." Dustin pointed to the word and Florie read it.

"Once ...upon ... a ... time," she said, looking up with a wide grin.

"Very good," said Lark. "Keep goin'."

"There ... was ... a ... prin-prin ..."

"Princess," Dustin helped her out.

"Princess," said Florie, looking back down to the page, starting over again. "Once ... upon ...a ...time..."

Lark realized if her daughter kept doing this, they were never going to get through the story. She looked over at Dustin and nodded at the book, wanting him to read it. He knew what she meant.

"How about if the first time we hear this story, your mother reads it to you," said Dustin.

"Me?" asked Lark in surprise. She wasn't expecting that since Dustin had been the one tutoring the child, not her.

"Mother doesna ken how to read," said Florie.

"What? Really?" Dustin looked up in concern.

"Of course I do," said Lark. "Florie, why would ye say such a thing?"

"Ye never read me a story before."

"Oh," said Lark, realizing she hadn't. That must be why Florie thought she couldn't read. Lark decided mayhap she should have tried harder to spend special time with her daughter long before now. Through the years there had been so many people in her clan and her family helping out with Florie, that after a while she found it easier to just sit back and let them do it. After spending time watching Dustin with her daughter, Lark now realized how much precious time with Florie she had lost and regretted it.

She had been so distraught hearing gossip about her having a child out of wedlock that she had ignored the most important person in her life. Lark realized now that she had been the reason why Florie was so disobedient. The little girl had been silently crying out for Lark's attention for years, but Lark had been focusing on all the wrong things that didn't really matter.

"I would love to read the story to ye, Florie, but only if ye sit on my lap."

For a few seconds Florie didn't move, and Lark felt her heart sink. Her child didn't want her.

"I love ye, Mother," said Florie, plopping down on Lark's lap now with the book in her little hands.

"I love ye, too, Florie." Lark hugged her daughter to her chest and kissed her on her head. She glanced over to Dustin with tears in her eyes and mouthed the words, thank you.

She had Dustin to thank for strengthening her relationship with her daughter. Dustin was also the one who made her feel like a queen instead of a troubled woman.

"Once upon a time, there was a princess," Lark read aloud. "The princess was a little girl with blond hair and blue eyes. Her name was Florie."

"Florie? That's me!" Florie looked up at Lark with wonder in her eyes. "Am I a princess, Mother?"

"Ye are to me, sweetheart." She kissed Florie and continued to read.

LOVE LETTERS FOR LADY LARK

One by one, the others wandered over to hear the story Dustin wrote as well.

"Look at the pictures and flutterbys," Florie told the others, pointing out each one to them.

"Oh. Butterflies," said Sister Joan, seeming quite excited. "I am so glad to see that."

"This one looks like the one that sat on my arm," said Florie, trying to pick up the book to show the others.

"Yes," Dustin answered. "It is just like the one that sat on your arm the first day we got here."

"Look, Mother, there is the dragonfly we chased, too."

"Yes, it surely is," said Lark, looking over at Dustin who was smiling at them. Her heart was filled with love, and it was all because of this wonderful man. She wanted to spend the rest of her life with him. There was no doubt in her mind about this anymore.

Lark finished the story and closed the book.

"That was a wonderful story, Dustin," said Sister Joan. "You have a true talent with words. And drawings. Why did you draw butterflies?" she asked, curiously.

"Because they remind him of me," Florie answered for him.

"Mayhap on parchment I can convey my feelings, but I can't say I have the same skill with speaking aloud all the time."

"I'm sure ye have other ways of conveyin' feelings besides words," said Lark with a shy grin.

He looked at Lark and winked.

She felt the blush rising to her cheeks, loving being around him.

"Where is my daughter?" came the gruff voice of Lark's father from the entrance of the labyrinth.

"Uh oh," she heard Dustin say under his breath.

"I'm sorry, Uncle Storm," said Rook, following right behind

him. "I told Lark and the others they needed to leave, but they insisted on staying."

"Go play with Bandit, Florie," said Lark, closing the book and handing it to Dustin.

"I'll watch her," said Sister Joan, helping Florie from the swing, walking away to go after the dog.

"Da," said Lark, standing up and brushing off her gown. She could tell how angry her father was with her already.

Twice now in the past week, he had sent a messenger from Blake Castle telling her to get back at once. She, in return, sent the messengers back to Blake Castle saying she was not yet ready to leave.

The others had stayed with her to support her, and now Lark hoped she wouldn't get them all in trouble.

"Lark, I told ye no' to be here more than a day or two. It has been a week now, and ye need to return to the castle," spat Storm.

"But Da, I was spendin' special time with ... with Florie," she said, wanting to say Dustin, but not thinking right now would be a good time to tell her angry father that she loved a commoner.

"Pack yer things. We are leavin' at once. All of ye," he said, looking over to Raven and the others.

"Sorry, Uncle Storm," said Raven. "We'll go and pack our things now."

"Yes, we didn't mean to anger you," said Eleanor. "We were just all having a wonderful time and the gardens are so beautiful here that we didn't want to leave."

"Thank you," said Rose. "We try hard to make the grounds pretty."

"My wife is the best at that," said Rook. "Oh, did you want to see the–"

"Rook!" scolded Storm.

"Mayhap next time," said Rook with a shrug of his shoulders.

"The feast and celebration to choose yer husband is next week," Storm told Lark, taking her by the arm and escorting her through the labyrinth, following the others.

"Yes. Yes, I ken that," said Lark, looking back to see Dustin following with his bag over his shoulder. He wasn't looking at her or at Storm, and she knew why. The last thing Dustin wanted to hear was that she was to marry a noble. Lark needed to talk to her father about Dustin, but he wasn't making it easy for her to get a word into the conversation.

"Scribe, there is a stack of letters this big waitin' for Lark to read them," said Storm, motioning with his hands to show how big, most likely exaggerating since her father seemed to embellish things all the time. "I'll need them all recorded with the names of her suitors before they get to the castle next week."

"Yes, my lord," said Dustin.

"Da, I need to talk to ye about this celebration feast and the suitors." Lark wanted to mention her feelings for Dustin and was trying hard to work it into the conversation.

"No' now," said Storm as they exited the labyrinth. "Now go, and get ready. We need to get on the road anon."

Dustin started to walk toward the keep, but Storm stopped him.

"No' ye, scribe. Ye stay here. I want to talk to ye in private."

Lark's eyes met Dustin's. The last thing she wanted to do was to leave him here alone with her father. She was about to object, but Dustin looked at her and slowly shook his head. Lark turned and ran for the keep.

• • •

"Scribe, did ye ever find out who that secret admirer is who has been sendin' my daughter those silly love poems?"

Dustin hesitated, not sure how to answer. He could tell Storm he hadn't found out anything, but that would be a lie. Brother Ruford had raised Dustin not to lie. Not that he always listened. Then again, he could tell Storm the truth, but that would put him in a very bad light. To say this to a mad Highlander was probably just short of suicide.

"I did," he answered Storm, no longer caring. He wasn't about to cower away every time Lark's father was near. He loved Lark and she loved him and he was not ashamed of it.

"Ye did? Well, tell me. Who is it?"

"Nay, you don't understand," said Dustin. "I did. Me. I'm the one who sent those letters to Lark and signed them as her secret admirer."

Dustin didn't think Storm could be any angrier, but he was wrong. Storm's face turned bright red. Dustin saw his hand hovering over the hilt of his sword. This wasn't going well at all.

"Ye had better tell me I heard ye wrong, scribe. Because, I just thought ye said ye sent those love letters to my daughter."

Dustin released a deep breath and answered. "You heard me right, my lord."

"Why in the devil's name would ye play such a trick on Lark? Dinna ye realize she is frail and fragile? Ye willna get away with such deception."

"It was not a trick," Dustin told him. "You see ... I am in love with Lark, and I want to marry her."

Thank goodness that Sister Joan approached them at that moment, or Dustin was sure the madman would have drawn his sword and lopped off his head.

"My lord, the traveling party is ready," said the nun.

"Fine!" said Storm, turning to leave, but stopping and

turning back to Dustin. "Ye are relieved of yer duties, scribe. Ye can go back to the monastery and I never want ye to speak to my daughter again."

"But my lord," said Dustin. "Lark is in love with me, too. We want to be married."

"Her name is Lady Lark and ye will no' forget to use her title again. If ye were no' almost like a son to Brother Ruford, I swear ye would hang for this."

"Please, my lord. We want to be together."

"Nay!" Storm shouted. "Ye are a commoner and my daughter will marry a nobleman and that is all there is to it. Now leave right now, because ye willna be travelin' with us. I never want to see yer face again."

Lark's father stormed off, leaving Dustin standing there with the nun, feeling as if his life was over. Without Lark, he had nothing to look for to, and no longer even had the will to want to live.

"Don't let him upset you," said Sister Joan.

"Listen to what you're saying, Sister."

"I mean it," said the nun. "Sometimes, things are not always what they seem."

She was starting to sound like the old sorcerer now.

"Well, this is exactly what it seems," he told her. "I am a commoner and Lark is a lady. I don't know why I fooled myself into thinking that we could be together when we both knew it was not possible."

"Dustin, listen to me." Sister Joan seemed like she had more to say, but Dustin wasn't in the mood to listen.

"I am sorry, Sister, but I am done listening to everyone. Please, give my regards to Lark and Florie. Tell Lark I tried, but I failed. Tell her that I am very, very sorry that things had to end this way."

CHAPTER 18

"Da, is it true ye told Dustin to leave and that he is no longer needed?" Lark had heard the news from Sister Joan, not to mention, everyone heard the yelling. She had still been inside the keep, and when she came out to the courtyard, she saw Dustin in the distance, riding away.

"Aye, that's right," said Storm mounting his horse.

"Da, I love him! We want to get married. Didna he tell ye?"

"Blethers, Lark, why do ye think I had to send him away?"

"Nay, this canna be happenin'."

"Get on your horse," Storm commanded. "We're leavin'. Move on out," he called out to the guards. The caravan headed out the gates.

"How could ye do such a thing?" Lark's eyes filled with tears.

"Ye have to marry a noble or yer reputation will always be tarnished," he so blatantly reminded her.

"I dinna care. I want to marry Dustin. Florie likes him too."

"Get on yer horse, Lark. And I dinna want to hear another

word about this." Storm rode off in a puff of dust, leaving Lark standing there.

"I'm sorry, Lark," said Rose, coming to her side and putting her hand on Lark's shoulder. "Mayhap he'll change his mind."

"Rook, do somethin'," Lark called out to her cousin who was watching from a distance.

"I don't know what you think I can do," Rook called back with a shrug. He turned and headed back into the keep.

"Rose, I love Dustin. What am I goin' to do? I dinna want to marry a noble. I want Dustin, even if he is a commoner."

"I wish I knew what to tell you," said Rose. "Your father seems pretty upset. Do you think you can talk about this with your mother? Would she be able to help you?"

"Yes. Yes, I believe she would," said Lark, mounting her horse. "Thank ye, Rose. That is exactly what I will do." Lark took off on her horse to catch up with the rest of the traveling party.

She didn't even speak to her father at all on the way back to the castle. It wasn't until they'd entered the courtyard of Blake Castle that she jumped off her horse and ran over to her father.

"When is mother arrivin'?" asked Lark.

"Yer mother will be here with yer siblin's for yer weddin'."

"Well, I want to send her a missive and ask her to arrive early."

"Lark, it's no use," said Storm. "By the time the letter gets to her in Scotland and she comes here, it will be at least a week anyway. Ye'll just have to wait to talk to her until she arrives. And I warn ye, she will no' change my mind, if that is what ye are thinkin'."

"My lord, where is the scribe?" asked Orrick, approaching them holding a large pile of letters. "I wanted to give these to Dustin to record them, but I don't see him."

"He's no' here. Just give the letters to Lark," said Storm, heading quickly to the keep.

"I'm sorry, I don't understand," said Orrick. "Did Dustin stay behind at Rookrose Manor for some reason?"

"Nay," said Lark. "Da dismissed him. He sent him back to the monastery and told him he can never see or speak to me again."

"Why not? asked Orrick. "Did something happen?" He handed the letters to Lark.

"Yes," she told the sorcerer. "He found out that Dustin and I are in love and want to be married. Please ask Sister Joan to watch Florie for me. I need to be alone right now."

Lark ran off to her chamber, not wanting everyone to see her cry. She entered her bedchamber, slamming the door behind her. Then the tears came like a flood. She looked at the letters in her hand and angrily stormed over to the hearth, throwing them in, and lighting a fire.

Then she ran back to the bed and threw herself down upon it, crying her eyes out. That's when her hand felt something under her pillow. She pulled it out and wiped her eyes, realizing it was a missive that looked a lot like the ones Dustin had sent her.

She opened it up with shaky hands, wiping away another tear, reading it aloud.

"Dinna fret, my love. I will no' give up. I will no' stop tryin' until we can be together. Forever. Dustin." At the bottom of the letter he'd drawn a little butterfly.

Lark realized the writing looked rushed, and that somehow Dustin had written this to her and got back to the castle before them and sneaked it under her pillow.

She held up the letter and kissed it, holding the parchment to her heart. He had signed it with his name this time and that meant a lot to her.

"Everythin' is goin' to be all right," she tried to convince herself, rocking back and forth. Dustin wasn't giving up so easily and neither would she.

There was still a week left before the doomsday of choosing a noble to wed. She wasn't sure how she would change her father's mind, but somehow she had to do it.

Lark finally knew happiness in her life after so many years of feeling unworthy, dirty and despised. Dustin filled that void in her heart. He had helped her to realize she was worthy of being loved, and no gossip or wagging tongues could ever make her feel differently again.

Dustin loved her.

She loved him, too.

He didn't care about her past, and accepted her for who she was. He treated her better than anyone ever had. He even cared about her bastard daughter. Lark wouldn't let him get away. She couldn't. Dustin was the answer to all her prayers, and she'd almost made the mistake of believing that she had to marry a nobleman to make things right in her life.

She knew better now. It didn't matter if the man she married was a noble, a commoner, or even a rag picker. All that mattered was that she and Dustin were in love and they filled the voids in each other's lives.

"Tomorrow will be a better day," she told herself, falling asleep with Dustin's message in her hand. Tomorrow would look brighter. She had faith that things would work out now because Dustin said he wasn't giving up, and that was good enough for her.

Now, if only she could think of something she could do to help him.

~

"Dustin, why are you here instead of at the castle?" asked Brother Ruford as soon as Dustin had entered the walls of the monastery. They walked together in the cloisters as they spoke.

"I've been relieved of my duties," he said, feeling like he had taken a beating, even though no one physically touched him at all.

"Why? What happened?"

"I'd rather not talk about it." He headed for his cottage, not wanting or needing to explain to Ruford that he'd been too honest with Storm MacKeefe and now he was going to pay for it. Ruford had warned him not to break Lark's heart and he might have done just that before this was all over.

Dustin hadn't been back long when there came a knock at his door.

"I told you, I don't want to talk about it," he called out from the bed, thinking it was Brother Ruford again. There was no need confiding in the man since he wasn't going to be able to help him.

He heard the door squeak open and looked over to see Orrick standing there.

"Orrick," he said, sitting up on his bed. "What brings you here?"

"May I come in?" asked the old man.

"Yes. Please." Dustin jumped up and welcomed the sorcerer into his abode.

"I heard what happened," said Orrick.

"Yes, I'm sure everyone knows by now that I made a fool of myself in front of Storm MacKeefe."

"Is that what you think?" asked Orrick.

"I am a commoner, Orrick. I told the man I was in love with his daughter and wanted to marry her. What the hell did I think he was going to say?" Dustin blew a puff of air from his mouth and sank atop a chair.

Orrick slowly walked over to the table. "You did the right thing," said Orrick. "It is good to tell the truth."

"Is it? Look what it got me. Banned from the castle without a job, and forbidden to ever see or speak to the woman I love again."

"So, what are you going to do about it?" asked Orrick, sitting down at the table with him.

"There is nothing I can do," said Dustin, running his hand through his long hair. "I'm just a scribe." Then Dustin had an idea. "Orrick? Can you do something to help me? Use your magic, mayhap?"

"I could, but like I already told you, that would be wrong. Don't you agree?"

"At this point, I'm not sure what to think. I'm grasping at everything and anything that can keep me and Lark together."

"Like I told you, Lord Corbett doesn't like me to use my magic anymore, so when I do, I have to do so hidden away in my tower room. He's afraid it'll frighten others."

"Well, believe me, there is nothing as frightening as a Madman MacKeefe who wants my head on a platter."

Orrick laughed heartily.

"What's so funny?"

"I have known Storm MacKeefe for a long time, and I assure you he is not the mean, angry man you believe him to be."

"You could have fooled me." Dustin scowled, playing with a dish on the table.

"Must I remind you that everything happens for a reason?"

"Aye. And the reason for this is to ruin my life as well as Lark's."

"Then do something to change that."

"What? What can I possibly do?" Dustin's hands waved wildly in the air and he got to his feet and started pacing.

"Well, to start with, I'd think you'd stop hiding away in the monastery thinking this is going to protect you."

"I am not doing that," Dustin ground out. "I'm here to think up a plan. Plus, I was told to stay away from Lark, and I was relieved of my job. I have nowhere else to go."

"It seems to me that Lord Corbett hired you as castle scribe, and Lady Lark hired you to tutor her child."

"Yes, that's right."

"So, Storm tells you to leave and you do it?"

Dustin stopped pacing and nodded. "You're right, Orrick. He didn't hire me and neither can he dismiss me, either. I'm going back to the castle where I belong." He started to pack up his bag.

"Before you do that, you might want to think of what kind of problems going back might cause between Lord Corbett and Laird MacKeefe."

"But you were the one to suggest it."

"Just saying."

"You're right," said Dustin, sinking back onto the chair. "It will also only cause more friction between Lark and her father. That is never going to win the man over."

"Then use your assets to get what you want."

"Assets? What assets?"

"Your talents. Your skills," said Orrick.

"The only skill I have is being a scribe."

"Exactly. You have the gift of being able to use your written words to your advantage, so use them."

"Yes," said Dustin with a nod. "You're right. But how? In what manner?"

"That, Dustin, is something you are going to have to discover on your own." Orrick got up and headed for the door.

"Wait," said Dustin. "Before you go, I'd like to ask you to bring something to Lark for me."

"Shouldn't a messenger do that?"

"Nay," said Dustin, hurriedly opening a piece of parchment and pulling out his bottle of ink and quill. "If I use a messenger, it'll surely be intercepted by her father." He scribbled some words onto the page, then blew on the ink to dry it. Folding up the parchment, he stuck it into the children's book he wrote for Florie and handed Orrick the book. "Please deliver this personally to Lark. And tell her ... tell her I love her."

LARK HEARD a knock at her chamber door, and thought it was Sister Joan returning from her walk with Florie. They had asked Lark to join them, but she was too upset to go. Plus, she was so angry with her father that she didn't want to see him or talk to him at all.

"Who is it?" she called out, not wanting to open the door if it was her father.

"It is Orrick, my lady."

"Orrick?" she asked, thinking it was odd for him to come to her room. She jumped up and ran over and opened the door. "Orrick, what is it? Is everything all right?"

"My lady, I was asked to give this to you." He pulled a book out from under his robe and handed it to her.

"It's the book that Dustin wrote for Florie." She took it with two hands, feeling as if she were about to cry. "Did you see Dustin? Where is he? Is he all right?"

"He is at the monastery, my lady. He asked me to tell you that he loves you."

"He did?" She held the book to her heart. "Oh, I miss him so much, Orrick. What else did he say?"

There came the sound of voices from down the corridor and Orrick's head snapped around. "Someone approaches, my lady. I must go now." Orrick hurried away just as Raven and Eleanor came walking toward her chamber.

"Lark," said Eleanor. "We came to comfort you."

"No one can comfort me, but ye are welcome to join me in my misery," said Lark, holding the door open and nodding for them to enter. When the women were inside the room, Lark closed the door.

"Cousin, we heard what happened," said Raven with concern in her voice.

"Yes, and with the way tongues wag I am sure everyone in the castle kens that Dustin and I are in love by now." Lark plopped down on the bed.

"I heard my father talking to yours," said Raven. "Uncle Storm is worried that the suitors will hear the gossip about you and Dustin when they arrive. And that they won't want to marry you after all."

"I heard them talking about adding even more to the dowry to make the deal sweeter," said Eleanor.

"More? How much more can they possibly add?" asked Lark, feeling helpless to change her horrible situation. "Before ye ken it, they are goin' to bribe the nobles with this castle, too."

"Nay. My father would never do that. Not with Blake Castle," said Raven. "Lark, you need to talk to your father. Explain to him exactly how you feel."

"I did!" Lark's hand went to her head which was starting to ache. "There is no talkin' to my da. He thinks he is right and willna listen to a word anyone has to say. I wish my mother were here. She is the only one who can possibly get through to him. I ken my mother would help me and realize exactly how I feel."

"She'll be here soon, I'm sure," said Eleanor, putting her hand on Lark's arm. "What is that book you have?"

"It is the book Dustin wrote for Florie. I'm sure she'll be glad to have it, but it only makes me miss him more." Lark tossed the book down on the bed and something fell out.

"What's that?" Raven pointed. "Something fell out of the book."

"It did?" Lark reached over and picked up the folded piece of parchment.

"It looks like a note of some kind," said Eleanor.

"It is," said Lark, recognizing the parchment as the same that Dustin had used to write her love poems. "I think it's from Dustin."

"Open it. Read it," Raven urged her on.

"Yes, we want to know what it says," agreed Eleanor.

With shaking hands, Lark opened the missive from Dustin, scanning the scant amount of words scribbled across the letter. It looked as if he had written it in a rush again, and it certainly wasn't another poem.

"Well?" asked Eleanor. "Is it another love letter from him?"

"Nay," said Lark. "It just says to meet him at the castle's smithy tonight when it gets dark."

"At the castle's smithy?" asked Raven. "That's my husband's shop. Jonathon must be involved in this. I'm surprised he didn't mention it to me."

"I have a feelin' mayhap Jonathon doesna ken about it yet," Lark told her.

"Well, whatever we can do to help you and Dustin, we'll do it," said Raven. "No matter what the consequences."

"Yes," agreed Eleanor. "I know how important it is to be with the one you love. I will help you, too." Eleanor put her arm around Lark.

"Thank ye both for stickin' by me. That means the world to me," said Lark.

"It'll all work out." Raven tried to console her, sitting on the other side of her and putting her arm around Lark, too. "After all, it worked out for me and also for Rook when we both fell in love with commoners. So, why shouldn't it work out for you as well?"

"Because, I'm the one with the tarnished reputation. I need to marry a noble more than either of ye did. Uncle Corbett and my da are both countin' on me to try to bring back honor to the family name. Since I've done the opposite already, it is crucial that I change things. Or, that is what they think, anyway."

"Who cares what others think?" asked Raven. "I know that I don't. We will find a way to make this right for you and Dustin, I swear we will."

"Yes," agreed Eleanor. "After all, isn't that what family is for?"

CHAPTER 19

Lark entered the smithy that night, slipping into the shop along with Raven, closing the door behind them. Jonathon stood across the room at the forge, working the large bellows to fan the fire. When he saw them, he removed a long pole with metal attached and laid it on the anvil. To Lark, it looked as if he were forging a sword.

"Is he here?" Raven asked her husband.

Jonathon motioned with his head to the bedroom. "My brother and Gerold are already sleeping," he told them. "Be quiet about it, and make it fast. I don't mind helping out, but I don't want the lords Corbett and Storm breathing down my neck. I've got enough irons in the fire and don't need more." He chuckled softly at his jest of irons in the fire.

"Thank ye, Jonathon." Lark walked over to the bedroom door and knocked softly.

The door opened and Dustin looked out.

"It's safe," said Lark. "No one saw us."

"Lark," said Dustin, stepping out into the room. He pulled her into his arms and kissed her deeply.

"Och, Dustin, I missed ye so much."

"God's eyes, it's only been a day, not a year," came a grouchy voice from inside the room.

Lark looked over to see Jonathon's brother, Avery and Gerold, the ten-year-old apprentice boy peeking out at them.

"Avery, give them some privacy," growled Jonathon.

"You and Lady Raven are out there, so it's not private," Avery called back.

"I'm purposely pounding on the anvil to make noise as a distraction so no one hears them. Now close the damned door," said Jonathon.

"Fine." Avery closed the door with a soft thud.

"Dustin, why are ye here?" asked Lark.

"I wanted to tell you that I am not going to let your father scare me away, Lark."

"Really? What do ye plan to do?"

"I'm not sure yet, but I promise, I will think of something. In the meantime, tomorrow I am returning to the castle as Lord Corbett's scribe."

"Oh, Dustin, that is risky. Did ye talk to my uncle about it already?"

"Nay, but Lord Corbett is the one who hired me, and I am returning to my job. As well as the job you hired me to do," he added.

"Dustin, ye are no' really comin' back as Florie's tutor?"

"Why not?" he asked. "Unless you are dismissing me from my position as well?"

"Nay! Never. Just be careful. My da has a temper and I canna say he will take kindly to this idea."

"I'm willing to risk everything to be with you, Lark. I swear, somehow I am going to convince your father that we belong together."

"Oh, Dustin. This is why I love ye." She kissed him again.

Raven was at the front door, peeking out. "Someone's coming," she announced. "Oh, no. It's my father and also yours, Lark," Raven reported.

"Dammit," Jonathon ground out. "This isn't going to bode well for me. Sneak out the back door, Dustin. Hurry. And don't let anyone see you."

"I'll see you tomorrow, Lark. Sweet dreams my goddess, until we meet again." Dustin kissed her once more.

"Go!" spat Jonathon, sending Dustin running for the back door. He had just left when the door opened and Corbett and Storm walked in.

"What's this?" asked Storm. "Why are ye two still awake and at the smithy at this late hour?"

"Aye, what is going on?" asked Corbett. "My guards told me they saw you two sneaking across the courtyard."

"Father, this is my home. I don't need to sneak to the smithy to see my husband," said Raven.

"My lords," Jonathon greeted them with a nod, sticking the sword back into the fire. "Was my noise keeping you awake? I am working late on Sir Albright's sword, but I can stop now if you wish."

"Nay, nay, continue," said Corbett.

Storm looked around the room suspiciously. "Lark, what are ye doin' here?"

"I couldna sleep," she told him. "And remember, I am no' talkin' to ye." She turned the other way and crossed her arms over her chest.

"Ye'll forget all about that scribe once ye meet the noblemen who will be arrivin' for the feast and celebration startin' tomorrow."

"Tomorrow?" Lark spun around. "Why so soon? The feast of fools isna supposed to start for a week yet."

"Dinna call the nobles, fools," growled Storm. "And I think

ye misunderstood how this works. Ye will actually choose and marry the man in a week's time. But until then, ye will spend time with yer suitors and get to ken them. After all, ye are choosin' a husband, Lark, and this is a position for a lifetime. Ye'll want to find out as much as ye can about each one of them so ye can make the right decision."

"Hrmph," she spat, not sure how to answer that. She didn't want any of the greedy nobles and didn't need a week to decide. She'd already determined that Dustin was the only man she wanted to marry. However, she didn't think it would be wise to revisit that issue right now. If so, her father might discover Dustin had been there and send the dogs after him.

"Get some sleep, Lark. Ye'll need to be well-rested and lookin' yer best when the nobles start arrivin' on the morrow," Storm told her.

Lark felt doomed. This was all happening too fast. Now, it only meant that Dustin had little or no time to figure out a plan. With each minute that ticked away, so did her hope of ever getting to marry the man she truly loved and cherished.

WITH HIS TRAVEL bag of supplies over his shoulder, Dustin entered the great hall the next morning, surprised to see it so crowded. He wasn't expecting this. It looked like there were at least half a dozen Scottish men standing around Lark. The same amount of English nobles, men he'd never seen before, were scattered around the room deep in conversation with Lord Corbett as well as Lord Storm.

"Dustin!" Florie spotted him from across the hall, breaking away from Sister Joan, and running to him, jumping into his arms. "Ye came back. I kent ye would."

"Hello, Florie," said Dustin with a chuckle, giving the little girl a quick kiss on the cheek. "How is my little princess?"

"She's not a princess, she's just a bastard child," came the rude remark of one of the English nobles. He, and another noble drank their ale, looking down their noses at Dustin. It was evident they were there trying to win Lark's hand in marriage.

"I am too, a princess!" shouted Florie, looking angry as well as sad.

"We've heard all about the wild child from hell," said the other. "She is almost as naughty as her lusty mother." That made them both chuckle.

Dustin didn't like this comment about Lark and Florie, but he bit his tongue. Storm and Corbett were looking over at the disturbance it was starting to cause. When they headed in his direction, Dustin put the girl down.

"Florie, we'll have a lesson later. Right now, I need you to go back by Sister Joan. All right?"

"All right," said Florie. "But I dinna like these mean men." She walked over and stomped her foot atop one of the noblemen, and kicked at the other.

Part of Dustin wanted to cheer aloud, but instead he did what was expected by scolding the child.

"Florie, that wasn't nice. Now go over by Sister Joan. Hurry."

"Aye, Dustin. I'll do it for ye." She ran off, knocking into Storm.

"Florie, what is goin' on here?" asked Storm, holding her by the shoulders.

"Those men were bein' mean to me, grandda," she said, shaking out of his hold and running into Sister Joan's arms.

"Mean?" Storm looked over at the nobles.

231

"I don't know what the child is talking about," said one of the noblemen.

"Me either," said the other. "She just went crazy and started hitting us and stepping on our toes."

"We're sorry about that," said Corbett. "We'll make sure it doesn't happen again."

"It better not," threatened the first man. "Because no man will want to marry the girl's mother if that child is so out of control."

They walked away scoffing about Florie.

"Scribe, what in the devil's name are ye doin' here?" asked Storm. "I told ye, yer services are no longer needed."

"No offense, Laird MacKeefe, but since Lord Corbett hired me as castle scribe, I thought he should be the one to tell me if he didn't want me here any longer," Dustin answered.

"Corbett?" Storm looked over at his brother-by-marriage. "Ye are no' goin' to let him stay, are ye?"

"Well, I'm not sure," said Corbett. "He was doing a fine job. Plus, I really do need a scribe. Especially since all the nobles are arriving and might want to send missives back to their families."

"I can do that, my lord," Dustin quickly offered, feeling hope that Corbett would keep him after all.

"Then again, if you really feel like he shouldn't be here, I might need to rethink this decision," added Corbett.

"I dinna want him here. He is only goin' to ruin things for Lark," said Storm.

"Excuse me, Lord Corbett," said Orrick, suddenly appearing and joining them. "I couldn't help overhearing the conversation. As your advisor, I think it would be in your best interest to keep the scribe for now."

"You do?" asked Corbett.

"Aye," said Orrick looking over at Dustin. "Not just for his ability to scribe, but because the child is so fond of him."

"Ye mean, Florie?" asked Storm.

"Aye," said Orrick. "Have either of you noticed that since Dustin has been coming to the castle, the little girl has been so much more well-behaved?"

"Yes, I have noticed," said Corbett.

"My granddaughter just stepped on a noble's foot and kicked another in the leg," scoffed Storm. "Dinna tell me that is no' bad behavior."

"Excuse me, my lords," said Dustin. "I must tell you that those two nobles called Florie a bastard child, and said some very unkind things about her. I feel as if Florie was only defending herself in the best way she knew how."

"They did?" Storm glanced over his shoulder and then back to Dustin. "They called my granddaughter a bastard child?"

"Yes. They also referred to Lady Lark as naughty and lusty," Dustin relayed the information.

"I'll kill them," Storm ground out, anger showing on his face.

"Storm, calm down," warned Corbett.

"I want them out of here anon," Storm continued.

"I'm not sure that is a good idea, my lord," said Orrick, surprising Dustin since he thought the sorcerer was on his side. "I mean, dismissing suitors before Lady Lark has made her decision will only cause the tongues to wag more."

"Orrick's right," said Corbett. "They'll be gone soon enough, so just try not to cause trouble with any of the nobles," he told Storm. "As it is, a lot of them hate Highlanders and I don't want a battle to start right here at my castle."

"Well, somethin' needs to be done," snapped Storm. "I willna put up with this."

"I have a suggestion," said Orrick. "What if you have the

scribe make a list of any of the nobles who offend you, Lady Lark, or even Florie while they are here? Then, you can secretly give the list to Lady Lark on the day of her decision, telling her not to choose those lords and why."

"Aye, a list," said Storm with a nod. "I suppose that is a good idea."

"So, I am still castle scribe?" Dustin asked Corbett.

"Yes, you are," said Corbett.

"And tutor to Florie as well?" asked Dustin.

"Now, wait a moment," said Storm. "I am no' sure I want ye near my granddaughter let alone my daughter."

"Lady Lark hired me to tutor her daughter," Dustin reminded him.

"True, and just like Orrick said, Florie is better behaved when Dustin is here," Corbett pointed out.

"Corbett, if I didna ken ye better, I'd think ye were personally tryin' to undermine me," complained Storm.

"How so?" asked Corbett.

"Ye ken this commoner wants to marry my daughter and yet ye fight for him to stay here."

"Believe me, I never wanted a commoner marrying the nobles in my family, and I still don't. I speak of the scribe's services only."

"The only services ye better be administerin' are those ye do with a quill in yer hand," said Storm, leaving Dustin standing there feeling somewhat happy because of the outcome. Still, it worried him that he might never be able to win the respect or gain the acceptance of someone as hard-headed as Storm MacKeefe.

CHAPTER 20

Lark sat up at the dais, totally exhausted from having to talk to all the suitors that had been showing up for the past three days. The hall was getting more and more crowded, and everywhere she went, some greedy nobleman was following her, trying to get her to choose him for his bride. One noble even followed her into the garderobe, trying to kiss her.

Lark had ended that with a punch to his jaw, reporting it to her father. Dustin added the man's name to the list he was keeping. In a way, Lark was glad so many of these nobles were turning out to be swine. That meant, their name went on the naughty list and that she didn't have to choose them for her husband.

She smiled inwardly thinking about the only kind of naughty she wanted. That included spending time alone and in Dustin's arms.

Ever since he returned to the castle three days ago, she felt as if mayhap there was still a shred of hope that they could end up married after all. She had found a love poem in her sewing basket yesterday from Dustin, and the day before she found one in her slipper when she got out of bed. He always drew a little butterfly at the end of the love letter, now that she knew it was him. The man was such a romantic!

She looked down over the dais to see Dustin sitting next to Jonathon and Orrick below the salt. Little Florie was with Sister Joan next to them. The nun was so good with Florie and treated her as if the little girl were her own granddaughter. Yes, Lark decided, she was truly blessed. Now, all she had to do was wait for her mother to arrive to help her try to talk sense into Lark's father so he'd let her marry Dustin.

"My lady, this is your food," said a kitchen maid, sliding a covered plate onto the table in front of her.

"Oh, I'm not hungry, but mayhap my father will want it." Lark picked up the dish to give it to Storm since he sat next to her.

"Nay, please, don't do that my lady," whispered the girl. "Dustin said to give it only to you."

"Dustin?" she whispered, looking below the salt to see him motioning for her to open the lid. "Thank ye," she said, waiting for the servant to leave. She looked over to see her father talking with Lord Corbett. So, she turned toward Raven sitting next to her, peeking under the cover and smiled.

"Oh, good, the smoked pork arrived." Raven took the plate, but Lark stopped her.

"Nay, Raven," she whispered. "This isna pork."

"Then is it the candied apples?" she asked.

"Sweeter than that, I am sure." Looking back at her father once more, Lark realized he was still busy talking. So, she put the plate on her lap, lifting the lid to expose a folded-up piece of parchment. There was a luscious big strawberry sitting next to it.

"Oh, Eleanor, look." Raven got their cousin's attention. Eleanor peeked over Raven's shoulder.

"Another love letter?" asked Eleanor excitedly.

"It is," said Lark with a smile.

"What does it say?" whispered Raven.

"Let me read it." Lark opened the missive and read it softly so only she and the girls could hear. *"My dear Lark,"* she read. *"Yer kisses are sweeter than this ripe berry and more luscious than the nectar of the brightest flower in the garden."*

"Oh, my," gasped Eleanor.

"There's more," said Lark, her back still facing her father. *"When we are together, beautiful music fills my heart and a satisfied calmness envelopes my soul."* There, at the end of the letter Dustin had drawn a little butterfly.

"My, that is romantic," said Raven. "I wish Jonathon would write me a love poem."

"At least you have a husband," said Eleanor. "I am surrounded by nuns and children my entire life. I'll never hear those kinds of words from a man."

"Eleanor, that was your choice," Raven reminded her. "Don't complain."

"What are ye lassies whisperin' about?" came Storm's deep voice from behind Lark.

"Och, nay." Lark's eyes flashed from her cousins over to Dustin and back again.

"What do ye have there? Whatever it is, give it to me. I have a feelin' I am no' goin' to like it," said Storm.

"What are you going to do?" whispered Raven. Eleanor quickly sat back in her chair and raised a goblet of wine to her mouth.

"I'll handle da. Dinna worry." Lark smiled as she folded up the parchment and shoved it down the bodice of her gown. Then she replaced the lid on the plate and turned back to her father. "This, da? I dinna want to give it to ye. Ye willna like it."

"This has somethin' to do with that sneaky scribe, doesna it?" Storm's brows were already furrowed.

"Now, really. Ye think everything has to do with Dustin," said Lark."Why dinna ye just accept the fact that we are in love?"

"Never! Now give me that." He grabbed the covered plate from her.

"Nay. Dinna open it," she played with him. "It willna make ye happy."

"I have every right to see what's under this lid." He ripped the lid off the plate and groaned.

Lark almost laughed aloud. She looked down to the other trestle tables below the salt to see Dustin looking up with wide eyes. She winked at him and smiled and he seemed to relax.

"I dinna want this thing," he said, making a face at the strawberry. "Get it away from me. It makes my throat itch."

"I told ye that ye wouldna want the berry," said Lark, plucking it off the dish and taking a big bite. "Mmm, it is delicious."

"I think they taste like slugs." Storm pushed the empty plate away from him.

"Well, that proves that everyone is different and that we all have our own preferences as to what we think is good," Lark told him. She took another big bite and looked back at Dustin, licking the juice from her fingers and watching him squirm. Unfortunately, it only made her thoughts run wild and aroused her as well. If only Dustin were licking her fingers right now, this would be so much sweeter.

～

DUSTIN WAS UP LATE that night, writing a letter in Orrick's chamber.

"What are you doing?" asked Orrick, settling into bed. "Are you still listing all the nobles who have offended Storm in some way?"

"Not at the moment," said Dustin, pulling out a list and chuckling. "However, it seems Laird Storm MacKeefe despises some of these noblemen even more than me. The list is getting quite long. I had thought of sabotaging this whole ordeal, but it seems like I won't even need to do so. It is happening by itself."

"Yes, before long, there will be no one left that isn't on that list."

"Good," said Dustin. "Then Lark won't have to marry any of them and can marry me instead."

"Is that really what you think?" asked Orrick with a yawn, reaching out to fluff his pillow.

"Nay, Orrick, it isn't. That is why I am writing this letter to Laird MacKeefe."

"What letter? What are you saying?"

"I figured talking to him wasn't getting me anywhere. So, I am writing a letter to him and his wife, telling them how much I love their daughter as well as little Florie. I am asking them to allow me to marry Lark."

"Do you think that will work?" asked Orrick.

"Well, you told me to use my skills and so I am. I am good with the written word. Hopefully, this will show them how much I really love Lark."

"You need to remember something, Dustin."

"What's that?" he asked, dipping his quill back into the ink.

"That nobles usually don't care about love. After all, love is certainly not why they marry. They marry for title, lands, or money, and most of the time to gain an alliance."

"That is not why two people should marry."

"I agree, but sadly, it is so."

"I still have to try," said Dustin, signing his name at the bottom of the letter. It felt odd since he was used to signing 'your secret admirer' every time he wrote a love letter to Lark. "Orrick?" asked Dustin.

"Mmmm?" the sorcerer mumbled from the bed.

"Can't you at least use your magic to scry for me? To let me know if Lark and I will end up being married?"

"We all have free will, Dustin. So, even if I see the outcome, you have the free will to change it and so does she. Therefore, I don't see scrying as being advantageous at all."

"You're right," said Dustin, sealing the missive and melting wax. He used a general stamp and pressed it into the wax on the letter. "I will make it happen," he said with a yawn. "I will not give up. I'll do it for Lark and Florie and me. They will be the family I never had and always wanted."

CHAPTER 21

.

The day of the feast was here, and that morning Lark's mother and siblings arrived at Blake Castle.

"Lark, your mother and siblings are here," announced Eleanor, sticking her head inside Lark's bedchamber.

"Oh, thank ye. Hurry, Florie. Yer grandmother is here," Lark called out to her daughter.

"I dinna want to get up," said the little girl, still in Lark's bed.

"Ye need to get dressed, quickly. I have to speak to Mother before it's too late."

"I'll help," said Eleanor, leaving the door open and heading over to Florie.

"Nay, I dinna want ye to help." Florie started having a tantrum and flailing her legs and arms in the air.

"What is the matter with her?" asked Eleanor.

"She kens I am goin' to have to choose a man to marry today," Lark told her cousin.

"I dinna want anyone but Dustin to be my da," wailed the little girl.

"Hello?" Dustin stuck his head into the room. "Good morning, everyone."

"Dustin!" Florie jumped out of bed and ran to him, wrapping her arms around his leg. "I want ye for my da."

"Lark?" he asked, looking up at her in question.

"She kens I have to choose a man to marry today. Dustin, have ye convinced my da yet to let us get married?"

"Nay, not yet," Dustin admitted. "Florie, can you go show Eleanor what dress you want to wear for this special day?"

"I dinna want to go."

"Well, if not, then you're going to miss out on all the fun. There are going to be games for the children, I'm told. The servants will hide treats wrapped up in parchment around the courtyard, and the children will find them. The winner gets a special toy, and all the children get to keep the treats they find."

"Really?" she asked. "I want to win the toy."

"Then you'd better hurry and get dressed," Dustin told her.

"Come on, Auntie Eleanor, help me pick out a dress." Florie took Eleanor's hand and dragged her to the adjoining room, the wardrobe, where all their clothes were kept.

"Thank ye," said Lark, putting her arms around him and kissing him on the mouth.

"Lark, we need to be careful." Dustin released her and looked over his shoulder. "There are a lot of people at the castle. I don't want your father getting angry with me right now because I am about to hand him this letter." He proudly held out a parchment to her that was folded and stamped with a wax seal.

"What is it?" she asked, donning her shoes.

"It is a letter to your parents telling them how much I love you and that I want to marry you and be a father to Florie."

"Oh, Dustin, that is so sweet. Do ye think it'll work?"

"Well, I purposely waited until your mother arrived, hoping she will be on our side."

"I am sure she will be. However, it still might no' be enough."

"If not, that's when I pull this out as my secret weapon." He held up a rolled up parchment releasing one end and letting it fall to the ground.

"That is a long list. What is it?"

"It is the list your father asked me to make. Every time one of the noblemen does something he doesn't like, or insults you or Florie, their name goes on this list. Your father won't let you marry the men who are named here."

"That is a lot of names," she said, eyeing up the scroll.

"Yes, it is. Actually, I checked and it has the name of every single nobleman on it who is attending this celebration."

"Every single one?"

"That's right," said Dustin. "So, according to this list, no nobleman here is allowed to marry you. Don't you see? Your father will have to let us get married now. Aren't you excited?"

"Well, I wish I could be, but I willna rejoice until I ken for sure that we will be married."

"Don't worry, Lark. It'll work. It has to. If not, I don't know what we'll do."

DUSTIN WALKED ALONGSIDE LARK, making their way to the courtyard. Sister Joan saw them and hurried over.

"Excuse me, Dustin, but may I have a word with you before the event starts?"

"Not now, Sister," he said, brushing the nun off. "I have something important I need to do."

"Mother!" Lark ran over and hugged her mother.

"Hello, Lady Wren," said Dustin with a nod.

"Lark, I canna believe ye're finally gettin' married." A young man with long brown hair hugged Lark.

"Dinna forget about me." A young woman with light brown hair hugged her as well.

"Dustin, this is my younger brother, Hawke, and younger sister, Heather," Lark introduced them. "Where is Renard?" she asked.

"He stayed back at the castle to protect it, since your grandfather is watching over the Highland camp," said Wren.

"Renard is my older half-brother," Lark reminded Dustin.

"Nice to meet all of you," said Dustin. When they looked confused, he told them who he was. "I am the castle scribe and also Florie's tutor."

"Oh, yes. Mother told us all about you," said Heather. "Ye are very handsome." The girl blushed.

"Heather, he's mine," said Lark.

"Yours?" asked Hawke. "I thought ye were goin' to choose a nobleman to marry today."

"She is," said Wren. "Darling, have you decided?"

"I have." Lark looked over at Dustin. "Mother, I love Dustin and want to marry him."

"Ye want to marry the scribe?" Hawke laughed. "He's a commoner. Da will never allow it."

"Lady Wren, I have written a letter to you and your husband, asking for Lark's hand in marriage," Dustin told Lark's mother.

"He didn't call her lady," Heather whispered to her brother. "He just called her Lark."

"Let me see the letter." Wren took it and broke the wax seal, scanning the letter quickly. "This is beautiful, Dustin. Is this really how the two of you feel about each other?"

"Yes," said Dustin.

"We're in love, Mother," said Lark. "And Florie adores Dustin. Can ye talk da into lettin' us get married?"

"Well, I don't know," said Wren. "Your father is a stubborn man. He has already determined that you will marry a nobleman and has gone to a lot of trouble, not to mention expense, to bring all the qualified nobles here for you to choose from. We wouldn't want to disappoint him."

"My lady, if I may show you this list, you'll see why your husband might be able to be persuaded." He handed her the scroll.

"What is this?" asked Wren.

"It is a naughty list," explained Lark.

"It holds the name of every noble here that Lord Storm told me he didn't want marrying his daughter." Dustin pointed to the list, running his finger down to the bottom.

"It does?" Wren looked at the list again and shook her head. "I don't understand."

"Lady Wren, each of the nobles invited here has somehow offended your husband, or spoken badly about Lady Lark and Florie," Dustin explained. "There is not a single one of your daughter's suitors that is not listed here."

"Really. Well, then, I don't see how Storm can say no to you two getting married. Except that Dustin isn't a noble," added Wren, sadly. "Still, I will go to him and show him your letter now." She left to find her husband.

It wasn't long before the herald blew a straight trumpet and made an announcement of a late arriver.

"Lord Gregoire Chastain of France," shouted the herald.

"God's eyes, nay!" cried Lark, her head snapping up, her eyes and mouth dropping open.

"Lark? What is it?" asked Dustin, thinking the name the herald called out sounded familiar somehow but he couldn't remember why.

"It is Lord Gregoire," said Lark. "What is he doin' here?"

"Lord Gregoire," Dustin repeated. "Isn't that the name of —"

"Yes," said Lark, taking a hold of Dustin's hand and squeezing it. "Dustin, this isna good. That man could ruin everythin' for us. He is Florie's father."

CHAPTER 22

Lark picked up her daughter, hugging her tightly to her chest. She couldn't stop from worrying that Lord Gregoire showing up here was only going to bring her strife.

"Dustin, I'm scared," she whispered. "I dinna ken why he is even here or how he kent about this."

"So, that's the man," was all Dustin said. He turned suddenly quiet and Lark didn't quite know what to think.

"Lord Gregoire, why in the devil's name are ye here?" Storm shot across the courtyard, followed by Lord Corbett.

"I heard there was a feast being given, hosting the suitors for Lady Lark, vying for her hand in marriage."

Lord Morcant made his way over to the Frenchman with Morcant's French wife holding on to his arm.

"Lord Gregoire, how nice to see you again," said Lady Adeline, Morcant's new wife who most people referred to as the French dragon. Lark's cousin Rook almost ended up marrying her, but thankfully Morcant took the woman off his hands. "Lord Gregoire is a friend of the family," said Adeline, a woman who Lark detested since she'd been so mean to her.

"It figures that they'd be friends," mumbled Lark, holding Florie and not letting her go.

"Mother, who is that man?" asked Florie.

"Never mind. He is no one ye want to ken," answered Lark.

"My wife told her parents about the feast after we received our invitation, right before they returned to France," explained Morcant.

"Aye, that is how I heard of it," said Gregoire. "I must say, Lark, I am surprised you would marry another man when I am the father of your child."

"Mother, is that my da?" asked Florie, holding on to Lark but looking over her shoulder.

"Yes, Florie. However, he is no' a nice man."

"Leave here anon," Storm commanded. His hand wavered over the hilt of his sword. The rest of the suitors and the crowd in the courtyard gathered around to see what the commotion was all about.

"Leave? Nay. I am here to win the hand of Lady Lark," the Frenchman said loud enough for all to hear. "After all, her bastard child is mine."

The crowd conversed softly amongst themselves.

"What's going on here, MacKeefe?" called out one of the suitors. "Are you going to choose a husband for your daughter or was this all a ploy to get us here and then dismiss us?"

"Aye," added another suitor. "I want that dowry."

"Me too," called out another man. "Let the Frenchman have the child, but I want the wench and the money that goes with her."

"Quiet!" shouted Lord Corbett, taking control of the situation. "Storm what do you want to do?"

Lark thought her father was going to fight Gregoire right there, he looked so angry. He surprised her by how he answered.

"We'll go ahead with the plan," said Storm. "Scribe, bring me the list of suitors."

"Aye, my lord." Dustin hurried over with the list and gave it to Storm.

"Is that the list of the men who qualify to be Lady Lark's husband?" asked Gregoire.

"Nay," said Storm, looking at the parchment. "This is the list of those who have offended me or my daughter and granddaughter and who are no longer in the running."

That didn't go over well. A lot of the suitors started to complain and shout. Once again, Lord Corbett had to silence the crowd.

"Lark, come here," commanded Storm.

Lark put Florie down, and looked over at Sister Joan. "Will you hold on to her please?"

"Of course," said the nun, holding Florie's hand.

Lark approached her father, not even being able to look at Gregoire. She despised the man and wanted nothing to do with him.

"Lark, ye will choose a nobleman now for yer husband. One whose name is no' on this list." Storm handed her the parchment.

"Excuse me, my lord," said Dustin. "I need to inform you that every suitor who has arrived is now on that list as a noble who has offended you, your daughter, or granddaughter in some way."

"Is that so?" asked Storm. "Ye are no' mistaken?"

"Dustin is correct," said Orrick making his presence known. "As advisor to the lord of the castle, I have studied the list personally. There is no noble here that stills qualifies to win Lady Lark's hand in marriage. Not by your standards, my lord."

Gregoire laughed. "Well, then I guess I will be marrying Lady Lark after, all. I am not on the list, I'm sure."

"Nay! I will never marry ye," spat Lark. "Ye abandoned me and my child."

"I only left because I had a wife at home. She is dead now, so you will be my wife from now on."

"Over my dead body," spat Lark.

"Lark, please," begged her mother. "Calm down."

"I've heard you want your tarnished daughter to marry a nobleman," said Gregoire. "We all know it is the only way she'll ever truly gain back respect. I am your man, MacKeefe. Let me see my daughter. Come here, child," he said, holding out his arms for Florie.

"Her name is Florie," said Lark through gritted teeth.

"Florie, come to your father." The man waited.

Florie broke away from the nun and ran to meet her father.

"Nay, Florie," whispered Lark, tears already filling her eyes.

"Are ye really my da?" asked the little girl, looking up at the Frenchman.

"Aye, so it seems. You'll be living with me in France now." Gregoire reached out for the little girl.

"Nay, I dinna like ye. I want Dustin to be my da." Florie bit the man's arm and stomped on his foot, before running over and clinging to Dustin.

"That whelp needs to be disciplined," yelled Gregoire. "And who the hell is Dustin?"

"I am," Dustin spoke up.

"The scribe?" Gregoire's laugh bellowed throughout the courtyard.

"I am in love with Lady Lark and want to marry her," said Dustin.

That caused a true stir in the courtyard now that everyone heard it.

"You are a commoner," spat Gregoire. "You can't marry a

noble. Even though, I'd hardly call that whore a noble after what she did."

"Lark, hold Florie," said Dustin, handing the child over to her and approaching Gregoire.

"No one calls Lady Lark a whore and gets away with it." Dustin punched the Frenchman in the face so hard that he went stumbling backwards and had to be caught by one of his guards. He was about to hit him again when Lark stopped him.

"Dustin!" screamed Lark. "Nay."

"He deserved it, Lark," hissed Dustin. "I won't let anyone speak that way about you, and neither can I remain silent anymore about how I feel about you."

"Behind you, Dustin!" Lark's eyes opened wide when she saw Gregoire yank his sword from his belt and lunge toward Dustin.

Storm intercepted, his sword crossed with the French-man's. Dustin stepped out of the way.

"Storm, there will be no killing today at my castle," warned Corbett.

"Just this one," said Storm. "I have been wantin' to kill him ever since he got my daughter pregnant."

"Nay. Put down the sword," Corbett said once more.

"Storm, listen to Corbett," said Wren.

"Get yer bloody arse out of here, and I dinna want to see yer face ever again," warned Storm, looking like it was taking all his control not to run his sword through the man's heart. "I warn ye, if I ever hear ye insult my daughter or anyone in my family again, I will run my sword right through yer blackened heart and then dance atop yer grave."

Gregoire slowly lowered his sword. "You'll regret this, MacKeefe. There is no nobleman now who will ever marry her, no matter how much money you use to bribe them. Let's go," he said to his men, and they turned and left the castle.

"We will leave too," said Lady Adeline in a huff since a fight almost broke out with the Frenchman.

"Nay, we're staying put," ordered Lord Morcant. "Adeline, if you know what's good for you, you'll stop telling me what to do."

"I'm sorry, husband," said Lady Adeline, sulking now.

"I don't care if that man is a friend of your family, you'll have nothing to do with him ever again," commanded Morcant. "Lords Storm and Corbett, I apologize for this unfortunate incident."

"It wasn't your fault he showed up," said Corbett.

"Mayhap not directly, but still, I feel responsible. I'm sorry. I can only hope you'll still allow us to stay and that this will not make an enemy out of us," continued Morcant.

"Of course, ye can stay and I willna hold it against ye," said Storm, sheathing his sword.

"So ... what will you do?" Corbett asked Storm. "It seems no one here is qualified to marry Lady Lark."

"Nay, they are no'," said Storm.

"What about me?" asked Dustin once again. "Laird MacKeefe, did you read the letter I gave Lady Wren, asking both of you for Lady Lark's hand in marriage?"

"I did," said Storm.

"Storm, they are in love. I think you should let them get married," said Lark's mother.

"Well, I am no' sure. Dustin is a commoner. He is no' a noble," said Storm.

"Yes, he is a noble," said Sister Joan, stepping forward with Brother Ruford at her side.

"Sister, what is this all about?" asked Corbett.

The nun looked over at Brother Ruford, seeming reluctant to speak.

"I will tell them," said Ruford. "Sister Joan is -"

"Nay, let me," said the nun. She walked up to Dustin, taking his hand. "Dustin, I have been trying to tell you something since I arrived, but haven't been able to do so."

"What are you talking about?" asked Dustin.

"I am ... I am your mother," she said.

DUSTIN FELT like he was in a dream. Had he really just punched a nobleman and now a nun was telling him that she was his mother and also a noble? None of this really made any sense, and there was no way it could be real.

"Ye're his mother?" asked Lark. "I dinna understand. I thought Dustin was an orphan, left on the steps of the church as a baby."

"Yes, he was." Lady Eleanor came forward. "Just like the other orphans I work with and try to find homes for."

"Nay, Lady Eleanor, it is a little different," said Ruford. "You see, Dustin was abandoned on the steps of the church as a baby, that is true. He had a note pinned to his blanket from his mother saying she would return for him. That is why I raised Dustin, waiting for his mother to come back someday."

"And she didn't," Dustin reminded him.

"Until now," said Sister Joan. "Dustin, I am truly your mother."

"Nay." Dustin shook his head, not wanting to believe this. How could a nun be his mother? How could she have left him and not returned for twenty-two years? "How do I know you are even telling the truth?"

"Dustin, I am so sorry to have abandoned you. I never wanted to leave you," said Sister Joan. "You see, I am an English noblewoman, Lady Joan Guildersleeve from Wareham. I was abducted by a dock worker and became pregnant nearly twenty-three years ago. When you were born, my father decided we would have to leave to save face. He moved my family to Ireland, but wouldn't allow my baby—you—to come with us. He made me give you up and leave you on the steps of the church in secret, and never tell anyone who you were. It broke my heart, but I was a troubled young woman and had no choice but to do as my father instructed."

"So, you're my mother? My real mother?" asked Dustin, still not knowing how to take this.

"Yes, Dustin, I believe she is," said Ruford. "I do remember the Guildersleeve family. They had a pregnant daughter, and one day they disappeared and no one knew where they went."

"Where is my father, now?" asked Dustin.

Sister Joan shook her head in shame. "My father killed that dock worker for what he did to me, since he took me against my will. And after your birth, he took me far away and put me in a convent in Ireland to be a nun for the rest of my life, saying no one would ever want me."

"Oh, no. This sounds a lot like what happened to me," mumbled Lark. "Ye poor thing."

"Why now?" asked Dustin. "Why didn't you come looking for me years ago?"

"I wanted to come back for you, I swear I did," said his mother. "However, my father forbade it. He died recently, and my mother, who is still alive, agreed that I should come back to England to see if I could still somehow find you. Even after all these years. It was God who brought us back together."

"I have ... relatives?" asked Dustin, so shocked by all this that he didn't know what to say.

"Yes, many. All in Ireland. I've spoken to them all, telling them I wanted to try to find you. They hold nothing against me or you. They will all want to meet you, son. Oh, Dustin, please don't turn me away. I have thought about you every day since I gave birth to you. I prayed I'd find you again someday, and now I have. My prayers have been answered."

"How can you prove that I am the same baby you left on the steps of the church?" Dustin didn't want to get his hopes up until he knew this was real.

"Well, I suppose I can't," said the nun. "Since I was forbidden to tell anyone about it, and I couldn't write it in the note, the only proof I have is this." She pulled a piece of fabric out of her cassock and held it up. "It is from my cloak. I ripped a piece of it and wrapped you in it as a baby."

"Let me see that." Dustin took it, running his fingers over the soft material. "This is the same cloth of my blanket I had as a child," said Dustin. "It was purple and I loved it and took it everywhere with me."

"That's right," said Ruford. "You were wrapped in it as a baby, Dustin. Just cuddling it seemed to calm you. Mayhap it held your mother's scent and you remembered it somehow."

"Mayhap," said Dustin, handing the cloth back to the nun. "But it still doesn't prove anything."

"Dustin, how can ye say that?" asked Lark.

"Lark, I need to be sure. Before I get my hopes up," said Dustin softly.

"Ruford, do you still have the note that was pinned to the baby?" asked Joan.

"Nay," the monk answered. "I kept it for years, but when Dustin became older, he wanted it so I gave it to him."

"I have it," said Dustin, thinking about the note that he kept in a jar at his home. It had been his only hope of being reunited with his mother someday, and he couldn't bring himself to get rid of it since it had her handwriting on it.

"Dustin, give me a piece of parchment, a quill and some ink," said the nun.

"Here? Now?" complained Storm. "What is this all about?"

"Storm, just wait," said Corbett.

"Do it, Dustin," said Ruford, even though Dustin didn't understand what this was all about.

Dustin pulled out the things from his bag. "Why do you want this?" he asked.

"I need to write something," said Joan.

Dustin set up the parchment laid over a book, and gave her the quill and ink.

Down on her knees, the nun dipped the quill in the ink, writing something, and then stood back up, handing Dustin the piece of parchment.

"Read it," she told him. "This should be all the proof you need."

Dustin took it from her and looked at it, and froze.

"Dustin?" asked Lark. "What does it say?"

Dustin read the note aloud. "It says, *Please watch over my son until I am able to return for him.*"

"That is exactly what the note pinned to you as a baby said," Ruford announced.

"Still, she could have guessed, or heard what it said," Storm spoke up.

"Yes, she could have," said Dustin. "However, she couldn't have known that my mother drew a little picture of a butterfly on the note as well." Dustin's heart stood still. This is something that no one would know except him and Ruford. Even if someone did know, they wouldn't be able to make the butterflies look identical.

"It is the same butterfly that I put on your note when I left you," said Joan. "Right after you were born, a butterfly landed on you, and you seemed to smile."

"A flutterby landed on me too," called out Florie.

"Let me see that." Ruford took the parchment from Dustin. "I think it is the same. Yes, I believe she's right."

"Mayhap you should look at the original note to compare it," said Joan.

"I don't need to," said Dustin. "I have that picture of the butterfly engraved in my mind, and have been drawing it in books and on manuscripts for years. I can assure everyone that it is the same."

Lark took the letter and looked at it, with Florie peering over her shoulder.

"That is the same flutterby that Dustin drew in my story book," said Florie.

"Yes," said Lark. "It is also the same one he drew on my love letters, too, ever since I found out they were from him."

"Do you believe me now, son?" asked Joan. Her eyes held worry, as if she were afraid Dustin would turn her away or not want her.

"Dustin?" said Lark, holding Florie, putting her hand on his shoulder. "I ken how bad it feels to be abandoned, but it wasna yer mother's fault. Please forgive her. Please, dinna turn her away."

So many things were happening so quickly that Dustin's head swarmed with thoughts of all kinds. He had a family? He had a mother? This is what he had wanted all his life. Plus, the woman was a noble. He felt like this was all a dream and he was afraid he'd wake up and it would all disappear in a puff of smoke.

"Mother," he said, slowly, testing the word on his tongue. It felt good. It felt right, and he was done denying that goodness could come to him as well. The old sorcerer kept telling him things happened for a reason. Now, he understood exactly why he'd been abandoned as a baby, and he no longer hated his mother for leaving him on the church stairs. "Mother," he repeated, this time louder, putting his arms around the nun in a big hug. This was so odd, but also so wonderful at the same time.

"Dustin," she cried, hugging him and kissing him, tears flowing down her face. "I waited so long. I am so sorry. I love you, and always have."

"Please tell me you'll leave the abbey now, Mother," said Dustin. "I am not sure how I feel about you dressed this way. It almost feels wrong just to hug you."

Everyone laughed, and it broke the tension.

"I don't want to be a nun," said Joan. "I never did. All I ever wanted was to be a mother, and someday, hopefully a grandmother too."

"Well, mayhap that can happen today," said Dustin, looking back at Storm. "What do you say now, Laird MacKeefe?" asked Dustin. "I am half-noble, so that is better than none at all. Will you let me marry your daughter? I love her and Florie and want to spend the rest of my life with them. If you say no, I don't know how I'll ever go on without them."

"Please, Da," begged Lark. "I love Dustin and want him to be my husband."

"I want him to be my da. I love ye, Dustin. Da," said Florie, melting Dustin's heart.

"Well ... honestly, I was about to tell ye that ye can marry my daughter, even before we discovered ye are half-noble," said Storm. "I have to admit, this makes it a little easier to accept." His frown turned to a smile, and that was nice to see.

"Oh, thank ye, Da!" cried Lark, first hugging and kissing her parents and then hugging and kissing Dustin right there in front of everyone.

"So, we have no chance at the dowry?" called out one of the nobles.

"It's over?" asked another.

"Nay, no chance at all for any of ye," shouted Storm. "My

daughter, Lady Lark will be marryin' Dustin. Lord Dustin," he corrected himself. "Any of ye who dinna want to stay for the weddin' celebration can leave right now."

"Let's go," grumbled one of the suitors.

"No reason to stay if the money is off the table," complained another.

One after another, all the noblemen who were there trying to marry Lark just for the money left the castle.

"I'm sorry, Lark," said her mother. "I'm sure it's not easy to see that all these men wanted was the dowry, after all."

"It doesna matter," said Lark. "I didna want any of them and I am so glad they're gone."

"The dowry is yers now, Lord Dustin," said Storm. "As well as the title of lord since ye are half a noble."

"Thank you, my lord, but I can't take the dowry. That is never what I was after," said Dustin, picking up Florie and putting his arm around Lark. "I am a richer man than money can ever buy now that I'll have not only a wife and daughter, but a mother and extended family as well."

"Dustin, that is so sweet," said Lark, kissing him. "I am so happy. Da, when can we get married?"

"Well, I will have to find a priest," said Storm.

"No need. I can officiate the wedding," said Ruford, stepping forward, holding his prayer book. "I have been a monk and abbot for so long now that the bishop has granted me the privilege of officiating marriages."

"Then let's do it right now," said Dustin, not wanting to wait, because if he did, he was afraid he'd wake up and find out everything was just a dream, after all.

CHAPTER 23

Lark quickly changed into one of her best gowns and joined Dustin in the courtyard where everyone awaited the joyous occasion. Dustin was dressed in the clothes of a noble, and he looked more handsome than he ever had before.

"Lark, I lent your future husband some of my clothes I left behind when I moved to Rookrose," said Rook, waiting for the event to start with a tankard of ale clasped in his hands.

"He looks so handsome in those clothes," Lark answered. "Thank ye, cousin."

"Lark, Florie helped me pick a wedding bouquet for you from wildflowers outside the castle walls." Rose, Rook's wife who was a gardener, held out the bouquet to her.

"Thank ye both," said Lark, sniffing the flowers. "They are beautiful. I especially like that there is so much lavender and larkspur in it."

"I picked it, too," said Florie, tugging on Lark's gown.

"Yes, you too, sweetheart." Lark kissed her daughter atop her head. She looked up to see Dustin's mother standing there with a slight smile, dressed in a normal gown now, and no longer wearing the robes of a nun. It was obvious Lady Devon or someone had lent the woman a gown.

"Florie, why dinna ye go hold yer Grandma Joan's hand durin' the weddin'," Lark told her daughter.

"Ye mean Sister Joan?" asked Florie. "She looks different now."

"That's because she isna a nun anymore, sweetheart. Now, she is yer grandmother."

"I thought Lady Wren was my grandmother." The little girl seemed confused.

"We both are," said Lark's mother, reaching down to take Florie's hand. "You are so lucky to have two grandmothers now, Florie."

"I am. I'm lucky!" shouted Florie. "Come on, Grandma Wren, let's go stand by Grandma Joan so she doesna feel sad."

"Good idea." Wren reached over and kissed Lark on the cheek. "You are getting a good man, Lark. I am happy about how things turned out for you."

"Thank ye for convincin' Da to let me marry Dustin," Lark told her mother.

"Sweetheart, I didn't really have to do much. Once I showed him the letter Dustin wrote, and told him you and Dustin were in love, I think that was enough for him. All he cares about, same as me, is that you are happy. Your father is stubborn and has a lot of pride, but your happiness is really what is the most important to him."

"Lark, come on. Everyone is waiting." Raven pulled her away and over to her father. Eleanor watched from the side.

"Lark, can I escort ye to marry the scribe? I mean-Lord Dustin?" asked Storm.

"Aye, and thank ye, Da. Even though ye dinna ken Dustin well, I am sure ye will like him in time."

"I like him already," said Storm. "He seems to care about ye and Florie more than anyone. I am glad he is marryin' ye instead of one of those greedy nobles and especially instead of that bloody Frenchman."

"Me too," said Lark. "Do ye really mean it when ye say ye like Dustin?"

"Of course, I do. Any scribe who can punch a bloody Frenchman like that is all right by me."

Storm walked her through the crowd of people to where Brother Ruford was waiting with Dustin. Jonathon stood next to Dustin.

"Here ye go, Lord Dustin," said Storm, handing Lark over to him. "Thank ye for always supportin' her. I ken ye will be a good husband for Lark."

"Thank you, Laird MacKeefe," answered Dustin. "I am honored to be her husband."

"Dustin," whispered Lark. "Ye look as nervous as I feel right now."

"I am, but I'll be better once our vows are taken and I have a cup of whisky in my hand."

Lark giggled. "I'm sure my da brought some Mountain Magic along."

"What's Mountain Magic?" Dustin whispered back.

"Let's just say it's somethin' my great grandda brews that will make anyone forget about all their troubles."

"Are you ready?" asked Ruford, looking like a proud father. Of course, since he was like a father to Dustin, Lark realized how happy Ruford was for this moment, too.

DUSTIN AND LARK said their vows, proclaiming their love for each other in front of all the onlookers in the courtyard. Since there was no time to get a ring, Jonathon provided a small ring of metal from his smithy for now, and Dustin promised

Lark he would buy her a real ring as soon as he could afford it.

Then Lark and Dustin kissed with everyone cheering for them and their life together that had just begun as husband and wife.

"Congratulations," said Lark's father, being the first one to shake Dustin's hand. "Dustin, I really want ye to have the same dowry I was willin' to give any of those nobles."

"Are you sure?" asked Dustin. "I don't feel as if I should take it."

"You're a noble now," said Lord Corbett. "Also, Lady Lark's husband. Of course you should take it."

Orrick pushed to the front of the crowd to speak. "Dustin, as an advisor to Lord Corbett, my advice to you is to take what is offered and stop talking! You talk too much."

That made everyone laugh.

"All right, then I guess I accept," said Dustin.

"Are ye my da now?" asked Florie, tugging on Dustin's tunic.

"Yes, Florie, I am." Dustin picked up the little girl and kissed her on the cheek.

Raven and Eleanor came over to congratulate them as well.

The minstrels started playing a snappy tune and the servants served drinks for everyone. A true celebration was happening within the walls of Blake Castle, and it was as if a miracle had occurred. Orrick had told Dustin that everything happens for a reason, even if we don't know at the time why, but just to accept it. Now, Dustin understood his advice perfectly.

"There will be a grand feast to celebrate the wedding of Lady Lark and Lord Dustin," Corbett announced. "Everyone, please head to the great hall for food and dancing and games for the children."

"Oh, Lark, we are so happy for you," said Eleanor giving Lark a hug.

"Yes, we are," said Raven, holding her husband's hand. "Everything worked out for you, Lark."

"Yes, and it is better than I could have ever imagined." Lark leaned in to hug her new husband.

"Mother, come join us," Dustin called out. When she seemed hesitant, Brother Ruford took her arm and escorted Joan to the front of the crowd.

"Joan, you are his mother now," said Ruford. "And since I am the closest thing to a father that he's even known, I suggest we both get used to this."

"I already am getting used to it," said Joan, brushing away a tear. "Dustin, I never thought I'd see you again, and now I don't ever want to leave you, or you to leave me for the rest of my life."

"Then don't," said Dustin. "Live with me and Lark and Florie. It will help make up for the time lost between us."

"Yes, please do," added Lark.

"Wait a minute," said Dustin, looking over at Lark. "What am I saying? Where will we live? I don't think we can live at the monastery, and my cottage is much too small for all of us."

"Dustin, ye are a noble now. Ye will live like one as well, so get used to it," said Lark, laughing.

"You are welcome to stay here at Blake Castle for as long as you want," offered Lady Devon.

"Och, nay," said Storm. "My daughter and her new husband are comin' back to Scotland where they belong."

"I'll miss you, Dustin," said Ruford, making Dustin feel as if he would be abandoning the man who was like a father to him if he left England. On the other hand, he couldn't take Lark from her family in Scotland either.

"I don't know what to say," said Dustin. "I want to stay

here with Brother Ruford, but go to the Highlands with Lark's family as well. I'm torn."

"Mayhap you can come back to England for extended visits," said Corbett. "That way, we can all visit with you. You can stay here at the castle when you do, and for as long as you'd like."

"You are welcome to stay with Rose and me at Rookrose Manor too," offered Rook.

"Aye," agreed Raven. "You have to come back because we'll all miss you."

"Yes, we will," added Eleanor.

"Then that is exactly what we'll do," said Lark. "Dustin, do ye want to live at Hermitage Castle when we go back to Scotland or with the MacKeefe clan at their Highland camp?"

"I think ... I think I want to live everywhere," said Dustin. "After all, my family just keeps on growing and I want to see them all and experience everything I possibly can."

"Dustin, don't forget, we'll also want to visit our relatives in Ireland, too," said Joan.

"Yes. Yes, we will," said Dustin, kissing his mother, liking the way the words *our relatives* sounded to his ears. He went from having no family to having an abundance of family, and he couldn't be happier since this had always been his dream.

"Oh, Florie, did ye hear that?" asked Lark. "Ye'll get to visit Grandma Joan's and yer da's family in Ireland too."

"Yay," shouted Florie. "Do they have flutterbys there too?"

"Yes, granddaughter, they certainly do," said Joan, smiling from ear to ear. Dustin thought she looked so much prettier not having to wear that habit anymore.

"Dustin, I am the happiest girl in the world," Lark told him. "It is all because of ye."

"Well, I am the happiest man in the world," Dustin told her. "I never would feel this way if it wasn't for you."

"This is all a miracle," said Dustin's mother.

"Yes, Mother, I guess it is. I don't think I ever really believed in miracles before, but now, I certainly do." Dustin hugged his mother as well as Lark and Florie, all at the same time. "I never could have dreamed that this would happen in my life. Honestly, it might not have ever happened if not for my *Love Letters for Lady Lark*."

FROM THE AUTHOR

I hope you enjoyed Lark and Dustin's story and will take a moment to leave a review for me.

Sometimes things happen in life and we think, woe is me, not knowing that maybe there was a reason for that happening. It's all about trusting that the universe will give us exactly what we need, not always what we think we want. Dustin and Lark both had hard pasts, and ones that are not easy to overcome. But sometimes the choices we made in our past, or the events that happened beyond our circumstances, can only make us stronger. Learning from mistakes or unfortunate situations is what it is all about. As long as we can walk away with our head held high and knowing that we've learned something from the events in our lives, that is all that really matters.

Brother Ruford was first seen in the first romance novel I ever wrote which is *Lord of the Blade*, Book one from my *Legacy of the Blade Series*. Orrick also appears in that series and shows up in several others.

If you'd like to read more about Lark's brother, Hawke, you can do so in **Highland Storm**, Book 1 of the **Highland Chronicles Series.** I often have characters from one series showing up in another. I also like to write about the children of my heroes and heroines years after the initial story, to let you know what happened in the next generation.

The next story in my **Below the Salt Series** is **Dancing on Air**. This is Lady Eleanor's story and one where I will be pushing the envelope again, but have been very excited to write it. She falls in love with the executioner's son, but that is all I am going to tell you for now. It is a story you won't want to miss.

This series follows the generations of the Blake family. If you'd like to read about Corbett Blake and his wife Devon, you can find their story in **Lord of the Blade**, book 1 of my **Legacy of the Blade Series.** Be sure to read the **Legacy of the Blade Prequel,** to find out what makes Lord Corbett Blake such a hardened man. The stories of his long-lost siblings can be found in **Lady Renegade, Lord of Illusion,** and **Lady of the Mist**. Orrick, the sorcerer's story from the Legacy of the Blade Series is the last book and one of my favorites, called **Keeper of the Flame.**

Stop by and visit my **Website**. You can follow me on **Amazon, Bookbub, Goodreads, Facebook** and **Twitter**. I also have a **Private Readers' Group** on Facebook that I invite you to join.

If you would like to stay informed of my new books and also sales, please be sure to subscribe to my **newsletter**.

Thank you,

FROM THE AUTHOR

Elizabeth Rose

ABOUT ELIZABETH

Elizabeth Rose is an Amazon All-Star, and bestselling, award-winning author of nearly 100 books and counting! Her first book was published back in 2000, but she has been writing stories ever since high school. She is the author of fantasy/paranormal, medieval, small town contemporary, and western romance. You'll find sexy, alpha heroes and strong, independent heroines in her books. Sometimes her heroines can even swing a sword.

Her earlier fantasy romance novels started out with her **Greek Myth Series**, inspired by the TV shows *Legendary Journeys of Hercules* and *Xena: Warrior Princess*. One of the books, **The Oracle of Delphi** was featured on the History Channel during a documentary of the Oracle. Elizabeth joins Oliver Heber Books with her **Portals of Destiny Series** which brings back characters from some of her other fantasy series, making guest appearances.

She loves adding humor to her work, because everyone needs to laugh more in life. Her **Bad Boys of Sweetwater: Tarnished Saints Series,** focuses on 12 brothers, a bunch of kids, and lots of humor. This small-town romance series was inspired by people, places, and things in her own life. The location is the lake and small town of Michigan where she grew up visiting her grandparents.

Living in the suburbs of Chicago with her husband, Elizabeth has two grown sons and one granddog – so far. A lover of nature, she can be found in the summer swinging in her 'writing hammock' in her secret garden, creating her next novel. Her secret garden is what inspired her medieval series, **Secrets of the Heart**, which of course centers around a secret garden too!

Visit elizabethrosenovels.com where you will find book trailers, sneak peeks at upcoming covers, excerpts from her books, as well as original recipes of food that her characters eat in her stories. If you'd like to sign up for her newsletter, join her private readers' group, or follow her on social media, just copy and paste the following links.

Join Elizabeth's Newsletter
Join Elizabeth's Facebook Group

Also by Elizabeth Rose

Medieval Series:

Legendary Bastards of the Crown Series

Seasons of Fortitude Series

Secrets of the Heart Series

Legacy of the Blade Series

Daughters of the Dagger Series

MadMan MacKeefe Series

Barons of the Cinque Ports Series

Holiday Knights Series

Highland Chronicles Series

Pirate Lords Series

Highland Outcasts

Medieval/Paranormal Series:

Elemental Magick Series

Greek Myth Fantasy Series

Tangled Tales Series

Portals of Destiny

Contemporary Series:

Tarnished Saints Series

Working Man Series

Western Series:

Cowboys of the Old West Series

And More!

Please visit http://elizabethrosenovels.com

www.ingramcontent.com/pod-product-compliance
Lightning Source LLC
Chambersburg PA
CBHW020122120726
47903CB00007B/2068